Mela was sitting in the dark in a dingy rooming house with a young man she scarcely knew. They were waiting to spy on a dangerous criminal!

"You were going to tell me what you think about me," Mela said.

"Would you really like to know?" Peter asked. There was something in his voice and something in his closeness. And suddenly Mela felt almost shy.

He reached out and took her hand again. "Mela. . . ." he began. But what he was going to say she never knew. At that moment the front door slammed, and footsteps started up the stairs!

A HEART
IS BROKEN

Barbara Cartland

PYRAMID BOOKS • **NEW YORK**

A HEART IS BROKEN

A PYRAMID BOOK

Published by arrangement with Robert Hale & Company, London

© Barbara Cartland 1944 and 1972

This revised edition first published in Great Britain 1972
Pyramid edition published May 1974

The author wishes her readers to know that this book, originally called *Yet She Follows*, was written in the Spring of 1942.

ISBN   0-515-03358-8

Printed in the United States of America

Pyramid Books are published by Pyramid Communications, Inc. Its trademarks, consisting of the word "Pyramid" and the portrayal of a pyramid, are registered in the United States Patent Office.

Pyramid Communications, Inc., 919 Third Avenue, New York, N.Y.   10022

A Heart is Broken

Chapter One

"I'm sorry, Mela old girl, but it's no use. I've got to come clean and tell you that I care for someone else."

I just stood and stared at Tim. I had been longing to see him, waiting impatiently—and it seemed to me for years—until he could get leave.

Actually he had only been in Winnipeg for three months, but the only things to cheer me up were his letters, and when they had begun to get fewer and fewer I told myself it was because he was working and had no time to write. After all, they keep them pretty hard at it in the Air Training Units.

Of course I was stupid—I suppose any girl is when she is in love. If I had read Tim's letters unblinded by my own feelings I might have guessed sooner. Instead of which I just went on loving and loving him.

I was mad about him. I still am. It's no use people telling me that "love dies in a night" or burbling about "Time, the Great Healer", or any of that sort of nonsense. Love doesn't die because of what people do. One loves them because one can't help it.

I adore Tim. I adored him even when he said goodbye for the last time and walked out of the door, rather pink about the face with the little muscle at the side of his jaw twitching as it always does when he's nervous.

I knew he was worried and unhappy at having to tell me the truth but it made me love him even more, if possible, because he minded.

Anyway, I suppose it was some satisfaction to know he cared enough to be upset.

But no—nothing was really any consolation. Nothing could lessen the blow or make me feel better about it. It was just the end of everything—the bottom had dropped out of my world.

At first it was hardly painful at all. Rather like being struck down and feeling numb.

"I met her when I first got to Winnipeg, Mela," Tim was saying, "and when I saw her—I can't explain—but an electric current seemed to flash between us and I knew without doubt she was the one girl for me. I'd always thought you the finest person in the world. We've been such pals, haven't we, Mela?"

He waited for an answer but I couldn't speak.

"But this was different," he went on, "it sort of knocked me out—but Jeeze! it's hell having to come here and tell you!"

I stood looking at him and all I could think about was that there was a tiny spot of blood on his collar and that his uniform wasn't really blue.

It isn't a good colour for the Air Force at all, I thought. Too much grey in the mixture.

And my mind ran on, thinking of the most idiotic things and all the time my heart was telling me—

'This is the end! It's over, Pamela MacDonald. Tim doesn't love you any more.'

I couldn't believe it. I wanted to put my arms round his neck, pull his dear face down to mine and kiss him —one of those long, exciting kisses which used to make me feel breathless, shaken, and somehow a little shy. But I couldn't do that now.

The Tim who was talking to me wasn't the same Tim I'd loved and who had loved me. This was another man—a man who loved a girl called Audrey Herman who lived in Winnipeg.

When Tim had gone I stood for a long time looking out of the window. Our house in Montreal is high up on the hill and on the horizon the mountains were covered with snow and I thought how last year Tim and I had gone ski-ing in the Laurentians.

What fun it had been!—the sunshine and the snow, and Tim laughing and teasing me, saying that my cheeks felt and looked like frozen apples.

But they hadn't been frozen when we'd sat in front of

8

the blazing fire in the little log cabin which Tim's parents had built in the forest. After the others had gone to bed, we used to sit up and talk. We made plans about all the things we'd do when Tim had made enough money for us to get married.

We were awfully sensible about it and decided to wait until we could be really comfortable. We weren't going to rush into anything. Not like some of my friends, struggling along without a maid and without a car. Of course, things would have been better if it hadn't been for the war.

Daddy had been hit and so had Tim's father, so there wasn't the nice, fat allowance which we might have looked forward to in ordinary times; but still, Tim was doing well.

His father's business is one of the oldest firms on the Stock Exchange, so even in the worst slumps he has always managed to keep his head above water.

And then, quite suddenly, Tim decided that he must join in. We had talked it over very carefully when the war started and come to the conclusion there was no reason why he should enlist.

Tim has always been rather more pro-American than pro-British. I didn't mind, although I was supposed to be opposite, having an English mother who loves her own country. Not that after twenty-five years in Canada she's any reason to love England except sentimentally.

Her English relations, with the exception of Uncle Edward, have treated her pretty badly. I've often planned how, when eventually I meet my grandfather, I'll tell him what I think of him. I'd like to show him my father and say—

"'There's a fine man for you. There's a man who's worked, who has been successful and kept his wife happy into the bargain. Now aren't you ashamed of yourself for forbidding your daughter to marry 'a common Colonial'?"

Yes, that's what he called my father when my mother wanted to marry him, and then he chucked him off the estate and told him to go back to Canada as quick as he could. He went all right—but my mother went with him.

How I would have loved to have seen my grandfather's face when he woke up in the morning to find her gone and only a note left behind to tell him what had happened!

I expect the butler took it in to him on the silver salver, and his porridge couldn't have tasted so good that morning when he realised that—perhaps for the first time in his life—he had been outwitted.

I suppose really it was Scot meeting Scot, for my father was Scottish although his family had been in Canada for two generations. They had emigrated with only a pound or so in their pockets and they worked like beavers to make good.

Well, they succeeded, Daddy had a decent education and I suppose he's one of the greatest experts on forestry in the country. Yet when he went over to England they talked about him as though he was a lumberjack.

Of course, he was young in those days, but even so you'd have thought the English would have seen some difference between him and the men who just fell the trees. But they didn't.

Well, Mummy crossed the Atlantic and when they got to Canada they were married, and from that day to this Uncle Edward is the only one of her relations who has ever spoken to her.

He is different, of course. He was considered the black sheep of the family for years—which is funny now when you think that he is the one member of the family who has got a position in the British Government—and a pretty important one too.

But even England has woken up to the fact that stuffy old people don't get her anywhere and that if they are going to win this war they will want go-ahead men who can forget tradition and class distinctions.

Uncle Edward's go-ahead all right—he's done strange and exciting things all his life. He's been in a gold rush, and in the Relief of Ladysmith, and he was torpedoed in a mine sweeper in 1917—and that's only a few of the adventures he's had.

I'd rather listen to Uncle Edward telling me stories than read any thriller that you can buy on a bookstall.

However, one swallow doesn't make a summer and one Uncle Edward doesn't make all English people seem marvellous to me. In spite of all that Mummy's said—and she's always been a little bit home-sick for her own country—I've hated a lot of the English people I've met and a good deal that I've heard about England.

So frankly I didn't care a jot when Tim decided that he wasn't going to chuck up his whole career to rush off and fight simply because England said we ought to.

After all, England was a long way away, and there's certainly something to be said for those who argue that Great Britain pays precious little attention to us until she wants something. But, of course, Mummy gets absolutely livid when I talk like that.

"England's not only our Motherland, Mela," she has said to me frequently, "she's the greatest power for good in the world today."

I can't argue with Mummy when she talks in that strain. She feels it all so deeply. Besides, if she thinks like that—let her. But I don't agree. I get sick of being told that "this must be best because it's English"—"buy British for value," and all that sort of sales talk.

It's always seemed to me a lot of nonsense that *Home, Sweet Home* should make Canadians who haven't seen the shores of England for forty years—if at all —sob ostentatiously into their handkerchiefs.

I think Canada's fine. It suits me, and all I ask for is a cosy little apartment in Montreal and Tim coming home after work, hooting his horn as he turns the corner of the street so that I shall be ready to run down and meet him as he arrives.

But that's a dream that can never come true now and I wonder what's going to happen to me?

I suppose really my dreams began to fall to bits the

day that Tim told me he was going to join the Air Force. He had been a bit restless all the month. The papers had been full of the Battle of Britain.

The radio said: "*115 Nazi planes . . . 185 German planes destroyed . . . London in flames . . . bombs raining death . . . women and children buried alive . . .*"

People like Mummy walked about with white faces saying—"Can't they stick it?" I used to wonder why they felt so keenly. I'd have been awfully sorry to see those Germans win, but somehow it didn't seem real.

I just don't believe that it would make all that difference to us, if Hitler did conquer England. Why, for years we've been speculating as to whether it wouldn't be better for the capital of the Empire to be in Canada.

People talked about asking the Royal Family to come and live over here. If anything would make me violently pro-British it would be the Queen's smile.

I saw her when they came to Canada. Daddy was presented to her and he said it was the proudest day of his life. And he meant it, too.

After I'd seen her I just hugged myself. I said:

"I'm Scottish too, and Scottish on both sides."

Which is true, because Mother's family have been lairds in Sutherland since the days of Bonnie Prince Charlie, and as for Daddy's family—I believe there's still a lot of MacDonalds in Scotland.

I was always sorry that Tim didn't see the King and Queen. He was in the States at the time and he couldn't get back. Perhaps if he had it would have made him join up sooner; because, personally, the Queen would make me want to fight for England, while the Battle of Britain left me rather cold.

Well anyway, while I was feeling interested but not emotional, so to speak, it took a lot of people quite differently, and Tim amongst them.

"I've got to go, Mela," he said, and he said it desperately, as if he was being compelled against his will.

"But why?" I asked. "Why now? We've talked it all

12

over. You decided not to volunteer. Of course, if it's a case of conscription it's a different thing. And now, suddenly, for no reason . . ."

"There's a reason, all right," Tim interrupted, "but I can't put it into words. It's those boys in the air—standing up to those devils—beating them at their own game without enough 'planes, without enough ammunition! They're game enough but they want help and I'm going to give it them."

I knew it was no use arguing with Tim. He'd made up his mind and that was that. Needless to say I wasn't enthusiastic. And what puzzled me was why he should suddenly change his mind and his life—or rather, our lives—overnight.

Dunkirk hadn't made him want to rush off and defend England against invasion. I couldn't see why a battle in the skies, which so far appeared pretty indecisive, should make such a difference to him.

But there it was—and there was nothing for me to do but grin and bear it. Really I was a tiny bit piqued, too. I felt that I should have been a good deal more important to Tim than a little island away across the Atlantic, but evidently I wasn't to be considered.

It surprised me, too, the way Mother and Father took it. I quite understood Mummy getting all sentimental and saying how proud and glad she was—she has always to my mind, been a bit silly about England —but from Daddy I did expect a more level-headed attitude.

Instead he said—"Good boy!" and held out his hand to Tim. He put an accent on the "good", which showed me he was particularly pleased.

Everyone was unusually nice to me, too, as if I'd done something commendable. And when I tried to say I couldn't quite understand Tim's point of view, they took up the attitude that I was miserable because he was going away and that I must try to be unselfish and bid him God-speed with a brave heart!

No one would see that while I minded him going personally—and I suppose selfishly—what puzzled me was why he should want to go.

It was no use trying to talk to my friends. Most of their young men or their husbands had joined up at the very beginning. I'd known that in a sort of way they despised Tim, but I didn't care.

We were perfectly happy together and, what was more, a great many of his American friends thought it very sensible of him to keep on with his job and not start flag-wagging because there was a war going on in some other part of the world.

"Your boy's got sense," one of them said to me. "Look what happened last time. You're too young to remember, but when the boys came marching home again what did they find? Their jobs had got filled by someone else! And let me tell you it's no fun being a hero on an empty belly."

But sensible or otherwise, Tim went off to Winnipeg to be trained as an airman and I learnt for the first time in my life what it was to be lonely.

Tim had been about ever since I grew up. There had been other men, too, when I first left school, who'd given me a rush and made a fuss of me. Some of the boys had wanted to marry me, but there had never really been anyone but Tim.

I think I loved him from the first day that he tipped me out of his toboggan head first into a six-foot snowdrift. It soon became pretty plain, too, that there was no one else in Tim's life, though he didn't say anything for a long while.

We just played around and had a good time.

Then one night coming home from a party, Tim stopped the car. It was a moonlight night and the stars were twinkling nearly as brightly as the lights of the city. Tim threw away his cigarette and turned towards me; he didn't say anything but he looked at me and suddenly I felt strange and breathless.

Tim's arms went round my shoulders and his lips were against mine; then I knew that happiness hurts, but it is so wonderful that one is afraid even of moving lest such ecstasy should vanish for ever. . . .

But it didn't vanish. Not where I was concerned, at any rate. Everything went on getting more wonderful until the day that Tim said he had got to go and fight for England.

That certainly increased the grudge I have always borne against that country, but still I had to put a good face on his going, and I kidded myself that perhaps he'd be no use as a pilot and they'd throw him out.

When Tim wrote that he'd got leave and was coming to see me I walked on air. I'd had a pretty gloomy three months one way and another. There had seemed very little to do after Tim had gone.

I suppose I ought to have made an effort and gone to work at the Red Cross or helped with some of the evacuees, but I didn't see why I should. Any time I want work they are only too pleased to give it me at the McGill University.

I find it quite simple to translate a German treatise into French or vice versa. I've translated one or two books and everyone's been very complimentary about them; so it's nice to think I can make a few dollars any time I want to.

Tim always said he wanted to support his wife and where Tim was concerned I wanted to be supported— so why worry about a permanent job?

Mother took all the credit for my ability.

"You're just like your grandmother," she said. "She was a brilliant woman. She travelled all over the world and could speak at least six languages as if she were a native of the country. It's funny how talents like that skip a generation. I was always a terrible French scholar and never even tried to learn any other language."

I didn't want to be beholden to any grandmother who was unnatural enough not to want to see her daughter after she had run away with the man she loved.

Mother tried to tell me that Victorian wives didn't

15

dispute their husband's decisions, but I took that with a grain of salt. If my grandmother had really cared for her daughter surely she would have written to her, if only once a year?

"Do you think there's anything in this hereditary theory of Mother's?" I asked Daddy.

"I shouldn't be surprised," he said. "Your mother's mother was a fine woman."

"You ought to hate her for the way she's behaved," I said.

Daddy laughed.

"Why should I?" he asked. "After all, she produced the one thing on earth that I wanted more than any other. I am very grateful to her for that. Besides, my dear Mela, a victor should always be magnanimous to those he has defeated."

I snorted. It was all very well for Daddy to feel philosophical about it, but somehow I couldn't. It was annoying, too, not being able to boast at school about my smart relations.

All girls—and boys too, for that matter—boast to each other, and there was a smug child at my school who used to tell us that she was a direct descendant of Louis the Fourteenth.

I used to itch to say that my family was related to Mary, Queen of Scots, for Mother had told me that we were and that a picture of her hangs in my grandmother's castle. But I couldn't tell them that without admitting that Mother had been cut off from her family for demeaning herself by marrying "a lumberjack".

So I had to keep silent, but I nearly burst with the effort at times.

Oh well, I'm thankful I take after Father—and until the war came I don't suppose I gave my English relations so much as one thought a year, but after that it was England, England, England all the time, and although Tim and I decided we wouldn't let the war affect our lives, it did and it has!

It has taken Tim away from me as surely as though

16

he had been killed by a bullet . . . it's ruined my life and it's destroyed my happiness both now and for all time.

"My heart is broken," I told my mother.

She came in from shopping as I was still standing in front of the window. I suppose I must have looked miserable, for she came in talking cheerfully, then stopped and put her basket down on the table.

"Why, Mela darling," she said suddenly, "whatever is the matter?"

Then the calm numbness which had paralysed me ever since Thn had told me that he loved me no more —cracked. I gave a big gasping sob.

"My heart is broken!" I cried. "Oh Mummy, Mummy, I'm so utterly miserable!"

Chapter Two

I expect at any moment to wake up and find it isn't true —to find that I have dreamt the whole thing and that I am in my own pink and white chintz bed, and not feeling rather sick and muzzy on the last lap of my journey to England.

The muzzy feeling comes from having too many cocktails before I left Lisbon.

"They will give you Dutch courage," my escort said.

Not that I needed it, for I haven't been frightened, not for one minute, since I left New York—but I could quite see, even in the few hours I was there, that to drink is the thing to do in Lisbon. Most of the people have nothing else to occupy their time.

Some of them have been waiting three or four months to get either a seat in an aeroplane to England or a visa to get them taken on board an American ship. Some of them, I'm told, will just have to sit drinking in Lisbon until their last penny is exhausted.

Nobody seems to worry about what will happen to them after that.

I wished in a way that I could have stayed a little longer, but it was awfully flattering to be told that a special priority seat had been kept for me on the very next aeroplane to England, which would be leaving exactly three hours after the ship docked.

It's a windy day and the aeroplane is heaving up and down, and I only hope I shan't be doing the same very shortly! I'm a pretty good sailor on the whole and I've never yet been air-sick, but the longest journey I've made was from Montreal to Toronto.

I suppose really I ought to feel frightened. At any moment a Messerschmitt might come swooping out of the clouds and shoot us down, but somehow I can't

18

work myself up into feeling dramatic. I couldn't on the boat, not even when we got into the danger zone and were told it would be wiser to sleep in our clothes.

The whole thing was like watching a film and I couldn't take it seriously.

Besides, life seemed to go on pretty much as usual. There were the innumerable meals which always seem to overlap each other; there were men talking business just as if they were in their offices—one wonders why they bother to come to sea to do it; and there was a stewardess who said—

"Don't you worry about submarines, honey"—as though she was talking about mosquitoes in the cabin!

The steward laughed when I asked him if there had been any incidents on any of the other trips.

"That would be telling," he said, and winked at me.

So I ate, and slept, and read all the magazines and books that Daddy had given me at the last moment in case I felt lonesome, and altogether it was very uneventful and very dull.

Only when we got to Lisbon did things begin to happen. It was there they spoke of Uncle Edward with something approaching reverence. I had realised that he was pretty important, but apparently in Lisbon, which is supposed to be neutral, British Cabinet Ministers really have some standing.

I was escorted from the ship to the aerodrome as if I was Royalty, my luggage was looked after. I was given my ticket—which I was told had been paid for in England—and altogether I found myself what Tim would have called "pretty big cheese!"

A very nice young man took me out to lunch and said he had been told to look after me—and they certainly picked the right sort of person to do it. He was full of talk and chatter about Lisbon and about the people passing through there.

He made me laugh at the tales of how some of the society women were absolutely furious at not being given priority seats and how a famous playwright who was on a job for one of the Ministries refused to go at all unless he could take his valet.

"I really can't trust the pressing of my clothes to anyone but George," he kept on saying, and so in the end they had to find an extra seat!

The time seemed to pass almost too quickly—in fact, I was really sorry when he said I'd have to be getting aboard the 'plane.

"I'll tell Uncle Edward how wonderful you've been to me," I said, and the young man blushed with pleasure.

"It's been a great honour to look after you, Miss MacDonald." he said. "What's more, I wish all my duties were as jolly as this one has been."

I shall certainly have to get Uncle Edward to recommend him for promotion—if there is such a thing in that particular service. Perhaps he might even slip him a medal of some sort, second or third class.

"I wonder if Uncle Edward has altered at all now he's so grand?" I asked myself.

It must be nearly three years since I saw him and then he was quite an ordinary Member of Parliament who, I understood, was frowned on pretty consistently by the Chamberlain Government because he asked uncomfortable questions which nobody wanted to answer.

He always said Mr. Churchill was wonderful, even in the days when everyone thought he was finished and was not likely to hold an important office again, and when he became Prime Minister, he made Uncle Edward Minister of Propaganda.

I just couldn't believe my eyes when Mummy brought me his cable. He sent two; one was official asking me formally to come as his secretary, and the other was to Mummy saying:

"Delighted to see Mela, and although we are breaking things rather than mending them in England just now, I'll do my best."

This was a joke, of course, because Mummy had

wired him that I'd got a broken heart and she wanted me to get away.

I suppose it was pretty beastly of me to worry her so much; but once I'd begun to tell her about Tim, I just broke down and cried like a child. And that's not a very good simile because I can't remember crying very much in my childhood.

I've always been very happy—I expect really I've been spoilt. I've certainly always had things when I wanted them. This is the first time I have ever come against it and I'm pretty ashamed of being so bowled over, but I can't help it.

I love Tim. I want him all the time, every minute, and now that I'm going off to England to forget him it's making things worse. I keep thinking:

"How interesting this is. What will Tim think when I tell him?"

Then I remember that I won't be able to tell him and when that happens I just start crying all over again.

I stood on the top deck of the ship looking at the sea, bleak and grey, and I wondered why I didn't chuck myself in. After all, I have really nothing to live for now. All the natural things in life are barred to me for ever —a husband, a home and children—that was what I wanted and that's what I'm never going to get.

Yet somehow the idea of committing suicide is so rediculous. I've always felt there was something theatrical and unreal about the accounts in newspapers of love-pacts and people putting their heads in gas ovens or jumping off the Empire State Building in New York.

I couldn't do any of those things and I don't think it's because I don't love Tim enough—it's going to be far harder to live without him than to die for love of him.

I keep thinking it would be just perfect if a bomb fell on me in London. I could then die a heroine's death and perhaps Tim would be sorry when he heard about it.

It's terribly annoying in many ways having been brought up in the twentieth century—or perhaps I should say in twentieth-century Canada. Maybe they do things differently in other countries. If I tried to drift about and go into a decline nobody would be at all sympathetic.

I'd like to fade away wanly in black velvet and pearls with a few violets in my hand; but the point is that no one would come in with hushed voices and visit me and I shouldn't have a Salon of adoring friends hanging on my dying words. They'd just say—

"Oh, don't let's go to see Mela—she's such a crashing bore!"

Besides, I'm not really the fading type. I wonder how many times I've looked in the glass this week and wondered what Audrey Herman has that I haven't. I've always thought myself pretty good-looking on the whole. Of course one notices one's own worst points more than other people do.

Strangers have raved to Mummy and said I was "the prettiest thing in years" and though I didn't allow myself to get too puffed up about that, I'd have been a fool if I hadn't realised that I certainly had points over some of my friends.

I've got lovely hair, for instance. It's a mixture of Father's and Mother's and I shouldn't have asked for any other colour if I'd had the choice.

Mummy was red—Scottish red—not that nasty sandy colour but the rather deeper tones which make you think of autumn leaves, and Daddy is a sort of golden brown, so I, with what I call consummate tact, compromised between the two.

I'm what Hollywood calls a "a chestnut blonde". I'm too fair to be red and too red to be fair. And with that I've got dark eyelashes. Genuine ones. No stranger believes it, but they've always been that colour since I was a baby. I've got, too, the whitish sort of skin that goes with red hair, a turned-up nose, and grey-blue eyes, the colour of the Atlantic the only day there was a glint of sun.

The colour of eyes isn't important, though. I think

my generation seldom notices anything but the expression in them. Mother was describing her family to me one day and I realised then that I'd not the slightest idea of the colour of anyone's eyes except my own.

"In my day," Mummy said, "we used to notice eyes particularly and all the novelists harped on them. I think it must have been the fashion, but you are all in much too much of a hurry to sign *Two Eyes of Grey* to someone you love."

I know Tim would have yawned his head off if I'd ever tried to sing to him, and anyway his eyes were brown—and brown rhymes with town, which doesn't sound very romantic but makes you think of going places and having fun—and we certainly did that, both before and after we were engaged.

Oh, dear!—it's depressing to think that all my memories are in the past and that now I shall always think of love in the past tense instead of in the future.

I'd got so used to thinking "when we are married I'll do so-and-so" that now I find myself still doing it. If I see a dress I like or a nice piece of furniture, I find myself thinking—

"I'll have that when I'm married. I wonder if Tim will like it!"—

Then I remember!

I didn't get many clothes to come on this trip. I just couldn't bear to go round the shops, in fact, Mummy bought me two or three dresses without my even seeing them. I couldn't rouse myself to do anything but cry.

I cried the whole of the first night after Tim had gone. Mummy sat up with me until it was nearly dawn. I kept saying to her—

"Do go away and leave me alone"—

But when she got to the door I'd ask her to stay.

I despise myself for it—at the same time it just shows the thinness of the veneer of "we can take it," and "our generation's tough". I remember a girl who was at school with me saying—"No man will ever cause me a sleepless night"—and thinking how right she was and that I'd feel the same.

But that was before I met Tim—before I fell in love. Perhaps love is the same in every generation and it doesn't pay any account to the fashions or the affections of the period. If one comes to think of it, it must be.

That's why Mummy was prepared to go with Daddy after she'd only met him a few times and give up everything she'd ever known because she loved him.

It's funny, but one never thinks of one's parents as being "fraught with passion and emotion." When one talks about love for them one imagines it a nice, discreet, kid-glove affair—tea and buns in the drawing-room and hardly kissing each other except in a friendly way.

It's stupid I know, but I suppose we all imagine that love is more tremendous, more passionate and more overwhelming for us than for anyone else, and there's something faintly shocking in thinking that older people have felt the same.

Now I come to think of it, I see that Mummy must have loved Daddy violently with every breath she drew, just as I love Tim, and that's why she was so understanding. I think, too, she was a bit frightened as to what I'd do. I was pretty wild in some of the things I said.

"I'll get him back," I told her. "I'll go up to Winnipeg and I'll beat that girl Audrey Herman. Tim's just taken with a pretty face. He wants me really—he must want me."

I meant it at the time. Now I think I should have enough pride to leave him alone. And yet I don't know. Can one have pride where love is concerned?

If Tim so much as sent me a postcard with a few words of hope on it I'd go back this second, if it meant swimming the Atlantic. But I suppose there's no chance of that now or ever.

Mummy realised it quicker than I did—she cabled Uncle Edward first thing in the morning. It was pretty sporting of her really because I know it was hard for both her and Daddy to let me go when the time came, but Uncle Edward had said before the war—

"Send Pamela over to me when you're tired of her. She could be my secretary if she could spare the time in between sight seeing and turning the heads of all our young men."

"Would you like to go?" Mummy asked me.

"I'd love to," I replied. "and I'll work hard, I promise you that, Uncle Edward, if you'll have me."

"Perhaps next fall," Mummy said. "It would be a lovely experience for Mela and I'd like her to see England."

There was a wistful note in her voice and a funny look in her eyes which comes there when she speaks of England, and most of all of Scotland. It means she's homesick, but I know she'd never go back while she's not welcome.

"Next fall then, Uncle Edward," I said gaily. "I'll be with you, and don't forget to polish up the town band."

I didn't go because I'd met Tim. I never gave England a thought after that, as for going away—Mummy couldn't even get me to go down to Toronto for a week-end if there was a chance of seeing Tim in Montreal.

I suppose she felt now that my one chance of forgetting Tim was to go away, and although she didn't tell me what she said, I gather her cable to Uncle Edward was pretty desperate.

We got the reply in three hours, and exactly half-an-hour after it came, they rang up from Ottawa to say they were getting a special permit for me to travel to England.

Still, I couldn't be enthusiastic about anything. I just wandered about looking miserable and crying myself to sleep every night until Daddy said—

"For the Lord's sake, Mela, cheer up! No man in the world is worth being so miserable about and if that young man was here now I'd kick him hard in the pants!"

"I can't help it," I said, and started to cry.

"Leave the child alone," Mummy said. "Don't you see she's making herself ill?"

"She ought to have more sense," Daddy growled.

He didn't mean it unkindly. I knew that. He was only upset that I should be so miserable.

When the moment came to leave him on the dock in New York, I suddenly felt I couldn't bear it.

"I'm not going," I said. "I can't leave you. We'll get my baggage off and go back home."

He shook his head.

"Your mother would never forgive us."

But I wasn't thinking of Mummy at that moment, or really of Daddy either. I was thinking of Tim. I felt I couldn't go so far away, couldn't leave him behind and put a whole ocean between us. At that moment I felt I must have been crazy to consent.

I looked up at the ship towering above us and I knew it was relentless and stern—an instrument of torture specially manufactured to take me away from all I loved.

"I won't go—I won't!" I said—but it was no use.

And then I went up on the top deck as they started moving the gangways. I didn't tell Daddy, but I'd a sneaking hope right up to the last moment that Tim would turn up and stop me going. I'd crept out the night before and sent him a wire.

"Sailing Europe tomorrow," I'd said, and I'd added the name of the ship.

"If he cares at all," I thought, "surely he'll come or at least wire— 'Don't go until I see you.' "

But there was nothing and when the ship slowly drew out from the harbour I knew that my last hope had died, and then once again I didn't care what happened.

I went down to my cabin and locked myself in, but after an hour or so I felt hungry. It just shows that matter has an ascendancy over mind, whatever people say to the contrary. I'd cried so much that I could hardly see out of my eyes and yet when I went down to the saloon for dinner I ate heartily.

Going down to the saloon that evening made me pull myself together, only it wasn't the food that did it. It was something I overheard one of the officers say to another.

I was coming out of the dining saloon just behind him and he didn't see me. He stopped to light a cigarette, and as he did so he said to his friend,

"Pretty lousy lot this trip."

Now that particular officer had been sitting opposite my table at dinner. He was young and quite attractive and I knew then what a freak I must look. I'd been so unhappy that I hadn't bothered even to powder my nose or make up my lips and when I got back to my cabin I nearly had a fit when I saw my face.

It just shows that one can control oneself if one wants to, however impossible it seems, because after that I didn't cry nearly so much.

There were moments, of course, when someone started to play the piano in the lounge one evening and they played *Over the Rainbow*, which was one of the tunes we'd danced to all the summer.

Another time when I went out on deck just before I went to bed—it was very cold but the wind had dropped and the stars were shining. There was a sort of radiance over the sea and suddenly I felt—

"How wonderful this would be if I was with Tim on my honeymoon trip!"

We'd sometimes talked of going to Europe—it was to be a toss-up between Paris and Florida.

I ran below simply howling, but when I looked at myself in the glass in my cabin, I stopped. I didn't want to look "lousy" even if it was a relief to my feelings to sob my heart out.

I've cried very little since. I expect I shall become hard, cold and bitter, one of those withered women that people always avoid because they say such shrewish things to everyone they meet.

It's awful in a way to realise that my love life is finished at twenty-one, but it is, and I shall try and grow old gracefully with an atmosphere of wistful sadness about me so that people will say—

"Poor dear, her heart was broken when she was very young and she's never really recovered from it."

The awful thing is, I don't believe Tim will mind. How will he know? I wish now I'd had the sense to say that whatever happened we'd remain friends and correspond with each other.

I could then have written him long letters with an underlying meaning which would have shown him what I was feeling and suffering. But perhaps that wouldn't have worked either.

Oh, well, it's all done now; it's past and finished and there's nothing for me but to look forward to England and hope by some lucky chance I'm blown up in a raid.

Chapter Three

When the taxi stopped in front of 92 Smith Square, I just sat and stared through the window.

At first, I thought he had brought me to the wrong house, then the driver opened the connecting window and said—

"Looks as if there's been a spot of trouble 'ere!"

It certainly did! There was a heap of bricks and rubble on the pavement and although the front door was closed the rooms on either side of it were open to the rain; there were satin curtains lying, wet and bedraggled, across what had been the area railings.

Over the mantelpiece in what had obviously been the dining-room, I could see a picture with its frame smashed, but with the portrait of Uncle Edward himself still intact.

After a moment of bewildered amazement, I gave a cry of horror, and jumped out of the taxi. A policeman walked across the road to me.

"Can I do anything for you miss?"

"What's happened?" I asked.

"We've 'ad a spot of trouble round 'ere," the policeman replied.

It annoyed me the way both he and the taxi driver spoke as if someone had cut their fingers or been had up for exceeding the speed limit. This was serious—in fact, to me it was desperate. Where was Uncle Edward?

I was just going to ask further questions when another policeman—I think he was an inspector—came striding up.

"Are you Miss MacDonald?" he asked me.

"Yes."

"I'm sorry miss, but you're a bit earlier than we ex-

29

pected. I was told to look out for you. Will you come this way?"

He gave the taxi driver a number and then he and I walked about a hundred yards down the street to where there was a smaller house with a green door and green painted shutters. Not that I'd time to notice much at the moment. I was feeling agitated and upset by this unexpected reception.

The inspector was still apologising.

"You never know these days with aeroplanes. Generally they are two or three hours late. To tell you the truth, when Mr. Flacton told me to look out for you I didn't think I need start on the job for another half-hour or so."

I was just going to ask who Mr. Flacton was, when the green door opened and the inspector said—"Miss MacDonald"—to the butler, and added.

"The taxi with her luggage is coming up now."

The butler said pompously—

"This way, miss."

He led me through a little panelled hall into a large room overlooking a courtyard at the back of the house.

My first impression was of books—books in shelves from floor to ceiling—and then from behind a big desk at the far end of the room there rose, rather slowly, a man.

He was tall, dark and extremely goodlooking in a stiff upper class English way. I always feel there is something cynical and inhuman about those sort of men. He came slowly across the room to meet me and I saw that he walked with a limp.

"Are you Miss MacDonald?" he asked. "I'm Peter Flacton. I'm sorry that I couldn't get down to Croydon to meet you. If I'd been certain the aeroplane would arrive punctually I might have managed it, but sometimes they're so delayed."

As he stopped speaking, I came to the point.

"What's happened to my uncle?"

"Won't you sit down?" Peter Flacton said.

30

He pointed to a chair near the desk and as I crossed to it he limped back to his own chair.

"Perhaps I'd better explain who I am," he started.

"I don't think that's necessary," I said impatiently. "There's only one thing I want to know and that is—what's happened to my uncle? It's been rather a shock seeing the house when I arrived."

"You've seen the house!" he ejaculated. "I'm sorry about that. I told the inspector to meet you at the end of the road."

"Well, he didn't," I replied sharply. "The taxi took me to Number 92, and then I saw that it had been hit by a bomb. Was Uncle Edward injured?—that's what I want to know."

Peter Flacton hesitated, and then he spoke quietly.

"Your uncle was killed."

I stared at him, not being able for the moment to take it in.

"I'm sorry to have to tell you like this," he went on. "I wanted to prepare you for the shock. It's been a great shock to me too. You see, I was fond of your uncle. I was his P.P.S."

I said nothing, and he went on as if giving me time to compose myself.

"That means Parliamentary Private Secretary, in case you don't know. I'd done a lot of work one way and another for him before the war, then after Dunkirk when I got my leg smashed up, he asked me to go back to him. It's been wonderful working with him because I admired your uncle more than any man I have ever met in my life. Somehow I can't believe that his career is really finished.

"When did it happen?" I asked, and my voice sounded strange even to myself.

"The night before last."

"Does everyone know? Is it in the papers?"

"It was given out on the one o'clock news today, so it will be in the evening papers. We didn't release the information sooner for certain reasons."

31

"What reasons?"

Peter Flacton looked uncomfortable. He hesitated. Then as if he had suddenly made up his mind, he said:

"I'm going to tell you the truth, Miss MacDonald. I think you are entitled to it. I see no reason why I shouldn't, but what I am going to say is completely and absolutely confidential."

"You can trust me."

He looked at me as if he was confirming my words, then said:

"Your uncle was killed by a bomb. There was a raid on at the time, but we know with absolute certainty that no aeroplane flew over this particular area."

"What do you mean?"

"I mean," he replied, "that the bomb which exploded in Number 92 was put there with the intention of destroying your uncle's life.

"But who did it."

"We have no idea. Naturally, the police are working on the matter—that's why the news of your uncle's death was kept from the public. We don't want to lose the chance of getting some clue but, frankly, at the moment we have none."

"None at all?" I asked. "But surely German spies, or whatever they are, can't rush about London blowing people up?"

I spoke with a kind of horror. I was just beginning to realise how ghastly it was that Uncle Edward had been killed, and now that he was no longer there I knew how much I had looked forward to seeing him.

"It sounds fantastic to me," I added hotly. "I don't suppose you could blow up one of the chiefs of the Nazi party and get away with it."

"We shall do everything in our power to bring those responsible to justice," Peter Flacton said.

"That's all very nice, but what about Uncle Edward? That won't bring him back, will it? Didn't he have detectives to guard him? What were you all doing to let something like this happen?"

"Miss MacDonald," Peter Flacton replied frigidly, "I assure you this has been the most terrible shock and surprise to us all. At the Cabinet Meeting this morning the Prime Minister expressed not only his deepest regret but also his horror at the occurrence."

"That still doesn't explain how it was allowed to happen," I insisted obstinately.

Peter Flacton suddenly stopped being calm and explanatory.

"Damn it all! Do you suppose I haven't asked myself the question over and over again?"

He looked human for the first time, less stiff and correct and more like a man who was really upset at having lost someone he cared about.

"Well, why don't you do something?" I asked. "Why don't you catch the people? What's the point of sitting here and saying you're sorry. Why, in Canada the Mounties don't let people get away with murder."

"Well, it's a pity you didn't bring some of them over with you," Peter Flacton snapped, and we both stared at each other with angry eyes.

Then he seemed to remember his manners.

"I'm sorry, Miss MacDonald, I know this is a terrible shock for you, but I'm a little on edge myself and I haven't had much sleep since it happened."

"Don't apologise," I said. "I'd rather you did show a little emotion about it instead of the 'imperturbable British calm' I've heard so much about."

He looked for a moment as if he might smile, but instead he reverted to his impersonation of the perfect statesman and replied:

"May I assure you once again, Miss MacDonald, that every thing I can do will be done and that the whole nation will mourn your uncle's death. He has died in the cause of freedom just as surely as if he had been shot in battle."

For a moment, when I heard his words tears prickled my eyes, but I was still angry with him. He irritated me. I thought him rather smug and certainly very pompous, and the whole thing was so muddled . . . letting me arrive and see the house and then be told in a kind of disjointed way what had happened.

It appeared to me that if it was left to Peter Flacton to find Uncle Edward's murderers it was likely that they'd remain free for a long time, so I took off my gloves and said firmly:

"Look here, Mr. Flacton, I want to help. I am going to find out why Uncle Edward was killed and, what's more, I intend to do it quickly."

Peter Flacton couldn't have looked more surprised if I'd announced myself the murderer. His eyebrows shot up and he stared at me. He has dark, rather penetrating eyes.

"I'm afraid that will be impossible."

"Why?"

"Well, for one thing, I thought you would want to return to Canada. I have made inquiries about accommodation and I think we can get you a seat on the aeroplane that is leaving for Lisbon on Monday."

I really boiled with rage then. What right had this young man, whatever his Parliamentary position with Uncle Edward had been, to run my life? I spoke quietly, but I was very angry.

"I don't think you quite understand my position," I said. "I came over here to be secretary to my uncle. Because he has been killed deliberately and in a murderous fashion, that doesn't mean I am prepared to turn straight round and go home again without getting to the bottom of the mystery. I will find out who murdered Uncle Edward or die in the attempt myself."

"But I do assure you, Miss MacDonald, it is quite impossible for you to interfere in these proceedings."

"And I can assure you, Mr. Flacton, that it is not."

We were glaring at each other furiously by this time.

"What about Uncle Edward's other relations?" I asked suddenly. I didn't say "mine".

"Sir Torquil MacFillan has, of course, been informed," was the answer, "but he's in Scotland and will

34

not, I think, be coming south for the funeral tomorrow."

"Are there any others?"

"There's Malcolm MacFillan—he's in Libya with his regiment. Apart from him and various cousins who may or may not turn up, there's only your mother."

"Have you let her know?"

Peter Flacton looked embarrassed.

"I'm afraid not. I thought perhaps you'd like to do that."

"I will cable her," I said. "At the same time I shall tell her that I am staying over here."

"You can do no good."

"That remains to be seen. Now I insist on knowing every detail of what happened . . . where the bomb was put, and who are the most likely people to suspect."

"Good God, girl! This isn't an Edgar Wallace drama!"

Peter Flacton hit the blotting paper hard as he spoke. He had gone quite red in the face and it was with a feeling of satisfaction that I realised I'd roused him at last.

"Isn't it?" I asked coldly. "It's suspiciously like one."

"You don't understand things in England, especially in war time. You just couldn't walk about investigating a crime of which you know nothing. You'll get in the way of the police, and what's more, there are many serious aspects in the case which couldn't be discussed."

"You haven't told me everything, then?" I challenged.

It looked as if I'd caught him out. He hesitated.

"I was speaking generally, of course," he said lamely.

"Nonsense!" I retorted. "It's obvious that you haven't told me the whole truth. Now, suppose we begin."

"Please, Miss MacDonald, go back to Canada." He was pleading with me now. "Honestly, you can do no

35

good by staying here. If you could help, I'd be the first person to ask you to stay."

"Just how much authority have you got?" I asked. "After all, I'm Uncle Edward's niece. I'm apparently the only relation on the spot. Have you got any right to stop me taking an interest in the crime which has caused his death?"

"No, I suppose I haven't," Peter Flacton replied. "But can't you understand—or won't you understand—that there are reasons which can't be divulged to the ordinary person? And if justice is to be done this ghastly and dastardly action must be kept quiet."

"I'll believe that when I know the reasons."

"If I give them to you, will you go back to Canada?"

"No."

I got to my feet and collected my bag and gloves.

"Where are you going?" he asked.

"I'm going to 10 Downing Street. I am going to see the Prime Minister and ask him, not only to tell me the truth but to put me in touch with people who are prepared to avenge my uncle's death."

Peter Flacton looked simply astounded.

"But you can't do that!"

"Why not?"

"Well, you won't be allowed to see the Prime Minister for one thing."

"I'll see him sooner or later," I replied. "and I've a feeling that when he knows who I am he won't refuse to talk to me. He was fond of Uncle Edward and I believe that he, at any rate, would want this mystery cleared up. Good-bye."

I turned towards the door. Peter Flacton got up.

"No, stop! Don't go, Miss MacDonald. Listen . . ."

"Well?" I turned back towards him reluctantly.

"Come and sit down," he begged. "You can't rush away like this. I'll tell you what you want to know. If you are really determined to stay here and see things through you'd better know everything."

He spoke grudgingly, but I knew I'd won. I didn't let

him see my elation, however, but walked slowly towards the chair I'd just vacated.

"Well?" I said again as I sat down.

I looked across the desk at him and I saw that he looked harassed, like a schoolboy when he's come up before an examiner and doesn't know his piece. I couldn't help myself—I smiled.

He looked at me and then he smiled back.

"You're rather an unexpected person."

"Perhaps you haven't met many Canadians?"

"Well, no—are they all like you?"

I had to laugh—it sounded as though he thought me so fearsome.

"Some of them are worse."

"No wonder we gave your country its independence," he countered, and then I had to laugh again.

"You'd much better work with me, Mr. Flacton. I shall want your help and I'd rather have it given me willingly."

"Look here, Miss MacDonald," he said, leaning forward. "You don't understand. I'd do anything in the world for your uncle, but I believe that it would be his wish for you to go home."

I laughed once more, but this time scornfully.

"Uncle Edward's been my favourite relative," I replied, "ever since I can remember. I've admired him, I've always loved him, but I've never known him take the conventional view about anything. If I know my uncle he'd say: 'Mela stay here whatever anyone tells you. If you think you can do some good—go ahead'."

"Do you really think he'd have said that?"

"I'm quite certain of it, unless being a Cabinet Minister turned him into something different overnight."

Peter Flacton shook his head.

"He hadn't changed. He was just as human, just as understanding, and just as revolutionary in his methods. Perhaps that's why he was killed."

"What makes you say that?"

"I'm going to tell you the truth. It may be indiscreet

of me, I may be doing the wrong thing, but somehow you've convinced me that your uncle would have liked you to know."

"Go ahead," I said, drawing my chair eagerly nearer his desk.

"When your uncle was made Minister of Propaganda," Peter Flacton began, "he not only reorganised the method of sending news out of this country, he had also his own system of bringing news in. And by that I mean not only the ordinary straight stuff on international affairs, but information from occupied countries and from Germany herself."

He paused before he continued:

"He was doing brilliantly, in fact, so brilliantly that we ought to have been more anxious about him than we were. I see now that nobody ought to have known where he lived or where he slept."

"Anyway, what happened was this—your uncle received from Germany, through a source which only he, the Prime Minister, and myself know of, a document which would prove of immense value in our efforts to accelerate American co-operation."

Peter dropped his voice.

"It was so secret that I dare not divulge to you its contents, but it will give you some idea of its importance when I tell you that a battleship was to have carried across the Atlantic the person who was to give it into the President's own hands."

"This document was placed by your uncle in a special safe in his study. With it were two other papers of great importance."

"One was the list of our friends in three of the occupied countries—men who could be relied on both to work for us and to render any of our agents assistance; and the other was a report on the production of a factory in the North of England which is making a new and special device to combat the night bomber."

"And you put all these vitally important things in the

safe together?" I asked. "Surely that was putting all your eggs into one basket."

"It sounds crazy now," Peter Flacton agreed, "but it was a specially constructed safe, both fire—and bomb proof."

"Bomb proof!" I echoed. "Then the papers are all right?"

"I'm coming to that. You will remember that very few people knew about these papers. When I heard the noise of the explosion at two o'clock in the morning, I quickly put on a coat and rushed across the street."

He drew a deep breath as if he was remembering what a shock it had been.

"A fire was burning fiercely in the study and when, finally, the fire brigade arrived and we got the flames out it was to find your uncle's body burnt beyond recognition. But he had not moved from his desk and we thought he must have been killed instantaneously by the blast."

"But I don't understand," I said. "If the papers . . ."

Peter Flacton held up his hand.

"Let me go on. None of us who helped put out the flames had any idea that there was anything extraordinary about the bomb until two or three hours later. Then, just before dawn, one of the chiefs of the London area rang me up and after that things began to happen. To cut a long story short, this is what we have discovered. Your uncle was shot through the back while he was sitting at his desk. There was a window behind him, just as there is in this room here. Someone must have got into his own private garden, waited until he was working at his desk alone, murdered him, then entered the room and opened the safe."

"Was it forced?"

"No one knew the combination but your uncle. Even I did not know it. It had been forced open very skilfully and the police think by someone really expert at the game. When the papers had been removed a time bomb was set.

"It was a very large one—you've seen for yourself the damage done—in fact, it was so large that if it hadn't just happened that we know with absolute certainty that no enemy aircraft had been over this particular area, we'd have thought the damage was the result of no ordinary high explosive."

"How do you know that for certain?"

"That is one of the secrets of radio-location. Our idea is not to let the public, or indeed, the murderers, know that we suspect the damage to be anything but the result of an ordinary air raid. The announcement which has been made on the wireless has merely expressed deep regret at your uncle's death owing to enemy action."

"It's enemy action all right," I said a little grimly.

"I'd give everything I possess in the world to see someone swing for this," Peter Flaction said, and I liked the way he said it.

"We'll catch them," I said, "if it takes my whole life —I'm going to catch those devils."

I don't think he believed me, but he held out his hand and solemnly, as if we made a vow, I put mine into his.

Chapter Four

So much happened in one day that it was only when I got to bed that I could begin to sort out events in my mind. It was then that the realisation that I should never see Uncle Edward again made me want to cry, only I'd cried so much in the past ten days that the tears wouldn't come.

Instead, I felt a hot burning anger against those who had killed him and I swore to myself that I would avenge him even if I had to do it entirely alone.

I felt that Peter Flacton, with all the goodwill in the world, lacked the necessary drive and determination. Perhaps it is only his English way; at the same time, I must say I like a man to show when he's roused and when he's angry.

Poker faces are all very well in books —they're merely irritating in real life. But I could see that he meant to be kind to me—at any rate, after he had swallowed the initial pill of my staying in England and not taking his orders to go right back to Canada.

When I asked him where he suggested my staying, he said:

"Here. Unless, of course, you'd prefer to make your own plans."

"Have you got a room for me?"

"Not a very large one, but it's comfortable. And my aunt is keeping house for me. We have two other guests as well, so we shall be quite a party."

Then he took me upstairs to the drawing-room and introduced me to his aunt. She seemed a nice woman, rather elderly but dressed like a girl of eighteen. Her name is Lady Flacton and I learnt that she is only Peter's aunt by marriage and that her husband is a General.

41

There were two other people in the room when we got upstairs. One was a girl, small but very pretty, who sprang to her feet as we came in and exclaimed—"Oh, Peter!"—only she pronounced it "Pe-taire".

The other was a young man. He was dark, rather short, and I thought very good-looking. He had a kind of smiling face with lots of white teeth which flashed when he talked.

"This is Miss Pamela MacDonald," Peter said, and they all composed their faces into that hushed, compassionate look that people assume when someone's been recently bereaved.

When I had shaken hands with Lady Flacton, Peter turned towards the girl.

"This is Vilie de Majlo," he said, "and this is her brother, Max. They are living here with us and we are glad to have them—aren't we, Sybil?"

He turned to his aunt as he spoke. Apparently he always calls her by her Christian name. It made her feel old, she told me later with a simper, to have a nephew who was so grown-up and so distinguished.

I turned to look at Vilie and my first impresssion of her was that she was exactly like a small, fluffy kitten, but I wouldn't be surprised if later she didn't turn into a full-blown cat.

That sounds as if I need a saucer of milk myself, but I soon realised that one person in the household who wasn't pleased to see me was Vilie.

She and her brother told me the story of their lives almost at once. They were Yugo-Slavians, it appeared, and they lived in a huge and "so, so wonderful castle", and they were terribly happy and contented—and then Hitler invaded their country and they had to get away quickly. Vilie touched her dark hair when she told me this and said:

"My grandmother—she was a clever and beautiful woman, but alas! she was a Jewess!"

Anyway, after the most extraordinary adventures and drifting about the Mediterranean in a fishing boat, they were picked up by a British destroyer and taken to Cairo. From there they managed to get to England because apparently they had one desire, and one desire only, to find Peter Flacton.

Their cousin had been at Cambridge with him and had spoken about him so often they felt, in Vilie's words:

"We knew him already. So here we are, you see, so lucky and so happy to have found Pe-taire!"

She gave him a flashing glance from her dark eyes as she spoke.

When she talks she uses her hands and almost every muscle of her body to express what she is saying. Her whole body moves and one expression after another flashes across her heart-shaped face. She is fascinating, I can quite see that, and yet it is impossible not to realise that underneath that soft fluffy exterior there are sharp little claws longing to dig themselves into me for having intruded into the household.

I'm quite certain that neither of the men has the slightest idea that she feels like that, but I am a woman and I understood the tones and inflections of her voice. I also did not miss what was obviously a glint of anger in her eyes when Peter said I wasn't leaving on Monday.

"You couldn't get the reservation then?" she asked.

"That was all right," Peter replied, "but Miss Mac-Donald, having come all this way, wishes to stay a little longer."

"But how nice!" Vilie said, although I knew quite well that she thought it was nothing of the sort.

"I suppose she's in love with Peter," I thought scornfully. "She needn't worry herself—I shan't interfere with her plans!"

Max was different. As soon as his dark eyes met mine I knew he was interested in me. Not that I care what man notices me at the moment, there's only one man I want or will ever want. But I'm not blind and I knew as surely as if he'd said it out loud that Max

43

thought I was attractive and that he, for one, was really delighted to meet me.

I couldn't help being amused at the fuss Lady Flacton and Vilie made over Peter. They both cooed at him and their voices sounded like soft, warm treacle, and if I'd been Peter I should have felt pretty nauseated.

Well, after we'd talked for a bit, Lady Flacton offered to show me my room and she took me upstairs into a really attractive bedroom overlooking the square.

"How pretty!" I exclaimed when I saw a pink taffeta bed against bud green walls.

"I'm so glad you like it. I decorated all this house."

"How clever of you!"

"I've got a shop. I'm afraid it's fallen on hard times since the war, but I love decorating. It gives one a chance to express one's personality. I think that's so important, don't you, Miss MacDonald? To let the fundamental yearnings of one's nature come out."

I didn't know quite what she meant by that, but I agreed.

"Of course, Peter's been an angel to me," she went on. "I really don't know what I'd have done without him. We were terribly hard up before the war, but he introduced me to all sorts of charming and rich people and soon I was overwhelmed with commissions."

"Did your husband help you?" I asked.

She laughed.

"My dear, you've never met my husband. Out of war time he's the typical country squire and thinks only of shooting and dogs. No, he stayed in the country all the year round and I joined him when I could find the time. I had the sweetest little flat, but what with air raids and the servant problem, it was rather frightening in war time living on one's own."

She looked coy and what she thought was girlish.

"So, when Peter suggested that I should come and keep house for him, I was only too delighted. I didn't want to leave London, you see. I still do a certain

44

amount of work at the shop, although every other afternoon I help in the Red Cross depot near here."

"Mr. Flacton isn't married, then? I wondered if he was, having a house of his own."

Lady Flacton looked amused.

"Oh no, he's managed to escape that so far. And it hasn't been easy, I can tell you. Of course, as you've not been to England before you won't know that Peter is what we call a very eligible bachelor."

"Which means he's rich. I suppose?"

"Frightfully," Lady Flacton said in a tone almost of reverence. "His mother was an Australian and her father made absolutely millions by canning meat. Peter was the only child and when she died he was left a millionaire.

"Dear me," she sighed, "it makes me feel quite envious to think what a lot of rich people there are in the Dominions! But perhaps you're rich, too, Miss MacDonald?"

She said it with an innocent, half-humorous air, but I knew quite well she was longing to know exactly to the last sixpence how much I had got.

I know Lady Flacton's type, I've met it before. She's what Daddy always calls "a small-town busybody", longing to know everything about everybody and always feeling that everyone's in better circumstances than she is herself.

Mother says that people like that always make her feel sad—they miss so much in life in their efforts to miss nothing—but I, personally, have always thought them rather bores. Just to annoy Lady Flacton, I looked embarrassed and said:

"I really don't know what you'd call a lot of money over here."

That excited her at once. I could see that she couldn't make up her mind whether to try to sell me something right away or wait until tomorrow

"I'll keep her on tenterhooks," I thought rather unkindly. "Nobody here will know whether I am rich or

45

not and if I pretend to be wealthy and mean it will give her something to puzzle over."

"Well, nobody as pretty as you really needs money," Lady Flacton was saying, and I saw her eyeing my coat and skirt and wondering what it had cost.

The maid came in then and offered to unpack for me, so Lady Flacton, having told me that dinner was at eight o'clock and that there was a bathroom next door, left me alone. I must say I was surprised about the bathroom. Peter Flacton's actually got four in his house.

I've always understood that no house in England had more than one and then it was generally in some inaccessible spot where you had to queue up for it in the cold. The bathroom I use here is just like a Canadian one, blue tiles, a shower, and—more important than anything—really hot water.

While the maid was unpacking, I stood for some moments looking out of the window. I could see two policemen on duty in the street, an errand boy whistling as he went past on his bicycle and a few fat pigeons waddling about looking for food.

It was all very peaceful and very quiet and it was difficult to realise that I was in "the front line" of the war. At least, that's what everyone calls it.

I kept turning over in my mind what had happened and wondering where those precious papers were at the moment. Peter had told me among other things that they expected that whoever had the list of sympathisers in the occupied countries would try to get it back to Germany.

I felt we ought to be going out and doing something. It was maddening and typically English to be changing for dinner, going downstairs to sit through three courses in spite of rationing while it was of the utmost urgency to catch the thieves and murderers.

But they are brave enough—one's got to admit that. Just as we were having a cocktail, the sirens started. I'd never heard an alert before and I think the warning—

that ghastly banshee wail—is almost as terrifying as the bombs.

No one took any notice at all but went on laughing and talking.

Then there was a bump, followed by another . . . the room shook and the candelabra rattled, but still they went on talking . . . I held my breath—suddenly there was a terrific explosion!—an almost continuous noise of bumps and bangs.

I'm afraid I must have looked rather white because Peter suddenly said:

"I'm sorry, Miss MacDonald, I forgot you hadn't been in a raid before. Would you like to go down to the shelter? We're hardened and callous or I would have suggested it before."

"No, of course not, I'd rather stay here with you," I replied, hoping that my voice sounded quite normal.

"They're a long way off," Peter said reassuringly. "It's our guns you hear making so much noise."

"Oh, that's what it is!"

"Poor Miss MacDonald, I'm sure you're terrified," Vilie commiserated. "I was the first time I was in an air raid—but now . . ."

She shrugged her shoulders.

I could see she was longing for me to admit I was frightened, but that made me more determined that wild horses wouldn't make me confess the truth. I laughed rather squeakily.

"I've never been terrified of anything so far. And no Nazi's going to make me afraid."

I saw Peter look at me and suddenly my words sounded pretentious. I remembered that he had been at Dunkirk and all the ghastly stories I had heard of the evacuation came flooding to my mind.

Had he been afraid? I wondered, and for the first time I realised that being brave is not just being unafraid—but carrying on with a job despite one's fear. Maybe the English do feel emotional under that bland exterior—perhaps even imperturbability has its points.

In spite of the air raid, which didn't last long, I enjoyed my dinner. The food was good and Max de Majlo went out of his way to entertain me. He was most attentive and once or twice I thought that Peter Flacton looked amused when he paid me some quite extravagant compliment.

That rather annoyed me because if anyone was being obvious in their intentions it was Vilie. She was wearing a dress of yellow lace which made her look like a small, fluffy and feminine chicken.

She was also seductive in what I should call almost an old-fashioned way; she dropped her eyelashes, pouted, and when she walked! But I can't explain it, she is just thoroughly feline but I have to keep watching her because she's so utterly unlike anything I've ever seen before.

I wondered, too, what Peter Flacton really thinks about her. Any of the men I know would have felt embarrassed by her affectations, but then in Canada we're so hail-fellow-well-met and I knew that was different; this was making love in a European way, and it was difficult for me either to judge it or to compare it with anything I have ever encountered before.

All the same, Vilie made me feel as if I wanted to look people straight in the eyes and give them a hard gripping handshake, just to be the opposite to her, but it was rather difficult to do that with Max trying to whisper "sweet nothings", as Mother would have said, in my ear.

He asked if he could tell my fortune after dinner merely as an excuse to hold my hand. I knew enough to refuse to allow him to do that, but when I said "No" he looked quite astounded and I wondered if I had misunderstood him.

We chatted for about half-an-hour, then Peter got to his feet and said he had to leave as he had promised to see the Home Secretary at nine-thirty.

"I'll walk a little way with you," I said. "I need a breath of air."

"You are going out now!" Vilie exclaimed.

"Why not?" I asked. "I shan't melt in the cold."

Lady Flacton looked surprised too.

"You must be tired, my dear," she suggested. "You've had a long day and a very sad one. Wouldn't you like to go to bed early?"

"I am going to bed early," I said firmly, "but I'd like to walk a little way with Mr. Flacton. That is if he'll have me?"

"I should be delighted," Peter said.

"Shall I come too?" Max suggested. "and then I can walk back with you."

"There are one or two things I'd like to ask Mr. Flacton," I replied, and he looked crushed.

I ran upstairs, got my coat, and met Peter in the hall just as the butler was opening the door for him. When we got outside in the cool, dark night, I said:

"Have you got any news?"

He shook his head.

"I'm hoping the Home Secretary may be able to tell me something. I got a telephone message from him just before dinner."

"Have you any idea what lines he's working on?"

"I know very little," Peter Flacton confessed, "except that the best men in Scotland Yard have been put on to the case. I saw the Chief and one or two others this morning. I think we can safely leave it in their hands."

"I want to meet them—will you arrange that?"

"They won't like it," he said in a worried voice. "They hate people interfering."

"Then they'll just have to put up with it."

"There's another aspect, too, which worries me. I didn't think about it before, but now I've been worrying about it all the evening."

"What's that?"

"It may be dangerous," he said, "for you, I mean. Have you thought about that? The people we are up against, whether they are Germans or of any other nationality, will stop at nothing. That's quite obvious."

"The more dangerous the better as far as I'm concerned."

I suppose my voice was very bitter because I knew that Peter Flacton turned his head sharply towards me, although in the darkness he couldn't see my face.

"You sound unhappy."

"I am."

"You mustn't be," he said gently. "I know your uncle wouldn't have minded dying. He loved life but he always looked on it as a fleeting experience with so much more to come."

I was surprised at Peter Flacton's words. They were not what I would have expected from him.

"I'm not unhappy about Uncle Edward," I answered. "At least—not entirely. I mind him being dead, of course, it has been a terrible shock; but there are other reasons why I'm miserable. Reasons that make me welcome danger, even death itself if it comes."

"Good heavens!—how awful!"

Peter Flacton sounded so startled that I almost laughed.

"Look here," he said, taking my arm, "you mustn't feel like that, you know. We must try to cheer you up. It's rather difficult at the moment because there isn't much going on and of course you're in mourning, but I may be able to think of something."

He sounded as if he was going to take me out to tea and give me an extra lot of chocolate éclaires or meringues! I wanted to say that nothing he could do, could alter my feelings, but I felt that might be unkind.

He was doing his best in a bungling sort of way and suddenly I thought how strange it was to be walking along through the dark streets of London, arm in arm with a man who was limping because his leg had been half shot away at Dunkirk.

In Montreal the lights would be shining, taxis and cars would be taking my friends to the theatre or to the cabarets. In Winnipeg, too, there would be lights and gaiety. I wondered what Tim was doing at the moment!

Peter stopped at the end of the Square.

"I think you ought to go back. I don't want you to get lost."

"All right. Shall I wait up in case you hear anything exciting?"

"No, don't. I may be late. If there's anything very sensational I'll come and tap on your door. And by the way, you will be careful what you say, won't you? I don't want to be unkind, but my aunt sweet though she is, is a terrible chatterbox."

"I gave you my word," I said stiffly. "I am not likely to break it."

"That's all right then. Oh, I forgot to give you a key before we came out. You will find one on my desk in the study."

"Thank you."

"Good-night," Peter said. "And don't be unhappy. You've got so much of your life yet to come."

He turned and disappeared into the darkness. As soon as he had gone I walked slowly back until I came opposite Number 92.

There was a policeman outside and when I stopped in front of the house it seemed for a moment as if he'd move me on, then he shone his lamp in my face and realised that he had seen me a moment before walking with Peter.

"Cold evening miss," he said.

"I suppose I couldn't go inside the house?" I asked.

" 'Fraid not, miss. It isn't safe. The ceilings of the ground floor will probably fall in."

At that moment I was aware of someone else standing near us. The policeman suddenly flashed his lamp and I saw a plump pink and white face distorted with tears.

"Can I help you, ma'am?" the policeman asked.

The woman murmured some incoherent reply, and

51

turned away, her handkerchief to her eyes. I wondered who she was and why she was so unhappy.

After a few more casual remarks to the policeman I went home. I rang the bell and waited for the butler to open the door. He was some time in coming and when he did, looked surprised to see me.

"Wasn't expecting you back so soon, miss," he remarked.

"Mr. Flacton was afraid I'd get lost if I went too far."

I started to go upstairs and then I remembered about the key on Peter's desk. I came down again and went into the study, switching on the lights. I found the key on his blotter and having put it in my bag I thought I'd take a book from one of the bookshelves.

I'd never seen a room with so many books in it; most of them were beautifully bound, but some in the far corner were ordinary novels. I was just taking down one of John Buchan's, whom Daddy knew when he was Govenor-General of Canada, when the door opened quietly and Vilie came in.

She was half across the room before she saw me; then she gave a start as if genuinely frightened.

"Why, what are you doing here?" she exclaimed. "I thought you'd gone out."

"I'm back," I replied unnecessarily.

"And now you're choosing a book."

Her voice was friendly again, the sharpness of her first exclamation had gone.

"Exactly. I don't suppose Mr. Flacton would mind."

She laughed.

"I can answer for him. He would be delighted. You see, I know so well what would please Pe-taire and what wouldn't."

"That must be very nice for him and must save him a lot of trouble." I spoke drily.

Suddenly she darted across the room and slipped her arm through mine.

"My dear, we must be great friends—you must let

52

me call you Pamela. It is such a charming name, so delightful, and you will call me Vilie—yes—Yes? While you are here we shall be just one happy family."

I thought it unlikely, but of course I had to agree.

"I'm always called Mela at home," I said.

"I hope, Mela, you will stay a long time," Vilie smiled. "When are you thinking of going back to Canada?"

I sensed that she was very anxious to know.

"Oh, I shall stay some time now I've come so far," I answered, and saw, with an almost mischievous delight, a flicker of disappointment in her eyes. "And now I am going to bed. I am very tired. Good-night, Vilie."

"Good-night, dear Mela," she replied, "I am so glad you are here."

I didn't answer. I went up to my room, but when I had shut the door I really had to laugh. Vilie's methods might deceive a man like Peter Flacton but they certainly did not deceive me.

Chapter Five

Sybil Flacton took me to the funeral. I'd much rather have gone with Peter, but he apologised and explained that he must go early so as to see the more distinguished mourners into their pews.

Lady Flacton meant well, but she's not a companion one would choose for such an occasion. She kept forgetting that she ought to be sympathetic and chatted away about clothes and other things which interested her.

I didn't really mind, but the service was rather an ordeal, because actually I'd never been to a funeral before.

Sybil also talked about Peter. I've discovered that he is her main topic of conversation. I can't quite understand why he should be such an absorbing interest in her life—unless it is because he has money.

She is the type of woman who would fasten herself like a parasite on to anyone who is rich. At the same time, she really admires her husband's nephew, and I've been quite interested in patching together the story of his life, which I have heard from her in bits at one time or another.

Apparently, Peter's father was brilliant—all the Flactons have been in politics since the days of the first Parliament, or very nearly as long—and Peter's father held, so far as I can make out, practically every post in the Government including that of Prime Minister.

But unfortunately, he died soon after he had taken office and everybody agreed that had he lived the history of England might have been quite different.

Having had to struggle when he was young against the difficulties of keeping up the family places without any money, he very wisely married an heiress. She renovated all the Flacton possessions, and made **them**, according to Sybil, absolutely wonderful.

At the moment, of course, the family place in Wiltshire has been taken over by the military, their London house, in which Peter has never lived as he thought it too large for a bachelor, is the headquarters of the Red Cross, and their place in Scotland is filled with evacuated children.

Sybil told me about the different houses and I must say her descriptions made me long to see them. They sounded so ancient and grand and just as I had expected English life to be lived among the so-called "upper class".

"Peter doesn't care much about any of them," Sybil added. "He just lives for politics. I think he will be brilliant, too, He had already made his mark before the war, but he was not in sympathy with Mr. Chamberlain's policy—he was far too go-ahead. Then as soon as the war started he went out to France with his Yeomanry. Now he's got his chance."

"You mean he will be offered a post in the Government?" I questioned.

"He's certain to get an Under-Secretaryship. It's supposed to be a secret, but I don't mind telling you he was offered one as soon as he got back from France, but he was so devoted to your uncle that he preferred to work with him. Peter's got one very strong characteristic—that's loyalty to those he loves."

I must say I thought rather better of Peter after hearing all this. He's a funny person, or perhaps it's just that I don't understand Englishmen, but he's so reserved—one might call it taciturn—or to use a good old Scottish word—dour.

Mummy used to talk about being "dour" and I never quite understood what she meant, but now I think that's what Peter is.

It's amazing, too, how he manages to avoid being embroiled in a flirtation with Vilie. She does everything she can to attract him short of throwing herself bodily into his arms—and for all I know she may do that too when they are alone.

I don't like her—I know that—just as I do like her brother, although he has involved me in an uncomfortable situation. But that is another story and, for the moment, I want to chronicle events as they happened.

Well, Sybil and I arrived at the funeral and, apart from the beautiful singing of the choir, I can't remember very much of the service because I was trying so hard to prevent myself from crying.

I can't bear people who are emotional in public and I know Uncle Edward would have hated me to make a scene at his funeral. I remember him saying once that he thought people talked a lot of nonsense about death.

He had faced death thousands of times in his life and never worried about it one way or another.

"It's always seemed to me," he said with a smile, "that death offers one pretty good odds of coming in a winner. If there is no after life, well, that's that, and we shan't know anything about it; and if there is, there's a possibility of it being one degree better than the one we have experienced here. It appears, therefore, that we can toss the coin and say. 'Tails you lose, heads I win'."

I kept thinking of him during the service and how he'd have mocked at Sybil Flacton snuffing into her handkerchief, knowing very well that she'd take good care not to cry enough to damage her mascaraed eyelashes or disturb her very cleverly made-up complexion.

She's good-looking and has that thin, rather graceful air of good breeding which seems predominant among English women of a certain age. In her black dress with a really lovely mink cape, which she told me Peter had given her, she looked very distinguished.

But she's so determined to do the right thing at the right moment that I knew long before we got to the service she'd make at least a pretence of crying.

Vilie and Max, I'm thankful to say, didn't come with us. For one thing, they hardly knew Uncle Edward; for another, their religion isn't the same as ours. Sybil and I were alone in the front pew, as Peter sat with the representatives of the Government and Members of Parliament on the other side of the aisle.

There seemed to be a lot of people in the church and we arrived almost the last. I couldn't look very closely at anyone, but as I came into the church I did see, sitting almost in the last pew, a face which seemed vaguely familiar. I couldn't think who it was for a moment, and then I remembered.

It was the woman I had seen the night before by the light of the policeman's lantern. I couldn't mistake that pink and white face, it was still blotched and marked by tears, and once again I wondered who she was and why she was so terribly unhappy about Uncle Edward.

When the service was ended and the coffin was taken from the chancel to the hearse waiting outside, we followed it down the aisle. Only intimate friends were to be present at the cemetery and I had learnt from Peter that we had to motor five or six miles to it.

Peter crossed the aisle and walked beside me as I followed the coffin. As I reached the last pew I had yet another look at the woman who had been crying. She was watching the coffin as it went past her and I have never seen so much sorrow expressed on a face.

She was dressed in black, but a frilly, flamboyant sort of black, with a lace blouse and two or three rows of very large and obviously false pearls. I noticed, too, that her curly hair under a jaunty little feathered hat was much too blonde to be anything but dyed.

She looked out of place in a church, somehow—although perhaps it was horrid of me to think that, because a church ought to be the right place for every sort and condition of person—but I can't explain the impression that she gave me better than by saying that she looked out of place.

I touched Peter's arm.

"Who is that?" I whispered, but he didn't hear what I said.

"What?" he murmured vaguely, and I realised then that he was feeling dreadfully upset.

One wouldn't have known it except for something in the set of his chin and the expression in his eyes. By this time we had passed out into the porch of the church and then Peter hurried me through the crowds and into the waiting car.

I didn't say anything when we started off. Sybil, who had joined us, was still sniffling into her handkerchief, but at the same time making remarks about whom she had seen at the church.

It was so like her to have missed nothing as she walked down the aisle. I knew few of the people that she mentioned so her remarks meant little to me.

As we neared the cemetery I said,

"Who else is coming?"

Peter told me the names of half a dozen of Uncle Edward's intimate friends and they were all men.

Nevertheless, just as the coffin was being lowered into the grave, I saw the woman who had been crying, come walking up the path.

She was carrying a big bunch of red roses. She moved round behind some of the other mourners and I couldn't see her for a moment; and then, as we stood with bowed heads, she stepped forward and threw the red roses on to the coffin.

I saw Peter glance towards her and looked surprised, but she turned round and disappeared quickly the way she had come.

As soon as we got back to the car I asked Peter who she was.

"I haven't an idea. I've never seen her before."

"She looked quite a common woman," Sybil said. "But perhaps she was one of dear Edward's past loves —he must have had many, he was such an attractive man."

"I think it's important to know who she is," I said suddenly.

Peter looked surprised.

"Important? Why?"

I remembered quickly that I musn't say anything in front of Sybil.

"Has Uncle Edward left a will?" I asked.

"I expect so," Peter answered. "In fact, his solicitor asked me at the church if you'd arrived, so perhaps there's some mention of you in it."

I said nothing more until we got back to the house. Then, as Sybil went in through the front door, I turned to Peter.

"I want to go to Uncle Edward's solicitors, and at once. Can you come with me?"

"I can't," he replied. "But why be in such a hurry? Mr. Jarvis will communicate with you if you are a beneficiary."

"Don't be so idiotic!" I said sharply. "You don't suppose I am going to see what Uncle Edward has left me, do you?"

"Then why . . .?" Peter began.

"Just give me the address, and I'll explain everything when I come back." I spoke coldly and I meant to be disagreeable.

After all, it is very annoying to work with someone like Peter Flacton who is not only maddeningly slow but also misunderstands one's motives. As if I should worry for one moment as to whether Uncle Edward had made me his heiress or not! There were other far more important things than that at stake.

"It's Jarvis, Jarvis and Webster, 200 Hanover Square," Peter said. "But look here, Mela . . ."

I felt that he needed to be punished for suspecting me of being mercenary and so I was determined to leave him guessing as to what I was up to.

"Can I take the car?" I interrupted.

"Of course," Peter said, "but won't you . . .?"

Again I cut him off in the middle of a sentence. I pulled the door shut, told the chaffeur where to go, and before Peter could say any more, we had left him behind on the pavement.

Jarvis, Jarvis and Webster's offices were exactly what I had expected English solicitors' offices to be from all the books I had read. They were dark and gloomy and rather moth-eaten. An elderly clerk told that he thought it would be quite impossible for Mr. Jarvis to see me if I hadn't made an appointment.

"Mr. Jarvis has just returned from my uncle's funeral." I said firmly. "Will you tell him that Miss Pamela MacDonald wishes to speak to him."

I was shown into a small and incredibly gloomy waiting-room. There was an aspidistra and one copy of *The Times* on the table in the centre of the room. It was obviously that every effort is made in this country to deter people from finding the law attractive.

After a few minutes, the clerk appeared and said that Mr. Jarvis would see me. He said it reproachfully, as if I had broken all the rules of the office by being allowed into Mr. Jarvis's presence without a previous appointment.

Mr. Jarvis himself, a small, withered, dried-up-looking little man, was, however, genial.

"I've come about my uncle's will, Mr. Jarvis," I said, coming straight to the point.

"Of course, of course, I thought that must be the reason for your visit. As a matter of fact, Miss MacDonald, I was going to get in touch with you. Mr. Flacton told me at the church you had arrived and then I saw you come in with Lady Flacton . . ."

"I haven't come about myself at all," I interrupted, "but I do want to know who are the beneficiaries of my uncle's estate."

Mr. Jarvis rang the bell and told the clerk to bring him Mr. MacFillan's papers. One might have thought that they would have had them ready, but it took at least ten minutes for them to be produced while Mr. Jarvis and I sat making desultory conversation about the weather.

He, of course, expressed his regret at Uncle Edward's death, but when I had thanked him for his sympathy there was nothing else left to say.

Finally, the will arrived and Mr. Jarvis proceeded to read it to me. To my surprise, Uncle Edward had left me quite a lot of money; most of it was to be held on trust until I was twenty-five or married, and another sum went to my mother for her lifetime and to come to me on her death.

When he had finished reading this part of the will, Mr. Jarvis stopped.

"There are one or two legacies," he said. "One to Mr. Hacton and some to various other friends. I don't think we need go into those."

"Oh but we must!" I insisted. "That's exactly what I have come for."

Mr. Jarvis looked surprised.

"I am sorry not to be more explanatory," I said, "but I am very anxious to know, for personal reasons, to whom my uncle has left his money. I wouldn't like you to think I came round here immediately after the funeral just to see how much I benefited myself. As a matter of fact, I hadn't thought of Uncle Edward leaving me anything."

Mr. Jarvis still looked doubtful.

"I can't see . . ." he hesitated.

"Mr. Jarvis," I said, "please believe me that this is a very urgent matter. Won't you read me the rest?"

I wasn't quite certain whether I was entitled to demand to see the will but at any rate I thought it best to keep on the right side of the old man, although he was being very difficult with his humming and hawing.

As soon as he agreed to read me the rest, I understood why. Uncle Edward left his books and certain pictures to Peter, legacies to the servants, and then the will stated:

"To Mrs. Rose Hewlett, of 119 Westminster Court, S.W.1, my oldest and most beloved friend, I leave the residue of my estate and all my personal effects, in some small token of appreciation for all the happiness she has brought me during the past twenty years."

"Thank you," I said as he finished. "Do you know Mrs. Hewlett?"

Mr. Jarvis looked embarrassed.

"I think I have met the lady once. You will excuse me suggesting it, Miss MacDonald, but this is an intimate side of your uncle's life which need not concern you."

"I quite understand, Mr. Jarvis." Getting up, I held out my hand. "Thank you so much. I shall be at Mr. Flacton's house for some weeks if you wish to get in touch with me."

Mr. Jarvis took me to the door. I was sure that he still believed I had come to see him to make certain of how much I benefited. I left him with that impression, but I had found out what I wanted to know.

The car was waiting for me and I told the chauffeur to drive to Westminster Court. When I got there, I dismissed him and went into the ornate red brick building. It had a quiet, old-fashioned atmosphere, the lift was very slow, and outside every flat door were brass knockers polished until you could see your nose in them. I had asked for No. 119, and this was on the top floor. I felt rather nervous as I got out of the lift; then I knocked determinedly on the door.

It was opened by an elderly maid with grey hair.

"Can I see Mrs. Hewlett?"

She looked doubtful.

"Who shall I say it is?"

I told her my name and waited in the hall while she went away. Some minutes passed before she returned.

"Mrs. Hewlett's a bit upset today," she said. "She's sorry, but could you come back tomorrow?"

Then I was certain that I'd come to the right place. I remembered Mrs. Hewlett might not recognise my name.

"Will you say it's the niece of Mr. MacFillan," I

said, "and ask her if she could possibly see me for just a few minutes. I won't keep her long."

The maid disappeared again and I looked round the small, square hall which was hung, surprisingly, with daggers and shields. They looked like the sort of weapons carried by Zulu natives, and then I remembered that Uncle Edward had lived in Africa at one period of his career.

The maid returned. She showed me into a big room overlooking St. James's Park. It was an extraordinary room, I have never in my life seen so many photographs.

They were nearly all signed and a large number of them were in silver frames. They covered the piano, tables, the mantlepiece, a writing-desk, and still more were arranged on little carved shelves on the wall.

There were a comfortable sofa and two or three armchairs which held cushions of all shapes and sizes. Some were black satin with hand-worked appliqué on them, others were in the shape of dolls dressed in taffeta frills, one or two were of red plush with heavy gold tassels hanging from each corner.

I looked round me in amazement. On the walls were dozens of pictures, oil paintings, water colours, and what I supposed to be rather good etchings, all jumbbled together and hung side by side, and over the mantelpiece there was the stuffed head of a stag.

I counted its points and it was a royal. Underneath, it had a small silver plaque which told me it was killed by Edward MacFillan Esquire, on Glenarrach Moor, September 9th, 1907.

I was looking at this when the door opened.

Chapter Six

I had been right. Mrs. Rose Hewlett was the woman I had seen crying outside Uncle Edward's house the night before, in church, and who had thrown a bunch of roses into his grave.

She had taken off her little fashionable hat and her furs, but she still looked somehow overdressed and slightly fantastic. Perhaps it was her hair which was the colour of the brass knocker outside the front door, or perhaps it was the georgette dress trimmed with tiny lace-edged frills and ornamented round the waist with a wide belt of jet beads.

Her face was still swollen and blotched with crying, but she had made an effort to improve the damage with a too-white powder and a dark red lipstick which had smudged a little at the corner of her mouth.

"I hope you will forgive me coming to see you unexpectedly like this, Mrs. Hewlett," I said.

"It's a bit of a surprise, I must admit that," Mrs. Hewlett replied. She had a low, deep voice which was somehow warm and charming in spite of being uneducated.

"Won't you sit down?" she asked. "And what about a glass of port?"

I shook my head. "No, thank you."

"Now don't say no, it'll do you good. Do me a bit of good too, now I come to think if it. I feel I need a drink after what we've been through, but it was a beautiful service, I'll say that for it—beautiful. When I saw all those important people mourning him I felt somehow he'd have been proud."

She took a handkerchief out of her sleeve and held it for a moment to her eyes.

"There! What must you think of me—making a fool

of myself, and I never was one to cry gracefully. Your uncle used to say to me: 'Rosy, don't cry. You're a pretty woman but you look a fright when you cry'."

She turned round and opened the door of a kind of sideboard at the end of the room which, like every other piece of furniture, was covered with photographs. She brought out a cut glass decanter and two glasses.

"Now don't say 'No', Miss MacDonald, it will do you good."

To please her, I let her fill my glass and then she filled her own and we sat down side by side on the sofa.

"How did you find out about me?" Mrs. Hewlett asked. "When Eleanor told me there was a Miss Mac-Donald to see me, I never connected it for a moment with your uncle. Now, of course, I remember that he told me a niece was coming over from Canada. Your mother wired him, didn't she?—said you had a broken heart?"

" 'What shall I do about this?' he said to me. 'Shall I let her come?' "

" 'Of course,' I replied. 'If the girl's unhappy at home the best thing is to get away. There's not a broken heart anywhere that can't be mended by another young man'."

"I shall never forget Tim," I said miserably. "My heart will never be mended."

Rose Hewlett looked at me.

"Is it as bad as all that?"

I nodded.

"Then I'm sorry for you," she said. "If you get it really bad it's hard—especially when you're young. But you'll get over it. You won't thank me for telling you that now, but you will. When you're young and you're pretty—well, the world's at your feet and you wouldn't be human if you didn't give it a bit of a shove to start the ball rolling. But when you're my age—that's when the pinch comes.

"Your uncle was the last man that will ever love me. I'm not saying I shouldn't have mourned him when I

65

was young, when we first met. I should have, but there'd have been other distractions. Now I've only got memories to live on for the rest of my life. Not that I'm complaining mind you. I've had some wonderful happiness with your uncle."

Her eyes filled with tears.

"And he with you," I said. "He's paid you a very lovely tribute in his will."

"That's kind of him, but I wish he hadn't done it. I asked him particularly not to mention me. 'It'll cause talk,' I says. 'You know what the world is.' But there—your uncle always was a pigheaded man, would have things his own way whatever the consequences—however much one might persuade him to do the opposite. What's he said?"

I told her, and slowly the tears brimmed over in her eyes and ran down her powdered cheeks.

"Bless him! God bless him! He was a fine man and we were very happy together."

She looked so pathetic that I put out my hand impulsively and put it over hers.

"I'm so sorry for you."

She gave it a squeeze.

"There, dearie, don't you go troubling yourself. You've got your difficulties and your own life to live. I shall get along all right, but the days are going to seem mighty long when there's no Eddie to come in in the evenings and have a chat."

"You saw a lot of him?" I asked, stupidly perhaps.

She turned to look at me.

"Now look here," she said. "I'm not making any pretences. Your uncle and I lived together as man and wife for over twenty years. He as much as says so, doesn't he, in the will? We had a lot of happiness—a good deal more, I dare say, than many poor devils get in their whole lives.

"We haven't always been together, of course. Sometimes he's had to leave me, like when he went to Canada, but on some of his trips I've gone too. All very re-

66

spectable, travelling under my own name and him under his and meeting in front of people as if we were just friends.

"But there have been times when I've nearly died of laughing when your uncle has come up to me on board ship or in a hotel and said:

"'Fancy seeing you, Mrs. Hewlett. Well, this is a surprise!'

"Act!—why, he could act better than most of them that gets their living by it. Sometimes I think that was half the fun for him—the pretending, the planning, the scheming so that we could be together and others wouldn't know what we were to each other.

"And then suddenly he'd change round and be the very opposite. He'd take me to Paris or the South of France and I'd travel with him and register in hotels as his wife."

"'It won't do you any good, Eddie,' I'd tell him.

"But no, the daredevil in him would out, he'd feel he'd want to defy public opinion—and defy it he would!"

"But you had a little home here?" I said.

Looking round the room, I tried to imagine Uncle Edward in it. He had always seemed a breezy person who liked a lot of space. I couldn't picture him, somehow, in the congested, essentially feminine atmosphere.

"When he first took it," Rosy Hewlett said, "he called it our little pied-à-terre, then gradually he started to think of it as home.

"'There's no place like home, Rosy,' he'd say when he came in of an evening.

"Then when he bought that house in Smith Square —had to keep up appearances in his political position —he had decorators and all to do it for him. When it was finished he took me round.

"'Well, what do you think of it, Rosy?' he asked.

"I didn't want to hurt his feelings and I hesitated, but he slips his arm through mine and gives one of his big

67

laughs—you know how he'd throw his head back and just let go.

" 'No need to say anything, old girl,' he says. 'Your face has told me what you think. It isn't like home, is it?

"It's all right for you, Eddie, I answered, but it's too darned grand for me.

" 'That's exactly what I think myself,' he says.

"We turned round and walked straight out of the house and came back here.

"He took off his shoes, put on the carpet slippers I always kept ready for him, and pulled out his pipe.

" 'Come on, Joan,' he said, putting his arm round me and pulling me down beside him. 'Come and keep your Darby company. We may have gone up a step in the world, but—by jove! we know where we're most comfortable!'

"And yet I think he was proud of his house in some ways. He used to tell me of the fine people he had to lunch and to dinner and what they'd said about his pictures. But always he'd seem happiest here.

"He had an old coat he used to slip on as soon as he arrived—it's hanging up now on my bedroom door—and he'd relax and sometimes when he was tired he'd sleep in the chair, and I wouldn't disturb him, but let him have his snooze out.

"Once he was late for the Prime Minister. He woke with a start and looked at the time.

" 'Rosy,' he said. 'you'll be the ruin of my political career.'

"But when I looked upset he gives me a kiss and said:

" 'I'm not certain that I'm not throwing away the substance for the shadow. You matter a damn sight more to me than all the Acts of Parliament put together.'

"And with that he snatches up his hat and was off before I can say another word. But that was your uncle all over—coming and going like a whirlwind. I never knew when to expect him or when I'd see the last of him. This place is so quiet now that it frightens me."

"Did you meet any of Uncle's friends?" I asked.

"Never had a look at them," Rosy Hewlett replied. "At one time I used to think it was because he was ashamed of me. I'm not a fool, my dear, and I used to wonder why such a clever man as your uncle had stuck to me all these years.

"I knew, too, I wasn't his class and I expected him to keep quiet about me, so to speak, but one day when I said something to that effect—I had a bit of a temper when I was younger—I can't remember what my exact words were but something about thinking his friends too grand for me, he turned and he took me by the shoulder and shook me.

" 'Never say that, Rosy.' he said. 'Never say that. I'm not ashamed of you—I'm ashamed of nothing in my life. I'm proud that you love me and humble enough to thank God on my knees for the happiness we've found together, but I'm a jealous man and I share you with no one.'

" 'You're my woman and I want you all to myself. I don't want you spoilt either by the flattery of those who won't appreciate you or by society who'd take you up if I said the word and laugh at you behind your back.'

" 'This place is our own—we're natural here, man and woman as God made us. Do you suppose I'd jeopardise that for a few miserable luncheons and dinners with those who—Heaven help them—think they're somebodies in a world of pretence?'

"I understood then what your uncle meant. He could escape here—although I don't know why—he was a clever man and I never made any pretence of cleverness. When I was young I was pretty enough and I could dance, too."

"Were you on the stage?" I asked.

Rosy Hewlett got up, and taking a photograph from the piano, put into my hand.

"That's me," she said.

I saw a pretty, round-faced girl dressed as Cleopatra. It was a funny, old-fashioned photograph, but I could see that she had a rather flashy prettiness which might have been appealing.

"Here's another," Mrs. Hewlett said, taking a photograph from the mantelpiece.

In this one, her hair was dressed over a frame and she was smiling toothily into the camera.

"Made quite a name for myself, I did," she said. "Mostly on the halls. They used to call me 'The Living Rose', because I had a stage set in which the curtain went up on me leaning out of a huge vase, all my skirts of pink taffeta hunched round my shoulders.

"Then, after holding the picture for a minute or two, I'd slip down a ladder at the back and come dancing on to the stage. Very pretty, it was. Your uncle used to come and see me night after night."

"Mrs. Hewlett," I said. "I've come . . ."

"Call me Rosy, dearie," she interrupted. "I can't stand being addressed as Mrs. Hewlett. Besides, it reminds me of Hewlett, poor fellow—and a lot of good he's done me in my life! If your uncle hadn't insisted on me keeping the name, I'd have changed it long ago."

"What happened to your husband?" I asked.

"You may well ask," Rosy replied. "Popped off a fortnight after we were married and I have never set eyes on him again. Shouldn't be surprised if he had another wife somewhere, but I couldn't prove it."

"How awful for you!" I said.

"Oh, I don't worry, dearie. There were a lot of men in my life in those days. That was before I met your uncle, mind. I was making quite a success in a small way and then I met a manager—at least that's what he called himself—and he thought up the idea of 'The Living Rose' and put me over big.

"I was getting as much as thirty pounds a week at one period and then your uncle came along and as far as the stage was concerned I sort of fizzled out. I ap-

70

peared a few more times, but it wasn't the same—my heart wasn't in it.

"Besides, we were travelling and no agent's going to worry with a turn who's here today and gone tomorrow. Have another glass of port?"

I shook my head.

"I won't have any more, thank you," I said. "Now I want to ask you something. Did Uncle Edward talk to you about anyone who might bear him a grudge? Had he any enemies?"

"A whole heap of them," Rosy replied. "Nobody gets anywhere in politics who hasn't."

"But did he talk about them?" I insisted. "Anyone in particular—anyone who might wish him out of the way? And not only people but in these last months of war were there any organisations or secret societies that might have had a grudge against Uncle?"

Rosy scratched her head.

"Well, that's a puzzler," she said. "I'm trying to think now. Yes, last month he was talking about someone. Now who was it? Some man or other was worrying him up near Glasgow."

"Near Glasgow?" I echoed.

"Yes, I think that was it, because he talked of going up to Scotland and I didn't want him to go to Glasgow because they'd been having bad raids there. Yes, that was it—something about a man near Glasgow."

"Can you remember any more?" I asked. "The man's name, for instance?"

"There you've got me," Rosy said. "He did mention it, but to tell you the truth, dearie, I got into the habit of not listening very much.

"Your uncle used to talk about so many things and I knew that he was making it clear to himself, putting it all out from A to Z, but not for me—for his own benefit. He had a habit of thinking out loud and he used to say:

" 'This is the only place I dare think, Rosy. Too dangerous these days, now I'm an important person. I

71

might give away Cabinet secrets and be shot at the Tower.'

"He was always one for a joke, was your uncle."

"Oh, but try and remember!" I insisted. "It's frightfully important that you should remember the name of the man."

"Well, now . . ." Rosy said—and then she gave an exclamation and clapped her hands together, "I've got it! It was Mosquito or something like that."

"An Italian name," I said.

"It might have been," she said. "I know I thought it funny at the time. Yes, I'm sure it was Mosquito."

It sounded strange to me. but I could get nothing else out of her. We talked for another half-hour and then I thought I ought to be getting back.

"I'll come and see you again," I promised.

"Do," she begged. "You've cheered me up no end."

I came away from Rosy's flat feeling that I'd seen a very different side of Uncle Edward's character. I wonder if Mother had any idea of what her brother was like or whether I was the only person who had seen him through her eyes as the gay adventurer; through Peter's as the brilliant if revolutionary politician; and through Rosy's eyes as the homely man liking his own fireside.

But Rosy had given me more than a new slant on my uncle. She had given me what I believed was a clue in the hunt for his murderers.

"Mosquito" and "Glasgow"—it wasn't much to go on, but still it was better than nothing. Who knew to what it might lead?

Chapter Seven

Peter really got quite excited when I brought him back my information.

"Glasgow!" he said. "The 'hush-hush' factory I spoke to you about is situated near there."

"Well, then, it's obvious that the people who killed Uncle Edward broke open the safe to get the particulars of this new invention."

"It certainly looks like it," he said. "Provided, of course, that Mrs. Hewlett has put us on the right track. By the way, what made you go and see her?"

I told him about seeing her in the street the first night I arrived and then at the funeral.

"Did you know about her?" I asked.

Peter looked embarrassed.

"Well, everybody did in a sort of way, and although I had not discussed it with your uncle I think he took it for granted that I knew he spent a lot of time with her. 'If you want me, ring me at Westminster 902', he used to say, but he never actually said where he was going."

I laughed.

"How very English! The old tradition, I suppose, that gentlemen don't discuss their womenfolk."

"And not such a bad tradition either," Peter said sharply. "If you'd heard, as I have, some of the younger men speaking about your sex you'd be grateful for those who have the courtesy to respect them."

I was surprised at him speaking like that, and then I smiled.

"You're quite right. And don't think for one moment that I was sneering at Uncle Edward. I think his love for Rosy was a very beautiful thing.

"Tell me about it," Peter said, and I told him most of

73

what she had said to me. He said nothing until I had finished. Then he sighed.

"Your uncle was lucky. I always thought so, but it seems he was even more fortunate than I knew."

"I wonder if it is entirely luck," I remarked contemplatively. "I can't help feeling that a lot of it was courage. I can't imagine the average man of Uncle Edward's standing or position having the pluck to go on with a love affair of that sort once he became important.

"I believe you're right," Peter agreed. "Most of us are cowards at heart—we're afraid to be unconventional."

"Well, I've got something unconventional to suggest to you now," I said. "I am going to do it anyway, and I hope that you'll help me."

"What's that?"

"I'm going up to Glasgow. You'll have to tell me, of course, where that secret factory is; then I'm going to work there or live near enough to find out what's going on."

"I think that will be quite impossible," Peter said with tight lips.

"I was certain you'd say that," I answered calmly. "I should merely have been surprised if you'd agreed. For heaven's sake!—stop doing 'the right thing' and let's do the sensible one for a change!"

"You can, of course, try to find out before we go if there's any well-known agitator with an Italian name, but if such a person isn't known to the police we are far more likely to get results on our own."

"And you think you look like a factory hand?" Peter asked scornfully.

I walked across the room and picked up the *Evening Standard* from the table.

"Look at this," I said, and showed him the picture of a duke's daughter working in a shell factory.

"I don't suppose she's any good."

I threw the paper down on the floor with an angry gesture.

"Oh, will you stop being so sneering and superior! I think you're one of the most odious men I've ever met in my life."

"I'm sorry," Peter said and he sounded it. "I didn't mean that. What actually annoys me is the publicity. Here we are engaged in total war, our backs to the wall and all that sort of thing, and yet the newspapers can't get away from the social angle."

He picked up the newspaper and looked at it disdainfully.

"Instead of putting in the factory worker who's had the best output since the war started they have to fill the pages of the press with photographs of some idiotic debutante who happens to have a title. What's it matter at the moment who goes into a factory? What matters is what comes out.

"I can see your point," I said. "but England has been socially minded for generations. A few years of war aren't going to change that overnight and I suppose that some of the girls who wouldn't demean themselves by working in a factory feel different about it when they realise that they may be working on the same machine with the 'daughter of a duke'."

"You're right," Peter answered. "And you're amazingly sensible in your outlook, Mela. I think we need people like you over here to show us how muddleheaded and how cluttered our brains have become with shibboleths that don't matter."

"You sound quite humble," I said. "I like you like that. It's the insufferable superiority of the English of which I've always been afraid."

"Sometimes I'd like to spank you!" Peter said grimly. "We are superior all right, but not insufferably so."

"If you'd ever met yourself," I teased. "you'd know what I mean."

He looked quite cross, then the clock struck six and I gave an exclamation.

"Listen! This is serious! I want to go up to Glasgow at once. I know my idea's a good one."

75

I took the *Evening Standard* from him because I'd remembered something. On the same page that showed the photograph of the duke's daughter there was also a picture of a canteen.

"That's the idea!" I exclaimed. "We could take a canteen there, you and I."

"I wonder if it would be possible," Peter said doubtfully.

"Possible! Anything is possible, if we make up our minds to it. First of all, go and ring up 'the powers that be' and find out if there's any known person of an Italian name. Then get permission—or whatever you have to get—for us to run a canteen for the 'hush-hush' factory."

"It would be best not to have anyone else with us, if you can manage it. You can drive it and I can dole out the food and drink."

"It's certainly an idea," Peter said. "I was just wondering what people would think."

"Which people?" I asked rudely. "And what the hell does it matter what they think, whoever they might be. This is war! You don't suppose the people who killed Uncle Edward worried what we should think about it."

Peter didn't speak and I went on:

"Well, I'm not going to worry what a few idiots think about me or about you. Besides, why should anybody know? There's no reason to put it in the paper that wealthy Mr. Peter Flacton, M.P., is taking a canteen to Glasgow."

"Of course not!" Peter exclaimed in horror. "I was only thinking about you, not about myself."

"I'll do all the thinking that's necessary about Pamela MacDonald. And between ourselves, she's a sensible young woman who can look after herself."

"That's obvious," Peter said mockingly. "Well, I'll do what you tell me. I shall have to tell the Home Secretary, and heaven knows what he'll say about it!"

"What's he like?" I asked.

"In appearance or character?" Peter countered.

76

"Both."

"He's tall, dark, thin, brilliantly clever, slightly crusty before breakfast, and a bachelor."

"Just my type. I'd better go round and see him myself."

"You'll do nothing of the sort. You're causing enough trouble as it is. Leave it to me. If you don't mind. I prefer my own methods.

I walked towards the door.

"I don't mind what methods you use," I said, "so long as I get what I want."

I didn't give him time to reply. I went upstairs. In the drawing-room I found Max alone, sitting in front of the fire reading the paper.

"Where's everybody?" I asked.

"Sybil's at the Red Cross," he replied, "and Vilie's gone with her. What have you been doing?"

"Lots of things," I replied evasively. "Is that tea, because I'd love a cup?"

"I'll ring for a fresh pot," he said, putting his finger on the bell.

I suddenly realised I was hungry and sat down to a good meal of scones, bread and butter, and eggless cake. When the butler had brought the fresh pot of tea, Max, lighting a cigarette, said suddenly:

"I shan't be here much longer. I'm joining the Free Yugo-Slavian Air Force."

"How lovely for you. Do you like flying?"

He ignored my question and asked: "Will you miss me when I have gone?"

"Of course," I said lightly. "But perhaps I shan't be here myself for very long. I too shall be working. If I stay in England I must get something to do."

"I think you are a very brave and a very lovely person," Max said in a foreign manner which in some strange way robbed the words of any embarrassment.

"I'm glad you think that."

I had finished my tea so I got up from the table. Max

77

suddenly threw his cigarette into the fire and, without any warning at all, put his arms round me.

"You're lovely, Mela," he said, "so, so lovely."

He was very strong and it was quite impossible to struggle against his encircling arms. I tried to move my head, but I was too late. I felt his lips on mine and he held me so close that I could hardly breathe. I started to struggle; even as I did so, the door opened and Peter came in.

Max let me go and we shot apart from each other with a violence that made us both look silly. Peter stood still for a moment, and it seemed to me that there was a glint of anger in his eyes.

"I hope I'm not intruding," he said icily.

There was nothing that I could say. My cheeks were flushed and I made a tremendous effort to appear natural.

"Have you come for some tea?" I asked. "They've just brought a fresh pot."

"No, I don't want any, thank you."

Peter turned on his heel and going out of the room again slammed the door.

I looked at Max.

"There—look what a position you've put me in now! What must Peter think? After all, we've only known each other about ten minutes."

"But I've been looking for you all my life," Max said caressingly.

"Don't be idiotic!" I remarked severely. "What am I to say to Peter, that's what I want to know?"

"Does it matter very much what you say?" Max asked. "Besides, it will do him good to be shocked. The English are so complacent."

It rather annoyed me to hear him speak like that. It seems ridiculous as I'm always running down the English myself, but somehow I didn't like a complete foreigner doing it. After all, whatever we Canadians may say in criticism of the old country it is keeping the controversy in the family.

"I don't think it's for you to criticise the English," I said rudely, but Max was quite unperturbed.

"Darling little spitfire! I'll believe whatever you tell me about them!"

He put out his hands towards me, but I edged away from him round the tea-table.

"Don't you dare touch me!" I said. "I'm annoyed with you."

Max laughed.

"Not really. You like me quite a lot."

He grinned like a mischievous boy and somehow it was awfully hard to be angry with him. Everything about him was naughty in the nicest way.

"Do be sensible," I pleaded. "You're making things very difficult for me."

"That's the last thing I want to do. I want really to make you very happy. Come and sit down, Mela, and let's think how we can be happy together, just you and I."

"I've got no time for happiness," I said, "or for discussions about it. And, as a matter of fact, I am very unhappy. I'm in love with someone in Canada whom I shall never see again."

"But how sorry I am for him!" Max exclaimed, and he said it in such a heartfelt manner that I had to laugh.

"I can't talk to you seriously," I protested. "I shall go upstairs now and have a rest before dinner."

I moved towards the door, but Max caught me before I got there.

"Don't be unkind to me, darling Mela," he said. "I will help you to forget your stupid Canadian friend. They don't understand how to make love, these men from the open spaces. Let me teach you what love is, and we will both be so happy together."

He put his arms round me and tried to kiss me again. It was really very difficult to resist him. I suppose I ought to have flown into a temper but his subtle, yet playful, way of making love was so different from anything I had known before.

79

Being a foreigner made it seem like a game; had it been a Canadian or an Englishman who was trying to kiss me I should have been angry and resentful because it wasn't Tim. Yet with Max I could only feel a sort of cosy warmth and a rather lighthearted amusement at his having fallen for me.

I let him kiss my cheek and then pushed him away.

"I'm going now," I said, "and if you can think of a good explanation to give Peter, you can tell it to me before dinner."

I went up to my room and took off my outdoor things. I thought I'd sit in front of the fire in my dressing-gown for a bit and read. I had just got undressed when there came a tap on the door.

"Who is it?" I asked.

"Mr. Flacton would be grateful if he could see you for a moment," the butler replied.

"Tell him I'll come down," I said.

I wasn't going to put on all my clothes again so I slipped on my dressing-gown and ran downstairs. Peter was in his study sitting at his desk.

"Oh, there you are!" he said. "I've got some news for you which I felt you'd like to hear at once."

He spoke very coldly and I realised he was still angry, though I couldn't see why it should matter to him whether Max kissed me or not—but then, everyone knows that Englishmen are prudes and I suppose he felt responsible as I was under his roof.

"Tell me the news," I said sitting on the arm of a chair near the desk, "and then I'll apologise for shocking you."

"You haven't shocked me in the slightest," he replied primly. "You must behave, of course, as you think best."

"Oh, don't be so smug!" I cried impatiently. "You know you were shocked, though why you should be I can't think. Max has got foreign ways and I really can't be bothered to have a scene. That's the explanation of what you just saw and there's nothing so very sensational about it."

Peter smiled cynically.

"I shouldn't have expected it of you, somehow."

"There's a great many things you haven't expected of me since I came here. So far as I'm concerned you seem to spend your time being either shocked or disappointed. Well, I dare say it's very good for you."

"I'm sure it is," Peter said, "but that's hardly the point, is it?"

I suddenly felt annoyed with him. If there's one thing I dislike it is people who talk to you in such a cold, distant manner that the air freezes round them. I don't mind a good row or people who lose their temper—what I hate is what Mummy and I call "repressions."

"Let's get this straight," I said. "I'm not here to be criticised about my behaviour either by you or anyone else. This is your house, I agree; and if you don't want me to stay in it I can quite easily leave, but as to allowing you to be a self-appointed chaperone, that's a different matter. I'm sorry, Mr. Flacton, but I am my own mistress."

"Very clearly put. And now shall we attend to business?"

"Please do," I said, in a voice which I hoped was as icy and as distant as his.

"Well," Peter started, "I've spoken to the Home Secretary and to the head of our Criminal Investigation Department. They can't think of anyone in the particular area in which we are interested with an Italian name similar to Mosquito, but they do agree that it might be an idea for you and me to make separate investigations to those being made by the police. There's always the chance that their men are known and avoided. They can see no possible danger in our undertaking the plan you suggested."

"The canteen?"

"Exactly—the canteen, and I have arranged for one to be put at our disposal in Glasgow. We can pick it up there in the morning and return it at night. They can keep it full of supplies for us and no questions will be asked as to where we take it."

"Well, that's splendid!" I said enthusiastically. "And when do we start?"

"I thought, if it was convenient to you, we might take the night train. It leaves at ten o'clock. If, of course, you have not other plans?"

I knew he was only being nasty and I jumped up and put my fingers on his lips.

"Don't!" I said. "Don't spoil things by being disagreeable. I am so pleased with what you've accomplished. Now at last things are beginning to move, and I feel certain that we shall discover something."

Peter caught hold of my hand by the wrist and held it.

"I wish I understood you," he said, and his voice was sort of strange.

I took my hand away and laughed.

"Thank heaven you don't! I can imagine nothing more depressing than being understood by an Englishman. But I'm grateful to you. Thank you, Peter, you've turned up trumps."

He looked really pleased at my praising him.

"Now what about clothes?"

"I've thought of that," Peter said proudly. "We will both be provided with a uniform when we take over the canteen."

"Efficient to the last detail! Well, I will go and pack."

"One minute. The only thing I haven't thought of is what we'd say to Sybil."

"That's easy, I'd thought of that already. You must say you are taking me up to stay with my grandfather."

"That's an idea, but . . ."

I wasn't to know what his objection was, for at the moment Sybil and Vilie came into the room. They both looked exceedingly surprised at seeing me standing there in my dress-gown.

"Is anything the matter?" Sybil asked.

To be annoying, I put on a bland expression.

"No. Why should there be?"

Sybil looked disconcerted.

"I just wondered," she said, "seeing that you . . ." She hesitated for words.

". . . Am in my dressing-gown," I supplied. "Oh well, Peter had something rather important to say to me and I ran downstairs just as I was. Peter likes it—in fact, I think you were just remarking what a pretty one it was, weren't you, Peter?"

He looked embarrassed, and there was a perfectly murderous expression on Vilie's face. She moved across the room and touched my sleeve.

"It's charming," she said. "But you must remember, Pamela, that in England people are very conventional —poor Sybil is quite worried as to what the servants will think."

She said it very sweetly, only I felt the claws pricking through the velvet. There was nothing left for me but to smile at Sybil and apologise.

"I'm sorry."

"It's all right, dear child," Sybil replied. "Only, as Vilie says we must remember what the servants might think."

"Dear Mela forgets things like that," Vilie said, "because they have so few servants in Canada."

"We don't have any," I retorted, perhaps unwisely. "We are a democracy and we think the word 'servant' rather degrading. We have 'helpers', however."

"How nice," Sybil said vaguely, but Vilie's eyes sparkled wickedly.

"How delightful," she cooed. "I'm sure that's the sensible way to put it. Now in my father's house in Yugo-Slavia we would have had thirty or forty 'helps'."

She was making fun of me and somehow I felt at a disadvantage. I was sure that Peter thought her wonderful and that everything she said was sparkling with intelligence and kindliness. Only she and I knew that we were fencing for an opening, waiting to deal each other a wounding blow.

It wasn't what she said, but somehow she managed to infer that I was gauche and uncultured, a person who wasn't used to living in the best places. Perhaps she was right.

Anyway, I didn't care. I put my chin in the air and walked towards the door.

"I'd better go and pack. Peter will explain to you that we are going away tonight."

I saw two startled faces staring at me and then I slipped out of the room. I felt triumphantly that I'd had the last word.

Chapter Eight

One has really got to hand it to the British, the way they take things calmly. I wish I knew whether it is "an instinct bred of centuries" or whether it is just lack of imagination.

We had two alerts while we were in the train and nobody took any notice of them, but when we arrived at Glasgow and got out on to the station feeling ready for breakfast and a bath—as one always is after a long night in the train—the sirens went again.

Various wardens called to us:

"Take cover."

As they did so a bomb shook the whole place so that I felt for a moment is if the ground moved beneath me.

"I think perhaps we'd better go into an air-raid shelter," Peter said calmly, and carrying my dressing-case, he led the way.

We went underground and found ourselves in a large, brightly lit shelter where there were all sorts and conditions of people sitting round. I must say it was all quite different from what I expected.

Everyone talked and exchanged opinions and no one seemed to take any notice of the bumps and bangs which we could hear going on up above us. Peter was rather surprising, too.

There was a fat, rather jolly sort of charwoman sitting next to us and she chatted to Peter and he to her. He wasn't a bit standoffish or even as formal and correct in his manner as he is with me in fact I liked him at that moment better than ever before.

There were some children romping about and one of them broke a little toy motor-car and took it to Peter to mend, and when Peter got it going again he gave a whoop of joy and rushed back to play with the others.

"They don't seem to worry, do they?" Peter said to me with a smile.

"Nobody does," I answered.

Then, looking at the people sitting round us who were all working folk—most of the elder women having a shawl over their heads— I said: "I think this is rather good for you. If the war goes on long enough you'll get really democratic."

"We have always been what you call democratic in danger," Peter replied. "It is only those who have never been in the front line who can't understand what a great equalising factor war is."

He spoke very seriously and somehow I felt I had made myself rather cheap, jeering at him. It's funny, but when you are here you can't help feeling that in the essential things the English know what they are about.

It's only that their manner is so infuriating—but still, I mustn't talk about the English now for I am in Scotland, although it is a very different Scotland from what I expected.

Glasgow horrifies me—the long streets of dingy, sordid-looking houses in poignant contrast to the richer quarters. Still, even in the better parts, there is a grimness about Glasgow. I can't explain what I mean—I feel that it is a city built by generations of human endeavour, by sacrifice and suffering. Perhaps I am wrong, but that is the impression it gives me.

When the "All Clear" went—which it did quite quickly, apparently it wasn't what they call a "serious raid"—we hurried out of the shelter and off to the hotel where Peter had arranged we should leave our luggage before going to pick up the canteen.

He was very quiet after we had got a porter and were moving along towards the Central Hotel where we were to stay.

"What's the matter?" I asked.

"I'm worrrying about you," he replied. "Are you quite certain, Mela, that this is a wise thing to do?"

"Good heavens!" I exclaimed. "What a fuss-pot you are! You ought to be a woman, Peter."

He took no notice of my gibe but said quietly:

"I wish you'd change your mind. I still don't think you realise what you are up against and, even if there's no danger, you're going to find it pretty dull and boring."

"Oh, do be quiet!" I said impatiently. "We've gone over this once, if not a dozen times. I've told you what I mean to do and if anyone backs out it will be you. I'm going through with it to the end."

"So be it," Peter said, and we went into the hotel.

When he had left my luggage there and booked me a room, he told the porter to get him a taxi.

"But why?" I asked. "Where are you going?"

"To another hotel."

"How absurd! Surely we can both stay here. I'll trust you."

I laughed as I spoke and it was Peter who looked embarrassed.

"It isn't a question of that. I've got to think of your reputation and—if I'm frank—my own as well. I have a constituency to consider as well as the ordinary conventions."

He paused, then continued:

"You see, in Britain, we have still got a pretty puritanical conception of what is right and what is wrong, and one thing my more eminently respectable electorate would never understand is an unmarried girl as pretty as yourself staying in the same hotel as a bachelor."

He was smiling at me before he had finished his sentence, although I could see that he was deadly serious.

"Oh, all right," I said, "if you feel like that about it, but it's a bit gloomy for me."

There was nothing more I could say. I felt rather wistful as I walked down the miles of corridors to the room Peter had taken for me.

Luckily, I had a sitting-room as well, which Peter explained meant that he could come upstairs and talk to me—otherwise we'd have had to sit permanently in the public lounge.

Well, I unpacked and put on the plainest and most sensible clothes I could find and waited for Peter. Very soon he came round to fetch me, and then we took a taxi to a small street not far from the docks where the canteen was to be waiting for us.

On the way we saw a lot of blitzed houses and they were quite pathetic. It made me almost cry to see the people turning over heaps of rubble in search of their small treasures.

There was a child crying over a broken doll and I wanted to stop the taxi and get out and buy her another, but Peter pointed out severely that we had more important work to do.

"Besides," he said, "you don't want to draw attention to yourself here. As far as anyone knows, you are just an ordinary young woman helping in the war effort, so don't say too much or your accent will give you away."

"My accent!" I retorted scornfully. "You should hear your accent!"

Peter's eyes twinkled.

"Which comes first," he said, "the chicken or the egg?"

But I refused to be drawn into an argument.

"Everyone knows that English people have accents," I said firmly, "so it's no use discussing it."

" 'Everyone', I could presume, being England's Canadian and American sons and daughters who left home to start on their own. Well, well, we live and learn!"

Of course, I could see that I was likely to be worsted in any discussion which followed on this subject, so I started to talk about something else and it wasn't long before we reached the depot.

An elderly woman, dressed in uniform and extremely efficient, handed over the canteen, made us sign various forms, and told Peter that he'd find a parcel addressed to him in the office. The parcel of course, contained our uniforms and I was rather pleased with my overall while Peter seemed to lose quite a lot of his dignity and pompousness in his outfit.

We filled up with petrol, were told to check the food-stuffs in the canteen, and then we set off, Peter driving quickly but, as I might have expected, steadily and with a certain amount of caution.

It's strange how the way a man drives shows his character. Tim, for instance, always tore along at what he and I used to call "a million miles an hour", skidding round corners, racing as soon as we got to an open bit of road where we were not likely to get into trouble with the speed cops.

But Peter kept an even pace and, although I saw it was far more sensible to do so when driving a heavy canteen, it rather irritated me. I was in a hurry to get there, but Peter took no notice when I tried to speed him up.

"I had an old Nannie," he said, "who used to say, 'Better be thirty minutes late this side of eternity than thirty years too early the other side'. She was a wise old woman and the older I get the more I find myself agreeing with her maxims."

"Very few Canadian children have Nannies," I said aggressively. "Most of them are brought up by their parents."

"I expect that's why they are so spoilt."

"We're not spoilt," I retorted.

Then I wondered if he was right.

I suppose in a way I have been spoilt all my life. I have always had everything I wanted and Mummy and Daddy have been too wonderful to me. Really, not being able to have Tim was the first time I had ever been refused anything that was really important to me.

"Why shouldn't one be spoilt?" I asked.

"I've often asked myself that question," Peter said slowly. "Perhaps the answer is to be found there—and there."

He pointed as we passed two almost completely demolished houses, their broken, shattered walls pointing grimly to the sky.

"You mean if people were spoilt they wouldn't be able 'to take it'?" I asked.

"Exactly," Peter said. "And they are magnificent—it's not all newspaper talk. I was down in the East End of London one night when there was a blitz and I have never seen such courage, such fortitude and such a spirit of 'We'll hold on, whatever goes'."

"I shouldn't have thought it mattered if some of those houses did go."

"However squalid they look, they're somebody's homes."

He spoke gently and I felt ashamed. I thought of what a home could mean—a home one had planned and thought of down to the last detail—a home, perhaps, one had just paid for.

To have it turned into a heap of rubble and broken brick must be nearly as bad as facing an empty future with nothing but tears and memories. For a moment there was a lump in my throat, and I couldn't see the road ahead.

"That's it," Peter said suddenly.

I had to swallow and blink before I could see where he was pointing and then, below us where the road curved down a long hill, I saw sheds and roofs of what looked like a kind of shanty town, wooden buildings stretching out over the valley.

We were only a few miles out of Glasgow but already the city was left far behind and we were in an undulating country of pinewoods and wild, heather-covered hills, bounded only by stone walls.

"Shall we be allowed into the factory?" I asked.

"Good gracious, no!" Peter said. "It's frightfully 'hush-hush'. We'll park just outside the gates. I've made inquiries and I find that the W.V.S canteen does that two days a week. This is one of their offdays so we shall have no opposition."

We reached the gates, which were closed and barred

with a sentry standing outside, and then we parked the canteen and Peter helped me pull down the front and make a kind of counter. We had hardly got everything ready before it was twelve o'clock and hundreds of men came surging out, some of them on bicycles, some of them on foot.

It appeared there were several cafés down the road while some of the workers lived nearby and went home to meals, but we were exceedingly busy almost at once.

The men crowded round, asking for tea, for cigarettes, for chocolates, and the meat pies and buns disappeared as if by magic.

It was only when the rush had subsided that I realised that we hadn't had a chance to talk to anyone, in fact it had been all I could do to understand what they were asking for with their strange accents and rough voices.

When we were quiet I pointed out to Peter that so far we hadn't been very successful. He stared at me.

"Good gracious, Mela, you didn't expect results as quickly as that?" he said. "We're new here and you'll find that our customers are shy or suspicious. When they get to know us a bit better they'll stop for a chat or to pass the time of day, and then's our chance."

"But it may take weeks or months!" I wailed.

"More than likely," Peter said calmly. "You can't hurry things. You'll learn that when you've been over here some time."

"I'm not complaining. I only want to get to the bottom of this mystery."

"It needs patience."

"Patience! Patience! Heavens, how sick I am of that word! I'm beginning to think that's the most important virtue of all."

"Perhaps it is—for you," Peter replied.

But before I could think of any really rude retort, someone came up and asked for a cup of tea.

After we had worked until half-past one and the men had gone back into the factory I was glad to have a cup of tea myself and eat a meat pie. They weren't bad in spite of the fact that we only charged a penny for them.

"Now what do we do?" I asked.

"Wait until the men go off duty. Some of them start going home at half-past five, but as they work in shifts I have arranged that we stay open until dark. What we must do now is go up to the village and pick up another consignment of pies and buns."

"You think of everything," I said grudgingly.

"I'm really very efficient," Peter replied.

"You don't give that impression."

"Of course I don't. In Britain we are brought up even as children not to show our emotions. It's a good thing, you know; you wouldn't like us all rushing about waving our hands above our heads and talking excitedly like the French or any of the Latin races."

I wasn't certain if he was teasing me or speaking seriously. After a moment, I said:

"As I've already told you, I find your imperturbable dignity hard to stomach."

"You'll get used to it, and then I hope you'll like it."

Peter dropped his voice on the last words and somehow I got the impression that he meant them very seriously. Impulsively, I put my hand on his arm.

"I'm not really grumbling," I said. "You've been a brick up to date. I do appreciate all you are doing, especially as I know it goes against the grain."

"You don't really think that!"

"Think what?"

"That I don't want to help! That I'm not interested! One day, Mela, I'll tell you just how much this all means to me."

"Tell me now," I said insistently, but at that moment we drew up at the restaurant and so we couldn't go on with the conversation.

By seven o'clock that night I was absolutely dead. As we drove back into Glasgow, I think I fell asleep for a moment with my head against Peter's shoulder. I know I woke up with an awful jerk as we reached the depot where the canteen lived. Peter got a taxi and drove me back to the hotel.

"What time do we start tomorrow?" I asked.

"Not too early," he replied, "about ten-thirty."

"Thank goodness! I've never worked so hard in all my life."

"You'll get used to it," he smiled, "when we've been here a few weeks."

I thought how much my feet ached from standing and my shoulders from bending forward to hand things over the counter. I groaned and Peter laughed.

"You asked for it."

"I know I did," I answered snappily. "But I'm so stiff I feel all my bones are atrophied."

"Well, you'll sleep well—that's one thing. I know I shall."

At the door of the hotel he held out his hand.

"Good-night, Mela."

"Good-night, Peter. If I wasn't so sleepy I'd thank you properly."

"You needn't bother to thank me."

We stood for a moment looking at each other. It was dark and shadowy in the porch of the hotel and the street outside was empty except for our waiting taxi.

For a moment I thought Peter was going to say something, but he didn't—he just pressed my hand, then he turned away.

I don't know why, but I felt rather forlorn as I crossed the big, empty lounge and waited for the elevator to take me up to my ugly cheerless bedroom.

Chapter Nine

It was three days before anything happened. I must admit that, with my usual impatience, I was getting rather fed up.

Canteen work can be very tiring and very monotonous, but what was still more deadly was staying at the hotel by myself, for although Peter had supper with me he would then hurry off, saying that he thought it better that we didn't give anyone the slightest cause for gossip.

I couldn't see who was likely to gossip about us because the hotel seemed full of serious-looking business men and officers of the Army and Navy; but I've discovered that Peter can be very obstinate when he wants to be and nothing I could say would alter him from the course he was determined to pursue.

So when something did happen, I was not only excited at being on the trail but also elated at feeling that my boredom and loneliness had come to an end.

We were serving to the usual crowd at twelve o'clock and doing a brisk trade in meat pies, when I noticed a little man leaning against the side of the canteen as he drank his cup of tea.

I don't know why I should have noticed him particularly out the hundreds of other men who were surging round, except that he was so extraordinarily ugly and he had a large wart on one side of his nose which gave him an almost comical expression—rather like one of the dwarfs in *Snow White*

I was handing out cups of tea, sandwiches, and cigarettes, and then I heard him speak to a man who came hurrying up. His voice was exactly what one might have expected, deep and husky with a kind of lilting intonation.

"I've been waitin' on ye, Jim," I heard him say.

Jim—who was a rather big, rough-looking man with a broken nose—said something I couldn't catch, then the little man with the wart on his nose said:

"Nat Grew is after expectin' the Reverend this evenin'. Can ye come doon about half eight?"

The words seemed to imprint themselves on my mind all the time I was saying—

"That will be twopence . . . Woodbines or Gold Flake? . . . No I'm sorry we haven't got any chocolate . . ."

Suddenly, like a blinding flash, it came to me!

Nat! That was the name for which we had been waiting.

The idea startled me so much that I dropped a cup and, as I did so, I looked to where the little man with the wart on his nose had been standing and saw that he and Jim had walked away together towards the factory gates.

One of the men said—"Hard luck, lass"—and another ejaculated—"Bang goes the profits!"—and it took me a moment or two to realise they were talking about the broken cup, then I filled another one and went on handing out the food.

It was only when the last man had been served that I could relax, turn to Peter and say:

"Peter, I've got it! The name . . . Nat! Don't you see? Rosy thought it was something like Mosquito—that was how it stuck in her mind when she wasn't really listening—but Nat's the name!"

I was so excited that the words were tumbling over themselves out of my mouth. When at last Peter did realise what I was talking about and I had repeated the conversation over and over again, he said slowly:

"You may be right. It's a possibility, at any rate."

"Right! Of course I'm right!" I insisted. "But Peter, how are we going to find out more—where Nat Grew lives and who 'the Reverend' may be?"

"Those are questions for the police to answer," Peter replied, and he started shutting up the canteen.

"The police!" I said. "Do you think they'll know anything? They won't butt in and frighten them away before we really discover anything?"

"They may know nothing," Peter answered. "It may be just a coincidence. At the same time, it strikes me as being quite a sensible explanation that 'Nat' was connected in Rosy's subconscious mind with the word 'mosquito'."

"Do you remember that game we used to play as children when someone thought of an object and you had to say quickly of what it reminded you?"

"Don't talk about games or children or anything except the fact that we may have got a clue," I cried. "Oh, Peter, do you really think we are on to the big thing at last?"

"Now don't get too excited," Peter said infuriatingly. "You've got to keep calm over this, Mela."

"Calm! Have I been anything else for the last three days—sitting round in this gloomy spot?"

"Have you been so very bored?"

"Bored stiff. Haven't you?"

Peter hesitated a moment and then he said:

"No, I can't say that I have. It's been something unusual, something rather interesting and out of the ordinary, and—I've liked being with you."

"Oh Peter," I answered, "you make me sound too rude and disagreeable for words. You've been awfully sweet to me—it's just that I'm in a hurry."

"You are. I've never met anybody in such a hurry as you. You'll have to learn how to make haste slowly—it's an old English characteristic."

"I don't want to do anything of the sort. I want to make haste intensely, quickly, passionately. I'd like to stick a pin into all of you, to put fireworks under your chairs, to galvanise you into action one way or another."

Peter laughed.

"You're like a small whirlwind. Do you know, I'm beginning to enjoy being blown around."

"Don't be so patronising," I retorted, "and couldn't you drive a bit more quickly."

We were on our way back to Glasgow by this time, but it seemed to me that Peter was driving with just the same level cautiousness as he had done on our way out that morning, when he had the whole day ahead of us.

"There's plenty of time," Peter said soothingly. "Besides, I want to get you there safely."

"Oh," I cried, stamping my foot, "you make me want to scream."

"Scream away then! Seriously, Mela, we've got to handle this with care. It's no use rushing into danger or into making fools of ourselves."

"I'm not frightened of doing either," I said scornfully.

"Well, I'd rather avoid both if possible, and I'm afraid you'll have to let me manage this my way."

I wanted to go on jeering at him, to rebel against his authority, and yet somehow—I can't explain why—I couldn't.

I took a look at his face in profile as he watched the road ahead and I realised that there was a look of determination in it and that, whatever I might say, he had every intention of doing things his way. In that moment, all unwittingly and reluctantly I conceived a new respect for Peter Flacton.

Despite all my protests, he dropped me at the hotel.

"I am going round to see the Chief of Police myself and I'll come and tell you about it afterwards."

Of course I wanted to go too, but it was no use, Peter got his own way, and I was left to kick my heels upstairs in the sitting-room until he returned.

When he did, I could see from the moment he opened the door that he had good news. Peter's face is not expressive, but in some funny way his eyes light up and one can tell by the atmosphere about him whether he is glad, or sorry, or annoyed.

"Tell me!" I said, jumping to my feet. "Tell me quickly! I can't wait another moment."

Peter shut the door quietly behind him, then he spoke in a low voice.

"You were right, Mela. Perhaps Nat Grew is the man we are looking for."

"What did the police say?"

"He's known as a pretty undesirable character and they wouldn't be surprised at him being involved in anything unsavoury. He's an Irishman, not a Scot, and before the war had various convictions against him.

"They were mostly for minor offences and, although the police suspected him on two or three occasions of being mixed up in political riots, they've never been able to catch him or pin anything on him.

"They know nothing about anyone called 'the Reverend' and they think it may be just a nickname."

"Well, what are we going to do about it all?" I asked.

"I'm coming to that," Peter said. "Nat Grew and some of his friends lodge down near the docks. The police think it more than likely that if they are holding a meeting of any sort it will be in Grew's lodgings—he and his friends are too well known to risk meeting in public where they might be under observation by a policeman."

He paused and looked at me searchingly.

"Now, the point is this. Are you game to try to get into the lodging-house? We may hear or see nothing. At the same time, there's always a chance of us being lucky. At least we should get to know some of the people by sight."

"But, of course, I'm game."

"I, personally," Peter went on, "was very against you going, but the Chief of police seems to think that it would be far better and far less suspicious if we go together—in fact, quite frankly, he didn't hold a dog's chance of me getting a room if I went there alone."

"Mrs. Mulligan, who keeps the lodging-house, is a difficult woman and he doubts if we shall ever get inside the place, but it's worth trying. As he pointed out to me, it was quite hopeless to send any of his own men down there. In that neighbourhood, he said, they can scent what they call 'a busy' a mile away."

"But of course we'll go."

"Well then, look here," Peter went on. "Your instructions are to exaggerate your accent."

He paused as if waiting for me to protest, but I was too intent on what he was saying to have time for arguments of that sort.

"He's given me the name of a well-known Communist in the States who was over here some years ago. He suggested that you say he gave you Mrs. Mulligan's address."

"And what about you?"

"I am coming as your brother," Peter replied, "and I'm keeping my mouth shut."

As he spoke, there was a knock on the door.

"Come in," I said.

A small pageboy carrying a large suitcase came into the room.

"This has just been left for you miss."

"Why whatever can it be . . ." I started to say, and then I caught Peter's eye.

"Oh yes, I was expecting it," I said lamely, and gave the boy sixpence.

When he had gone I turned to Peter for an explanation.

"Clothes," he said briefly. "You don't imagine you can go down to the dockside looking as you do now, do you?"

We certainly looked very different by the time we had dressed ourselves in the clothes sent round by the police. Peter had a simply ghastly American overcoat in a loud and common check with a belt and a cloth cap which made him look like nothing on earth.

I had a tartan suit and an imitation sealskin fur coat which made me look just like one of the women you see in East Side, New York. I must say the British police are thorough when they do something.

There were even two cheap suitcases with American

labels to stick on them and a note to Peter which said that a certain ship had docked that afternoon, on which we could presumably have been passengers.

We slipped out of the hotel by the side entrance, took a taxi out of the better part of the city, then got on a tram.

I don't think I have ever felt more self-conscious than I did sitting in that tram in those awful clothes, but it was a relief to see that no one took the slightest notice of me or of Peter. Carrying our suitcases we left the tram and turned down a dark, dirty street called Horseferry Row.

"You aren't nervous, are you?" Peter asked as we walked along.

"I've enjoyed myself more. I feel exactly as if I was living in a Phillips Oppenheim novel."

I wasn't going to admit to him that my heart was beating rather fast and I had that funny dry feeling in my throat which one gets when something is about to happen and one isn't certain whether it's going to be nice or nasty.

We found Number Sixty-five and knocked on the door. Nobody came to answer it and after a minute I knocked again and almost immediately it was pulled open and an aggressive-looking woman with red hair stood there.

She was thin and angular-looking in every way and she had a strange scar which reached from the side of her nose right down to her jaw. It gave her a most extraordinary appearance and I found it hard to look into her eyes and not at the scar when I was talking to her.

"Say!" I said, speaking in the most nasal voice possible. "Are you Mrs. Mulligan?"

"And what if Oi am?" she asked intimidatingly.

"Then I'm pleased to meet you," I said, and added in an aside to Peter. "We've come to the right place, big boy."

I then explained that I had been told to lodge here

100

when I came to Glasgow, mentioning the name of the Communist in New York.

"We've only docked this afternoon," I said. "Can you fix us up O.K.?"

She looked us up and down suspiciously and then slowly, as if reluctantly, she said:

"Oi've a double room on the third floor. Ye can take it or leave it."

I felt instinctively that Peter stiffened and quickly, before he could say anything, I responded with—

"Sure, that'll do us fine. My husband and I'll be very glad to have it."

It was impossible for Peter to back out then, and Mrs. Mulligan let us come into the entrance hall after a sharp reminder to us to wipe our feet.

The house smelt horrid. Peter told me afterwards it was really the damp that made it have such a strange odour but I think it was lack of scrubbing too. Anyway, as we walked upstairs I really felt quite sick at the prospect of having to be in such an atmosphere for long.

"Here ye are," Mrs. Mulligan said, throwing open the door.

It was an awful room, the only furniture being one brass bedstead, a chest of drawers with a cracked mirror on top of it, a washstand, and a hatstand with wooden hooks all round it.

"Seven-and-six a night, and pay in advance."

Peter gave her the money, pretending to be a little uncertain as to whether he had got the right amount— which I thought was very good acting on his part.

Finally, when she had snapped out that there was nothing to eat in the house and if we wanted any supper we would have to go out for it, she stamped downstairs again and Peter and I were alone.

"This is most unwise," Peter said.

"What do you mean?" I asked, pretending to look innocent, although I knew perfectly well what he meant.

"Pretending we are husband and wife," Peter said.

"Really, Mela, you do the wildest things without thinking of the consequences."

"I sat down on the bed and started to laugh."

"We might really be married the way you're nagging me."

"It's no joking matter. If we are discovered . . ."

"We shan't be," I interrupted. "Don't be so gloomy, Peter. The only people who are likely to discover us are Nat and Co., in which case he isn't likely to be conventional about it. A sharp knife between the shoulders is very likely his idea of settling the matter."

"Don't talk like that. I wish to goodness I'd never allowed you to get mixed up in this! Besides, having one room halves our chance of learning anything. If you ask me, all we'll do is to sit here all night—hear nothing and see nothing."

"You leave it to me," I said. "The first thing we are going to find out is where Nat's room is."

"Three floors down, I expect," Peter said gloomily.

"What a little ray of sunshine you are!"

I picked up my handbag and went toward the door.

"Where are you going?" Peter asked.

"Ask no questions," I replied brightly. "I'm going to explore."

Leaving him apprehensive and worried I went pattering downstairs to find Mrs. Mulligan. I discovered her in the kitchen where the smell was much worse than in the rest of the house. I must say she didn't seem overjoyed to see me.

"Well, what do you ye want?" she snapped.

"Oh, Mrs. Mulligan," I said in my best sugary voice, "have you got such a thing as some smokes, or is there anywhere near we could get some? My husband's just dying for a smoke and so am I."

"Oi might be letting ye have ten," she said. "They'll cost ye a shilling and a tanner."

"That's fine!" I remarked.

Pretending I hadn't realised that she was grossly over-

102

charging me, I got the money out of my bag and put it on the table.

"Tell me about Glasgow," I said. "This is my first visit here."

Mrs. Mulligan was not to be drawn.

"There ain't nothing Oi can be after tellin' ye won't find out for yerself in time. If ye asked my opinion ye'd much better have stayed in yer ain land instead of gallivantin' across the sea in the time of war."

"We had quite a good trip," I said. "I was frightened, but nothing happened to us."

"Some people are lucky—and some ain't," Mrs. Mulligan growled.

I felt there was nothing more to be said and then, at that moment, as I turned to leave the kitchen, I heard someone slam the front door and a voice shouted:

"I'm back, Mully, Bring us up sommat to eat when you've got it ready."

"Ori right," Mrs. Mulligan replied. "But ye are awful early, Nat."

I had heard all that I wanted. I was out of the kitchen like lightning. I saw a man going up the stairs just ahead of me.

He was dark, stocky, and very broad-shouldered. He went past the first floor past the second, and right up to the floor where our bedroom was. I heard him open the door on the opposite side of the passage and slam it after him.

Then I went hurrying upstairs and back to Peter.

"I've seen him," I whispered.

"Who?" Peter asked.

"Nat Grew," I replied. "And where do you think he's sleeping? In the room the other side of the landing! We can see who comes upstairs and watch for his visitors."

"My goodness!" Peter said, "that is a bit of luck. Are you quite certain it was him?"

"Quite certain," I replied, and I told him the conversation that had passed with Mrs. Mulligan.

"Well, now we wait and see," Peter said. "We shall have to be careful."

The blind was already drawn and the room was lit by one gas jet which had an emergency shade made by a piece of cardboard hammered on to the wall.

"We'd better sit in the dark," I said, "and then we can keep the door slightly open."

We turned out the light, then I picked up my suitcase and put it outside on the landing.

"Why are you doing that?" Peter asked.

"If anyone comes up the stairs," I replied, "I'm going to walk outside and bring in my suitcase."

"You must be careful. Let me do it."

"No. They are far less likely to take account of a woman than of a man."

We sat down to wait on the edge of the bed, the door ajar. It all seemed unreal, somehow, and I couldn't believe it was happening to me. Then, as we waited, the front door slammed and we heard foot-steps coming slowly up the stairs.

"I wonder who this is?" Peter whispered.

We listened to them passing the first floor and again the second.

"They're coming right up," I said, and got ready to go out on the landing.

Chapter Ten

As the man reached the top stair I opened the door boldly and went out.

The stairs were only dimly lit by a gas jet on each landing, turned low, but there was enough light to see and be seen and as I got outside the bedroom door I recognised the little man with the wart on his nose whom I'd first heard mention Nat outside the canteen.

He saw me, but I turned quickly and went back into the bedroom, closing the door behind me. With my ear against it I could hear him hesitate on top of the stairs. Then, after a moment, footsteps crossed the landing and there was the sound of the opposite bedroom door shutting quickly.

"Who was it?" Peter asked in a whisper and I told him.

"I wonder if he remembered seeing you before, I hope not. The slightest thing might make them suspicious and then it could be exceedingly unpleasant for us."

"What could they do?" I asked.

"Not much," Peter said. "At least—I hope not. I took the precaution of having a policeman within call."

"What do you mean?"

In answer he produced something from his pocket and put it into my hand. I could feel that it was a police whistle.

"There are two plain-clothes men up the road. At the sound of that they will come here—and quickly."

We had been talking very quietly but now I said "Shush" and opened the door again. Then we sat on the bed and waited.

"I'll go out the next time," Peter said. "We don't want to take any chances and if your friend with the

105

wart nose opened the door at the same time as someone was coming upstairs and saw you bringing in your suit-cases for the second time he would think it distinctly fishy."

"All right, but I thought you were nervous . . ."

The words died on my lips . . . the door of the bed-room opposite had been opened. Very quietly I pushed ours to, hoping whoever it was coming out had not seen it was ajar. We heard someone go downstairs.

"I bet you any money you like," Peter whispered, "they've gone to inquire who we are."

"Aren't you giving us an undue importance in their minds? After all, this is an ordinary lodging-house, ain't it?"

"Ostensibly." Peter replied. "Yet I don't believe that Nat Grew, if he's the man we think he is, would take any chances. In similar circumstances I should ask questions—wouldn't you?"

I longed to open the door and look outside but I felt it might be unwise. Then, after a few minutes, we heard footsteps returning.

"Let's hope Mrs. Mulligan has given us a good char-acter," Peter said facetiousy, but I knew he was anx-ious.

The footsteps went into the opposite bedroom and the door was shut. Very cautiously I opened our door just a crack; the landing was deserted.

"I wonder what they are planning" I said. "And I wonder, too, if this is really the man we are looking for. Why should Nat Grew, whatever sort of reputation he has got locally, want to murder Uncle Edward?"

"He may not be responsible for it personally," Peter replied, "but he might be in league with some big or-ganisation which is doing such things all over the coun-try."

"What—murdering people?" I asked in horror.

"Sabotage mostly," Peter replied. "My lips are sealed, so I can't tell you much, but I can say that the authorities have been seriously worried for some time about the amount of sabotage which is going on, and are of the opinion that such incidents are not isolated instances but part of a clever thought out plan radiating from one centre, perhaps even from one man."

"Oh, Peter, I do hope we get him!"

"So do I." Peter reached out in the darkness and put his hand over mine. "I think you are being fine about this. I admit your courage, Mela."

I felt as pleased as if he'd given me a medal.

"Thank you, Peter," I whispered, and then suddenly I began to laugh—but silently.

"Why are you laughing?" Peter asked.

"Can't you see the funny side of it? You and I, who haven't known each other long, sitting here in this sordid bedroom, in these ridiculous clothes, talking politely as if we were in a drawing-room. I love your compliments—I do really, Peter. At the same time I can't help feeling that the atmosphere is not quite right for them."

"I see what you mean. At the same time I mean every word of what I said. I do admire you."

"You didn't at first," I challenged.

Peter chuckled.

"I was terrified of you. I always am of people who want to hustle me into things without giving me time to think."

"I think I rather like being called a hustler," I said.

"I should hate it. It always makes me think of one of those sexless women in a masculine coat and skirt with a collar and tie—the type who run an office and bully the clerks who work under them."

"I don't think that sounds like a description of me."

"It certainly isn't that," Peter remarked.

I felt he was going to say something else, and it annoyed me that it was too dark to see his face.

"Tell me what you really think about me. The darkness will hide my blushes."

"Did you ever know how to blush?" he asked in an amused voice.

"Of course I did—and do. What are you suggesting by that remark—that I am hard-boiled?"

"Isn't 'a tough baby' the right expression?"

"Don't be so horrid," I laughed. "When the war's over you'd better come and stay in Canada and you'll see that we don't all talk like second rate Hollywood films."

"I shall keep you to that invitation."

"Now don't let's get off the subject," I admonished. "Go back to where we started. You were going to tell me what you think about me. Go on—be brave—you've got me at a disadvantage. I can't be angry because I daren't raise my voice."

"Would you really like to know?" Peter asked.

I had the impression—I can't really describe why—that the conversation had taken a serious turn.

It was something in his voice, something too that I sensed as I sat next to him. I don't know why but I suddenly felt as if I wanted to hear what he had to say and yet—I didn't. It was a queer feeling, almost one of shyness, which, of course, was absurd.

Then, as I hesitated, he reached out and took my hand again.

"Mela . . ." he began. But what he was going to say I never knew for at that moment the front door slammed.

We both stiffened and Peter's fingers gripped mine hard. We heard someone speak to Mrs. Mulligan. It was a man's voice, rather low, and we couldn't hear what he said, it was just a sound—and then slowly and deliberately we heard footsteps mounting the stairs.

"Wait till he's nearly on the landing," I admonished, "otherwise you may only see the top of his head."

"All right."

The footsteps drew nearer and nearer and then, just when I was afraid he was going to leave it too long, he opened the door and went out.

He was half-way through the door when suddenly he reversed violently, or that's what it seemed to me, and shot back into the room, almost knocking me over, and shut the door to with a sharp click.

"What's the matter?" I asked.

Then, as Peter didn't answer me, I picked up the box of matches where we had left it handy on the washstand and lit the gas jet.

"What's the matter?" I asked again, and turned round to see him standing with his back to the door.

"We've got to get out of here," Peter said.

"Why?" I asked.

"I know that man," he answered, "the man who was coming up the stairs."

"Who is he?"

"He's from my constituency," Peter said.

The tone in which he said it made me realise how serious it was.

"He's the man they call 'the Reverend' all right, and I know why he's got that nickname. He's a lay preacher and he's an ardent pacifist. He's been a fearful nuisance for years in the part of the country I represent and ever since the war started he's been working with some pacifist group who all ought to be interned."

"Pacifism!" I said. "Then you mean they are trying to spread it up here?"

"Exactly," Peter said. "But that's not what we are looking for and, whatever happens, he mustn't see us here. He knows me well and dislikes me intensely— nearly as much as I dislike him. We've crossed swords on several occasions. Come on, Mela, get your coat on."

"Are you certain he didn't recognise you?"

"I don't think so," Peter said. "He was looking at the other door as I saw him in profile and I had time to turn back before he looked towards me—at least, I think I had. One can't be certain of anything."

"Oh Peter, this is too disappointing!" I said, starting to put on my coat. "If this is only a pacifist organisation all our time has been wasted."

"I shouldn't say that," Peter replied. "There may be

more in it than meets the eye. This man Durbin is a trouble maker all right. The police may be glad to know about him."

"But if he's a pacifist he's not likely to be murdering anybody," I said.

"No, that true," Peter answered.

I started to put on my hat in front of the looking-glass.

"Hurry up Mela!" he said impatiently.

"All right," I replied. "but it sounds funny for you to be telling me to hurry—the boot's usually on the other foot."

We picked up our suitcases, opened the door quietly, tip-toed across the landing and started off down the stairs. As we got to the second floor landing, I stopped.

"What are we going to say to Mrs. Mulligan?"

"Good heavens!" Peter said. "I hadn't thought of that. What do you suggest?"

"We'd better say we've decided to go to London tonight instead of waiting till tomorrow. There must be a train about eleven o'clock.

"Sure to be," Peter said. "That's a good idea, Mela. You do the talking. I suppose we couldn't slip out without telling her?"

"We might try," I suggested.

There wasn't much hope of that. The kitchen opened off the hall and as we reached the bottom step of the stairs Mrs. Mulligan put her ugly scarred face round the door.

"Who's that?" she asked, and then, when she saw us, she looked aggressive.

"We have changed our plans, Mrs. Mulligan," I said. "I hope it won't inconvenience you but we thought we'd better not wait till tomorrow to go through to London but try to get the late train tonight. Of course, if there's any extra we owe you . . ."

I only got as far as that before Mrs. Mulligan started. For a moment I couldn't think what she was talking about. She came out into the hall, her arms akimbo, and she started off:

"Oi'll have ye ken that this is a respectable hoose and it's a respectable woman Oi am. Never have Oi let me rooms by the hour and it's not now that Oi'll be startin. Comin' here with yer fancy stories and fancy names! Oi might have been after guessin' as soon as Oi set eyes on ye both what ye was oop to."

She went on and on and it was impossible for us to get a word in edgeways. Also, she was standing between us and the front door and short of pushing her out of the way, there didn't seem to be much we could do.

"Will you please let me explain," I said over and over again.

But she wouldn't listen, she just ranted on, calling us all sorts of fearful things—in fact I've never heard such language and must admit half the time I didn't understand what I did hear.

Just then when it seemed she must stop for sheer lack of breath, Peter got really angry. Regardless of the fact that I'd put a restraining hand on his arm earlier in the conversation, he said:

"Now that's enough of that, my good woman. We will pay you anything we owe you and now we intend to go."

That started Mrs. Mulligan off again.

"Dinna ye 'my good woman' me," she said, "ye . . ."

Then came a stream of abuse from her mouth. The noise was terrific, so much so that neither of us heard someone come downstairs till he was standing only a few yards away from us, then very quietly a voice asked:

"Is there anything I can do to help, Mr. Flacton?"

Peter showed nothing of his feelings but I knew just what they must be. The man who had interrupted us was dark and cadaverous, with untidy grey hair falling across his forehead. He wore dark clothes with a badge of some sort in his buttonhole.

111

He had, I think, one of the nastiest faces I have ever seen: it was cynical, sneering, sardonic, and altogether untrustworthy, and yet one had the impression that he was trying to look like a saint.

Altogether I hated Mr. Durbin on sight, and I realised exactly what a fix Peter was in.

But Peter didn't have time to speak. Mrs. Mulligan did it for him.

"Ye may well ask if aught is the matter, Mr. Durbin," she yelled and started her tale of how we'd pretended to be man and wife, and just exactly what we were in her opinion.

"Perhaps you can persuade Mrs. Mulligan to make less noise and to let us leave quietly," Peter said slowly. "I have already paid what she asked and am ready to reimburse her further should she wish it."

"I expect Mrs. Mulligan is disappointed at losing such an important guest," Mr. Durbin said with a faint smile on his lips.

I could see he was enjoying himself enormously, imagining that he had got Peter exactly where he wanted him.

He hadn't once looked towards me but I knew what he thought and after all it wasn't surprising. I must have looked fantastic in that tartan coat and skirt and imitation fur coat.

"After all," Mr. Durbin went on, as Peter did not speak, "Mrs. Mulligan is very proud of her lodging-house. I do hope you haven't found it uncomfortable?"

"I think that is neither here nor there," Peter began, but Mr. Durbin interrupted him.

"On the contrary, Mr. Flacton, a reputation in this neighbourhood means a great deal. Perhaps you think little of such things but to Mrs. Mulligan it is a very important asset. If, as she says, she let the room to you under the impression you were a married couple, well, naturally she is upset to find she has been deceived."

I saw Peter scowl and knew there was only one thing

I could do. I stepped forward and put my hand on his arm, looking up at him.

"Won't you introduce me to this gentleman, darling?" I said in my most charming voice.

Then, looking directly into Mr. Durbin's eyes, I said:

"I'm afraid we haven't been married long enough for me to have met all of my husband's friends."

"Married!" Mr. Durbin exclaimed.

For a moment he looked genuinely astonished.

"Yes," I said coyly, "but we have been keeping it a secret for family reasons. I know we can rely on you, Mr. Durbin, not to mention it to the Press as yet."

"Of course, of course." Mr. Durbin said then to Peter he added grudgingly: "Congratulations."

"Thank you," Peter said. "And now, perhaps we can be allowed to go. We had planned to stay here tonight but my wife has changed her mind and wishes to go through to London."

"It's all right, Mrs. Mulligan," Mr. Durbin said, "you can believe what this gentleman says."

Mrs. Mulligan moved away from the door with an ill grace.

"Well, all Oi can say," she said, "is that it's a strange way of carryin' on. People shouldna change their minds."

"I quite agree with you," Peter said, "the fault is entirely ours."

He took a pound note from his pocket and handed it to her.

"Perhaps you will accept this in the nature of an apology."

She almost snatched it from him and went into the kitchen, slamming the door.

"Our landlady hardly has 'Ritzy' manners," Mr. Durbin said, smiling, "but then one can hardly expect that in these quarters. I shouldn't have expected you to have found your way here, Mr. Flacton?"

"No?" Peter said vaguely. "You mustn't expect to

keep all the good things to yourself, Durbin. Well, good-night."

I could see that Mr. Durbin was reluctant to let us go and yet there was nothing more he could say or ask. He stood on the doorstep and watched us go down the street. I knew his mind must be seething with curiosity.

We neither of us spoke as we walked away until we reached the end of the road. Then, when we were out of sight Peter took out his handkerchief and mopped his forehead.

"Well," he said, "that's torn it!"

"What will he do?"

"Spread the news everywhere he can. I suppose I can deny it and will do so—after all, it's his word against mine—but how much harm it will do me, remains to be seen. People always prefer to believe the worst."

"Will you have to resign your seat?"

"That again depends entirely on how many people believe Durbin and how much mud he can manage to sling at me."

"You'll just deny it, will you?" I asked curiously.

"I suppose so," Peter said wearily. "But there's one person to whom I shall have to tell the truth."

"Who's that?"

"The Prime Minister."

"But why? Why should you do that?"

"I had a letter this morning saying he wanted to see me immediately on my return to London."

"To offer you a position in the Government?"

Peter nodded.

"I suppose so, and I can't very well refuse it without giving him a reasonable explanation."

"I shouldn't refuse it then," I said quietly.

"Ministers of the Crown can't be involved in scandals," Peter replied bitterly. "It doesn't do them or the Government any good."

"Then I shouldn't be involved in a scandal."

"Involved!" Peter said with a laugh which had no humour in it. "I'm up to my neck in it, Mela. I assure you Durbin is a danger, he is also an avowed enemy of mine. It would be crazy to underestimate the harm he can do me."

"That's why he mustn't be allowed to do you any harm."

"What do you mean?" Peter asked.

He spoke irritably, and, under a street lamp, he put down his suitcase.

"Wait a minute—I must have a cigarette."

He offered me one but I shook my head, then as he lit his own I saw that his hand was trembling. There was something pathetic in that.

I thought of all Peter had been through, the wound he had got at Dunkirk, the plans he had made for the future, and of how, against his better inclination, I had got him into this trouble.

"Peter," I said suddenly, "I don't think you understand what I am trying to say to you."

"I'm sorry, Mela," he answered in a voice which attempted to be light. "Am I being obtuse? This has just knocked me out for the moment. I suppose I might have anticipated something of the sort but it's easy to be wise after the event."

He threw his match into the gutter where it sizzled and died.

"Well, what are you trying to say?" he asked.

His voice sounded cold and disinterested.

"I'm suggesting a way by which there need be no scandal, by which you need be afraid of nothing that man Durbin can say to you."

"Sounds like a riddle to me. All right, I'll buy it. What's the answer?"

I felt the words almost choke in my throat as I said them and yet I forced them out:

"The answer is that I should really be your wife."

Chapter Eleven

Peter didn't speak for a moment and I had the impression that he was absolutely staggered by the idea. Then, very quietly, in a strange voice, he asked:

"Do you mean that?"

"Yes, I do," I replied.

Suddenly I realised that my heart was beating abnormally fast. I felt queer—not exactly afraid—but as if I'd taken a tremendous leap in the dark and wasn't quite certain where I was going to land.

"You understand what you are doing, of course?" Peter said.

Again his voice was very quiet and serious, but I knew he was tremendously moved.

"Of course I do," I answered, looking straight at him.

He looked slightly fantastic in that terrible coat and cap but his expression was as enigmatic as usual and I thought that I must have been mistaken and that he was taking it all as a matter of course.

Yet my own feeling of strangeness remained—and it made me feel shy and inexperienced. Nervously, I began to talk.

"You see, Peter, I quite realise that I have got you into this fix. I know how much your political career means to you—Sybil told me about your father and that you are expected to be just as brilliant as he was. I've gone and made a mess of things for you."

I thought he would say something but he didn't and I continued:

"You'd never have come on this wild goose chase if I hadn't insisted. You'd have stayed in London and let the police do the work. I was wrong—I see that now—I suppose it's too big a thing for me to tackle. So, if I can put things right by marrying you—well, why not?"

"There are your feelings to be considered," Peter said.

His voice was calm, as if we were discussing two strangers rather than ourselves.

"I have considered them," I said. "You see, Peter, it's like this. I am in love with someone else, someone who doesn't want to marry me, and that's why I have come to England—to forget. It doesn't matter much to me what happens now—as far as I'm concerned the future is pretty blank—so if I can make myself useful and put things right, I'll be only too glad."

Peter didn't answer because at that moment a taxi came crawling down the street.

"We can't stand here talking like this," he said.

He hailed the taxi. We picked up our suitcases and jumped in.

"Well?" I asked after we had been going a little way.

"We've got to think," Peter replied. "We can't just rush into things like this—for your sake."

"I'm not rushing into anything," I said impatiently. "Really, Peter, what difficulties you do make! If you want to marry me, say so. If you don't—well, I suppose you're game to face the consequences. And judging by Mr. Durbin's face, they'll be pretty nasty ones."

"Look here," Peter said.

He turned round so as to face me, although it was very dark in the cab and we could neither of us see the other's face.

"Look here, Mela. I think it is the most wonderful thing anyone could offer to do, but I don't feel I can take advantage of your generosity."

"Oh, don't be stupid! Don't you realise that I meant what I said when I told you that the future's a blank for me. When I left Canada I vowed I'd never marry anyone—never . . . never . . . I loved someone with all my heart and soul—I still love him, I always shall love him whoever he marries and if he has twenty wives—so

117

what's it matter what I do? I might just as well marry you as sit about being miserable."

There was a long silence, then Peter said:

"You are very persuasive, Mela, but I don't think you are old enough yet to know your own mind. You'll fall in love again—fall in love with some decent chap."

"Never!" I replied defiantly. "Never! . . . Never! I've told you that and I mean it. If I don't marry you I shall never marry anyone."

Peter suddenly put out his hand and took mine. He held it very gently and then said slowly:

"You understand that if you marry me it is for always? A broken marriage could do me just as much harm politically as a scandal. If you regret it, there'll be no turning back."

His words were solemn and once again I had that strange impression of nervousness, of springing forward to unknown depths; then quickly, so that he should not thing I was hesitating, I said:

"I am still ready to marry you if you want me."

"If I want you!" Peter repeated the words after me— then his voice changed.

"Thank you, Mela," he said quietly. "I'm going to take you at your word."

"Good," I said briskly. "Now, how are we going to do it?"

Peter released my hand and lit himself a cigarette.

"It's got to be done as quickly and as secretly as possible, to be effective. That's an extremely difficult thing to do. The Press are everywhere."

Suddenly he gave an exclamation.

"I've thought of something—something which would solve that problem!"

"What?"

"Listen," he said. "The great difficulty owing to the laws of England will be to get married, even by special licence, without the newspapers getting to hear of it. But there are just a few private chapels where a marriage ceremony is allowed to be performed. One of these belongs to your grandfather."

"We can't go there!"

"Why not?" Peter asked. "I know Sir Torquil; and it's about time he was introduced to his granddaughter, anyway."

"On second thoughts, I rather like the idea," I said. "There's a sort of poetic justice in it—but do you think he'd consent,"

"I shall tell him the truth and I'm certain he'd do anything rather then allow a scandal about one of his family."

"Well, when do we start?" I asked.

"Tonight, if possible," Peter replied.

The taxi drew up at the hotel. Peter told the driver to go to the side entrance so we slipped in unnoticed and upstairs to my suite where we quickly shed the ghastly clothes which had been sent us by the police.

I took some time changing and when I came back Peter was on the telephone. He finished speaking and put down the receiver.

"We may feel we have been failures," he said, "but the Chief Constable is exceedingly interested. He says there has been a lot of pacifist propaganda going on in these parts for some time and they wondered who was instigating it. They intend keeping an eye on Durbin. Apparently they hadn't heard of him before but someone is paying for the literature and various other expenses connected with pacifist activity."

"Is Durbin well off?"

"No, but he might be the agent for someone far bigger than himself. Anyway, what we've reported will be useful. They are going to put some of their men on to watching Durbin and Nat Grew right away."

"I hope they catch them!" I said savagely.

"I don't know. Perhaps they've done us a good turn. 'It's an ill wind,' Mela."

He spoke quite gaily and I looked at him in surprise.

"Don't look so startled," he exclaimed. "Your

eyes are as big as saucers. "I'm feeling happy—do you grudge me that? After all, prospective bridegrooms are supposed to be, you know."

Now I was facing him in the lighted room in my own clothes I felt things were different. I didn't regret what I had suggested, at the same time I felt that it was all rather peculiar and it made it seem even stranger when Peter talked like that about being my husband.

As if he sensed my feelings he changed the subject.

"Listen, Mela, I've looked up the trains. There's one at midnight which will get us within forty miles of Mac-Fillan Castle by nine o'clock tomorrow morning. We can motor the rest of the way. I've already wired your grandfather, warning him of our arrival and I've tried to book sleepers on the train. The station-master has promised to do his best."

"What about the licence?"

"I've thought of that, too. As a matter of fact, the Archbishop of Canterbury is a distant relation of mine. I've put a call through now to his private chaplain. I shall tell him what I want and then, as soon as I have introduced you to your grandfather, I propose leaving you there and taking an aeroplane south to get the licence."

"Oh, must you do that?"

"I'm afraid so. Besides, you aren't nervous, are you?"

"Of course I'm not," I replied quickly. "My grandfather's far more likely to be afraid of me by the time I've finished with him. I have been saving up for a great many years for the day when I could tell him exactly what I think of him."

"Well, don't annoy him too much. Remember, it's of inestimable advantage to be able to be married in the chapel of the Castle."

"I won't forget," I said. But I started planning in my mind what I'd say to Grandfather.

How I wished I could have a talk with Mummy first!

120

But I expect that all she'd have done would have been to beg me not to be unkind but to make a good impression.

Personally I didn't care what sort of impression I made if I could make my grandfather realise what a wonderful person my father is and how utterly mistaken he has been about him.

I didn't have time for much more conversation with Peter. I had to start packing and there was only an hour before our train left. He hurried off to his hotel and even then he was ready before me. When I came into the sitting-room I found he had ordered some sandwiches and a bottle of champagne.

"What extravagance!" I exclaimed at the sight of the champagne.

"I thought you not only deserved it but that we ought to drink each other's health."

"But, of course—what a good idea! Besides, I'm hungry now I come to think of it."

I started to eat a sandwich as Peter opened the champagne and poured me out a glass, then, raising his own glass, he said:

"To the future, Mela—yours and mine—and may we one day find happiness!"

I had lifted my glass to his but now I found I couldn't meet his eyes. I don't know why—perhaps it was silly of me but I felt suddenly ashamed, as if I was doing Peter a mean trick instead of doing him a service.

I can't think why I should feel like that because, after all, I couldn't be kinder or more generous than saying that I will marry him to put right all the trouble that I've got him into, but if I'm truthful that's how I did feel—rather mean, small and sly.

Peter drank from his glass.

"Drink, Mela," he said, for I had forgotten what I was supposed to do and I was just standing there thinking about his words. I drank and tried to smile.

"I can't think of an original toast," I said, "so I'll just add 'Amen' to yours. Will that do?"

"Perfectly," Peter said.

There was a silence between us.

I felt awkward, I thought perhaps he did too, but after a few moments we were talking again quite naturally, and gradually—I dare say the champagne had something to do with it—I began to feel a sense of excitement and adventure creep over me.

After all, it was rather thrilling, and fun, too, to think how we would outwit that horrid man Durbin.

It was only when I got into my sleeper and was alone that I began to feel apprehensive. Here I was, starting a new life with a man who was really a complete stranger to me, and marrying—after I'd sworn I'd never marry anyone except Tim.

I wondered what Tim would say when he heard about it. I couldn't help hoping that all the papers at home would make a great fuss. Peter is distinguished and I suppose from a worldly point of view he is fifty times more important and a better "catch," as Mummy's generation used to call it, than poor Tim.

I told myself that I would never let the people at home outside my own family know why Peter and I married each other. They should just think it was love at first sight—they should never know the truth if I could help it.

There was one thing—I felt that Peter would be easy to handle. He'd be kind to me and let me have my own way, and somehow the years ahead of me didn't seem quite so grim and miserable as they had.

"I'll be a good wife to him," I thought sleepily. "I'll work in his constituency and, what's more, I'll stop Sybil and all those people sponging on him. I'm sure he's awfully weak with them and they get thousands of pounds a year out of him.

I wondered too what Peter thought about it and if he also was lying awake in his sleeper thinking about me. Had he ever been in love? Had there ever been anyone he had wanted to marry? I thought of Vilie's infatuation for him and it really gave me great pleasure to think how annoyed she'd be.

I suppose that's petty and catty, but if I'm honest I must admit it. I don't like Vilie and really no girl should make her intentions so obvious.

But there must have been other women in Peter's life. I thought of how I'd known all about Tim before we got engaged. I'd known most of the girls he'd had "a crush" on and he was absolutely frank with me, telling me exactly how much or how little he had cared for them and what they had meant to him.

I knew nothing about Peter. Then I remembered that he knew nothing about me either. Perhaps it was a good thing—at least there'd be something to talk about and to find out when we were married.

I decided I would go to sleep, but at two o'clock in the morning I was still lying awake while the train rumbled noisily on into the night.

I began to feel frightened—frightened of what I was doing. I felt that my life was rather like the train, seeing only a few yards ahead but rushing on into the unknown.

"It's all very well," I said to myself, "volunteering to save Peter's career, but just supposing that you are utterly miserable when you are married to him—what are you going to do then? Besides, you'll have to live in England."

"I'd forgotten that, of course—forgotten that I should have to stay in England all my life.

"I won't do it," I thought, "I was crazy to say I would. I'll tell Peter now that we'll get out at the next station and take a train back to Glasgow."

I got up and put on my dressing-gown and slippers; but when I switched on the light, suddenly things seemed different. I'd given my word. Besides, I liked Peter, I didn't want to let him down.

I thought of that sneering, triumphant look on Durbin's face as we stood in Mrs. Mulligan's smelly hall; I thought of the words she had used to describe us and her loud, vulgar voice, and of Peter, white and strained, the line of his jaw sharp and tense.

"I'll do it," I said, and, taking off my dressing-gown, I got back into bed.

I think I must have fallen asleep after that for the next thing I knew was the attendant knocking on the door and bringing me a cup of tea. And then I got up and drew up the blind.

My first view of Scotland thrilled me as no other place has ever done before—the real Scotland, I mean, not what I'd seen before of Glasgow and its surroundings. There was a pale spring sunshine over the moors and in the distance the tops of the mountains were covered in snow.

There were burns, crystal clear, running swiftly over grey rocks, and every now and then there was a glimpse in the distance of an emerald green sea.

I can't begin to describe how beautiful it was and it made me feel happy and excited again, and thrilled too at what lay, before me.

"At least I shan't die of boredom in my life," I thought, "anything's better than that."

I began to dress just as Peter knocked on the communicating door and asked if I was awake.

"I'm getting up," I said.

"We should be there in twenty minutes," he told me.

I started to hurry then and was soon ready. I took great care to make myself look attractive. I wasn't going to arrive at my grandfather's castle looking dishevelled or anything but smart and up-to-date.

"I'll teach him to be rude to my parents," I thought.

When I was ready, Peter opened the communicating door.

"Did you have a good night?"

He hesitated and I noticed that his eyes looked tired.

"I don't believe you slept a wink!" I accused. "What was worrying you—the past or the future?"

"Both," Peter said slowly.

Then steadying himself as the train lurched he asked:

"Are you quite certain you haven't changed your mind, Mela? There's a train back to Glasgow if you'd like to catch it."

I felt as if he knew of my doubts and indecision in the night.

"I've made up my mind, Peter," I said, "and I'm not in the habit of changing it."

"Bless you!"

He spoke as if he were relieved but before I could fathom if that was the truth he turned away to pick up my suitcase.

"We're just arriving," he said.

I put on my fur coat and followed him along the corridor. The attendant helped us and we stepped out at the tiny wayside station. It was very cold—but the air was crisp and invigorating and reminded me of the wonderful weather we got in the fall at home.

The train only stopped a few minutes and was moving out of the station by the time we had walked down the platform.

I watched it go, wondering if I ought to feel that it was my last link with the past, but I didn't. I felt at that moment no regrets, only an excited anticipation of what was going to happen now.

There was an old, rather dilapidated-looking taxi waiting for us.

"I wired to the local garage," Peter said. "I'm afraid it's the best they can do."

"As long as it gets us there."

The driver grinned at me.

"Dinna let it worrit ye, miss," he said. "Your motor got an awfu' lot of work in ut yet."

We got in and rattled off. Rattled is the right word, for every window and every joint in that car seemed to have a squeak and a creak of its own. The roads were terrible, Peter explained that the recent snows had broken them up and they'd be repaired later in the spring.

I didn't really mind about the roads, I was so taken up looking at the scenery. We drove along the coast and the cliffs went down sheer on to a sandy beach where the waves were breaking.

Suddenly Peter touched my arm.

"Look" he said, "there's the castle."

I looked ahead and over the undulating moors, high above the surrounding landscape I saw, at the head of a long valley, the grey walls for which my ancestors had fought and died.

Chapter Twelve

I shall never forget my first impressions of the castle.

As we drew nearer in the car it seemed to get larger and larger and more and more grim and austere in appearance until it dominated the whole landscape and I could see nothing else but its gaunt, grey walls with their narrow slit-like windows and great arched entrance.

The gates were open and we drove straight into the big square courtyard. There was no one about but I could hear several dogs barking.

I got out of the car and, for the first time, I felt nervous. Then I remembered that it was Mummy's home and how much she had loved it and somehow I felt braver, as if her spirit was beside me urging me forward.

A very old man came to the door. He was wearing a kilt and, for a moment, I wondered if it was my grandfather and then I realised that he was the butler or whatever the equivalent is in Scotland. Peter took my arm.

"I think the Laird is expecting us."

The old man led the way down a dark passage. I had a glimpse of oak panelled walls, of an ancient winding wood staircase, and then a door was opened for us and we entered the most enormous baronial hall.

The ceiling was very high and the walls were white, but they were almost entirely covered with weapons of every description, guns, pikes, pistols, shields and daggers, which I learnt later should be called a dirk and a skeandhu.

I stood staring until Peter urged me forward and then, at the far end of the room, before a huge log fire,

I saw someone sitting in a high-backed armchair. We walked a few paces and I saw—my grandfather.

He's a magnificent-looking old man, there is no other word to describe him. Although he's getting on for eighty, his back is as straight—if not straighter—than mine, and he holds his head high. His hair is white but his eyebrows over deep set, strangely penetrating blue eyes are still dark.

He too was dressed in a kilt and by his side lay two black retrievers who sat up at our approach, and growled. He said something to them in a deep voice and they lay still, watching us suspiciously.

Slowly, and with an indescribable dignity, he rose to his feet and held out his hand to Peter.

"You got my telegram, sir?" Peter asked.

"I was expecting you," my grandfather replied. "Welcome."

Then he turned towards me. He stared at me and I don't know why, but I felt as if my knees turned to water. I felt, too, that my heart was beating double time. But Peter was quite composed.

"May I introduce, sir, my future wife and your granddaughter, Pamela MacDonald."

"Pamela MacDonald," he repeated very slowly.

"We have come to ask your help," Peter said.

Then, very briefly, he explained what had happened since I arrived in England.

I thought he chose his words well. He explained my devotion to Uncle Edward and how I was determined to discover who his murderers were, then he went on to describe what had happened the previous night.

The old man looked at him while he was talking but occasionally his gaze turned towards me again. Finally Peter finished his tale.

"If you would help us, sir," he said, "we would be exceedingly grateful."

Without a word, my grandfather turned away from us and walked across the hearth-rug to tug at a long red bell-pull which hung from the wall. It was only a few minutes until the door opened and a kilted servant stood waiting.

"Fetch the Minister!"

The servant disappeared and then the Laird beckoned to us to follow him. He walked slowly across the floor to where at the far end of the room the wall was hung with pictures—portraits of men and women.

He stopped before one of them and then, as we drew near, turned to me and put his hand on my shoulder. He pointed and we all looked up.

The picture was that of a woman in eighteenth-century dress but I saw the resemblance at once. It was extraordinarily like me. The woman in the picture had the same coloured hair, the same coloured eyes, and the same shaped face as I have—or rather I have the same as she had.

"It's remarkable!" Peter exclaimed.

"She's a MacFillan," my grandfather said grimly, and I knew that he referred to me and not the woman in the picture.

I felt the pressure of his hand on my shoulder, and somehow at that moment much of my pertness and a great deal of determination ebbed away from me. All the things I had meant to say to my grandfather were lost.

It seems in retrospect both ridiculous and cowardly and yet it was neither of those things; it was something deeper responding to the call of centuries, to the blood from which I had sprung.

We walked slowly back to the fireplace and now I knew that my grandfather had accepted me, had acknowledged me as his kith and kin. We spoke of Uncle Edward, until the door opened and the Minister arrived. I learnt afterwards that his house was only a very short way from the Castle. He, too, was an old man, small and grey but with a kindly face and twinkling eyes which made me like him at once.

He knew Peter, it appeared, and almost at once after

the first moment of shaking hands they started talking about fishing and shooting.

I felt that they would never come to the point and discuss the purpose of our visit or realise that time was of importance.

However, at last my grandfather told Peter to explain why we were here. He did so, and added that he hoped to be back with a special licence by the following morning.

"There's an aerodrome near here, I understand," Peter said.

"It's in the very grounds," the Minister replied.

"All the better. If I go over and see the officer in charge I think I shall be able to arrange for them to take me south. This is one of the few occasions when being a Member of Parliament is really useful."

He turned to my grandfather. "I thought, sir, that you would look after Pamela until I come back."

"We will do that for you," my grandfather replied.

Peter shook hands with him and with me and turned towards the door.

"Thank you," I said. "Goodbye, Peter—good luck."

"I'll come with you," the Minister said. "I will return later and talk with you, Miss Pamela."

Peter went away and I suddenly had a wild desire to call him back, to ask him to take me with him. I hated being left alone without him to support me and, in a way, protect me.

I felt vulnerable here alone in this castle with Grandfather. He made me feel small and insignificant, and for the first time I understood why his family had always been afraid of him and I realised, too, how tremendously brave it had been of my mother to run away from home.

Here there was a mellow peace and a quiet as if the centuries had passed by leaving memories but with the emotions of individuals merged into a pattern. One felt insignificant and trivial—a mere drop in a flowing river.

When Peter had gone I looked towards the pictures. "May I look at them again?" I asked Grandfather.

He nodded and sat down in his chair as I walked across the hall.

It was funny to see family characteristics on so many faces but there was a distinct resemblance in the Mac-Fillans all through the ages. When I had looked at the pictures I discovered a case of miniatures, and in them too I could find an echo of my own nose, in the shape of my face, and even in the way my hair grew back from my forehead.

I supposed it was all more exciting to me than it would have been to many British people who are used to having reminders of their ancestors about the place—pictures, furniture, books, and all sorts of other things which had accumulated through the generations.

But my mother had come to Canada empty-handed and my father, not being the eldest of his family, had received very little from his parents, who in their turn had very little to give.

When I had finished looking at the pictures I walked back to my grandfather. There was a wooden stool by his side and I sat down on it.

"Did they interest you?" he asked.

I nodded my head.

"Tremendously," I said. "I'd like to hear about them and what they did."

He looked pleased.

"My mother has told me a little," I went on, "but, you see, it makes her sad to talk about her home."

I saw his lips tighten and for a moment I wondered if he would tell me not to speak of his daughter, then in a low voice he asked:

"How is she?"

"She's well and happy," I said, "but she misses her family. Haven't you missed her all these years?"

Even as I said the words I felt that they were greatly daring and wondered if he'd reply sharply. He didn't

131

answer for a moment, instead he bent down and stroked the black head of one of the retrievers.

"Ay," he said at length. "We've missed her."

"Why did you hate my father so?" I asked. "Was it because he was a Canadian, or was it because he was a MacDonald?"

Grandfather looked into the fire, at the flames that were licking round the great log stretched across two steel dogs. Then, after a moment, he began to speak.

I can't remember his exact words but he made the story as he told it seem real, he made it live, and he made it so poignant that it was hard to remember that he was talking about something that had happened not yesterday but centuries ago.

He told me how once the MacFillan clan had been quite a large one. They had built this castle where their chieftain lived and the clan settled in the valley. They were not sheep stealers or meandering robbers like so many of the Scotch clans, they had a fine chieftain of noble character who gave them laws which made them respect other people's property as well as their own.

They were happy and prosperous, they had a great many head of cattle and many sheep too, so that they were never in want.

Then one day they had a call to help another clan that was in distress about thirty or forty miles away. It was a call of friendship and could not be ignored, so the fighting men went off, leaving only a few youths or men who were too old to fight to guard their women and their livestock.

While they were gone, the MacDonalds came down over the hills; they looted and stole everything on which they could lay hands; they killed the youths and the old men and they carried off the young women and the children along with the cattle and the sheep. They set fire to the crofts and tried to burn the Castle.

When the MacFillans returned they found only the smoking ruins of what had once been their homes; they found a land stripped bare of everything which had made them prosperous and happy.

They had, of course, followed the MacDonalds, angry and bitter, vowing their vengeance. It had been some months before they could come to grips with them and then the battle which had been fought had gone against the MacFillans.

They were outnumbered and outmanoeuvred in a part of the country which they did not know. Only a few had escaped alive to return to their own valley.

Of the remnant that returned, the chieftain's youngest son was one. He inherited the Castle and became head of the clan, for his father and brothers had all been killed.

From him we were descended and as Grandfather told the story I understood how, all down the ages, the tale of the MacDonalds' treachery and cruelty had remained an open wound, for vengeance had never been exacted, retribution had never been paid.

If I had heard the same story in Canada I suppose I'd have laughed and thought it ridiculous, but hearing my grandfather tell the tale as we sat in that great room hung with the ancient weapons of war I understood many things which had escaped my comprehension in the past.

I could hear in the tones of his voice how deeply personal was his grievance, how to him all MacDonalds would be the same—treacherous, cruel, thieves and despoilers of women.

For his only daughter, whom he loved, to run away with a MacDonald was a bitterness almost beyond words.

Yes, I could see that, and somehow as he talked it was hard to understand how my mother could ever let herself fall in love with a MacDonald. She must have been brought up on that story.

I felt that had I heard it from the cradle I would have shrunk almost in horror from any man bearing the name.

133

As my grandfather finished speaking I seemed to come back into the modern world from a long, long distance. I put out my hand and touched his arm.

"Thank you for telling me," I said. "For the first time I understand your point of view. For years I have been thinking you cruel and hard. Now, though I still think it a pity, I do to a certain extent understand your feelings."

And then I started to tell him about my father. I told him how his people had gone to Canada, how he had started as a little boy to help in the lumber yards; I told him how he had worked his way upwards until now he was head of the whole department of the Government which dealt with the forestry; and I told him, too, how happy he had made my mother.

Grandfather did not interrupt me. When I had finished speaking he made no comment. Instead, after a long silence, he rose to his feet.

"Come along. I am going to show you the Castle."

Then he took me on one of the most exciting sightseeing tours I have ever been. He showed me the original walls; he showed me the turrets, now half-ruined, in which one climbed up narrow, twisted staircases to tiny, circular rooms through which one could look out over the whole countryside. He took me along the battlements and to the ruins of the old keep.

I discovered that the part of the Castle now habitable was very small compared with what it had once been, but while I was impressed by the magnificence and age of it I noticed something else.

I saw signs of poverty everywhere; the carpets and the curtains were threadbare and there were no modern conveniences such as we have taken for granted as being essential.

The only lighting was from oil lamps or candles; in the kitchen they cooked on an old fashioned open fire and used ovens which had been in existence for over a hundred years. There were, of course, no bathrooms and no water supply laid on in the house.

The water was fetched from a deep well sunk in the courtyard which had been discovered when the Castle was first built and which had enabled my ancestors in the past to withstand a siege from the Duke of Cumberland's forces.

I discovered, too, that there were very few servants. The old man who had opened the door—his name is Robert Munro—has been with my grandfather all his life. His wife, who is nearly as old as he is, does the cooking and there is another old woman who comes in to help sometimes.

Her name is Jeannie Ross and I learnt that she had nursed my mother when she was a child.

She cried when she knew who I was and put her hands on mine and blessed me, and told me that she had loved my mother all her life and never forgotten her.

Finally, we stood on the battlements again looking out over the moors while my grandfather pointed to the distant mountains and told me their names.

While we were doing so, I saw an aeroplane come over the Castle and swoop down and circle round the fields below, getting ready to land.

"It seems funny," I said, "to see something so modern here,"

Grandfather did not answer, he was still looking over his land and I thought that he was hardly aware that the world had altered since he was a boy. He pointed out the salmon river to me, silver as it caught the sunshine, winding its way slowly down the valley, and showed me where a family of young grouse were dusting themselves in the driveway.

Then he fetched what he called his "glass", but what I have always known as a telescope, and showed me a stag lying high up on the moors against the autumn burnings.

It was difficult to see and it took me some time to distinguish him, but then I was thrilled.

"This will be something to tell Mummy," I thought.

I remember how once she had told me that she used to watch the stags from her bedroom window and then try to stalk them all on her own without the help of a ghillie.

Soon it was time for luncheon and we went down to sit opposite one another at an ancient refectory table in a big dining-hall. The Minister had come back just before luncheon and my grandfather asked him to stay and eat with us.

He started to ask me questions about Peter and I found them rather difficult to answer. He was a kindly old man and I felt quite certain that he had got it into his head that we were two people who had fallen madly in love with each other the first time we had met.

He thought it all very romantic that we wished to get married in such a hurry and secretly.

But once or twice I realised that Grandfather's eyes were on me and wondered if he, knowing the true story, did not guess the real reason for my marrying Peter.

All the same, I felt it was greatly in Peter's favour that the old man like him. There was no doubt about that, and I felt that Peter ought to feel honoured. I couldn't help wishing that some of my friends in Canada could have seen me in the Castle and, what was more, the Castle itself.

It was impressive, there was no getting away from that, and although the luncheon was a small one and not particularly appetising it was served up on huge silver dishes which were engraved with the family crest.

As we finished luncheon the Minister said:

"By the way, Miss Pamela, when I went down to the aerodrome with Peter Flacton we found there were some Canadians there. I wondered if you'd like to go down this afternoon and have a talk with them. They have only recently arrived and I expect they are feeling pretty homesick. It would be a kindly action on your part."

I was just going to accept and then I realised that it

was a great mistake for me to see anybody until I was Peter's wife.

After all, one never knew how these things might be linked up and if Durbin was as dangerous as Peter thought, the fewer people who were introduced to me at this moment as Pamela MacDonald the better.

"I don't think I'll go this afternoon," I said.

I glanced at my grandfather, and as if he understood what I was thinking he said:

"No, let the child stay here. There's lots for her to see in the Castle."

I smiled at him and for the first time he smiled back.

"He's really rather an old dear," I thought.

Chapter Thirteen

I suppose everyone feels strange on their wedding day. I know I did on mine, and I felt, too, that my wedding had a strangeness peculiarly its own.

I was even rivalling Mummy, who, having eloped with my father, had not been able to get married until they arrived in Canada.

Peter did not get back to the Castle until nearly tea-time. We had been expecting him since early morning but apparently he had been held up with one thing or another.

When he did arrive, I had been so anxious about him that I forgot everything except my relief at seeing him safe and sound. I had thought of all the frightful things that could happen to him—an air crash on the way, or being involved in a fight with an enemy raider—and I suppose my imagination got beyond control, for I had worked myself up into a state of tense anxiety.

I felt isolated at the Castle, as though I were the imprisoned maiden of the fairy tale and Peter the knight coming to rescue me.

It sounds silly now but there was something in the atmosphere diffused by those old walls which was conducive to drama and romance—and one couldn't remain unaffected by it.

After twenty-four hours there I could understand why my mother had run away with the man she loved. Had she lived in an ordinary house, she might have thought it over and decided the risk wasn't worth it, but in the Castle her surroundings would urge her on to show courage, bravery and initiative.

All the MacFillans have been brave, all of them have shown individual courage. I could quite understand how

Uncle Edward could defy respectability and live with Rosy.

As I had said to Peter, that sort of thing requires courage just as much as going out to fight an enemy and Uncle Edward undoubtedly had inherited the courage of his forebears. Mummy was no exception to the family rule and I suppose that same courage constitutes part of my own make-up.

But that did not prevent me worrying about Peter.

I was genuinely glad to see him when he arrived. I was sitting in the big sitting-room with Grandfather when he walked in at the door.

We both got to our feet.

"Peter!" I exclaimed. "What has happened to you? I've been so worried."

"I'm sorry about that, Mela," he said.

But he looked more pleased than sorry and held both my hands very tightly for a moment. Then he walked across to Grandfather.

"I hope you haven't been anxious, sir."

"I felt no news was good news," Grandfather replied. "It was this young woman here who was trying to give herself grey hairs."

"I'm flattered," Peter said, and he looked at me.

"Have you got the marriage licence?" Grandfather asked.

"I have," Peter replied.

"Then the sooner the ceremony is performed the better."

With these words the old man walked across the hearth-rug, just as he had when we had first told him our need for haste, and rang the bell. Munro came to the door and was told to fetch the Minister. Peter and I stood silent.

He was looking at me and just for a moment I felt a sudden fear, a sort of shrinking within myself. Was it possible that the moment had really come for me to marry him?

But before I did so I had a surprise for him. Jeannie

Ross had been told that morning that I was going to be married and when she heard the news had produced from an old dower chest, where it was always kept, the most exquisite lace-veil I have ever seen.

She told me that it had been in the family for generations, that every MacFillan girl wore it when she was a bride, and that every MacFillan was christened in it.

Of course she wanted me to wear it and at first I thought I must refuse as I hadn't got a suitable dress, whereupon she looked very disappointed, and I felt that Grandfather would be disappointed too if the tradition was broken.

Then I looked in my cases and found that I had packed among other things what the Americans call a "hostess gown." It had been brought me from New York and was in white quilted satin with a tiny pattern of blue and silver leaves on it. I had often worn it as a dressing-gown, although it was useful to slip on for dinner when I was tired or in a hurry.

It seemed a funny thing to use as a wedding dress and yet I saw that the veil would look very pretty over it. The lace had become parchment-coloured with years, so that anything dead white would have been an ugly contrast.

As soon as the Minister had arrived and was talking to Peter, I slipped upstairs. Jeannie was waiting for me, my gown was laid out on the bed and she held the lace veil in her hands.

All the time I was changing she talked to me in her soft, Scotch voice and there were tears in her eyes as finally she pinned the veil into place, then stood back murmuring blessings.

I felt shy and self-conscious as I went down the oak staircase. Grandfather and Peter were waiting for me in the hall and as I appeared they both looked up.

I came down slowly, holding in my hand a prayer-book which Jeannie had told me belonged to my mother. As I reached the men I heard Grandfather murmur:

"She's a MacFillan!"

I knew he could not have paid me a greater compliment. I did not look at Peter although I was aware that he was looking at me . . .

I suddenly felt desperately shy, I longed to run away . . .

We walked down the long passages which led through the house to the chapel. As we reached the door, Grandfather turned to offer me his arm and slowly we walked up the narrow aisle to the altar.

The chapel is very old, and built into the Castle itself; but as the only church in the neighbourhood was burnt down about ten years ago it is used by all the local inhabitants who, the Minister told me, walk miles across the moors on Sundays to attend service.

Now, of course, there was no one there save ourselves, the Munros, and Jeannie Ross, who was to be one of the witnesses of our marriage.

I had seen the chapel in the daylight but now blackout curtains had been drawn over the windows and it was lit only by the candles on the altar and in a great wrought-iron chandelier which hung from the ceiling.

The effect was lovely and I felt, too, that there was a wonderful atmosphere in this tiny place, an atmosphere made sacred by the faith of those who had worshipped there.

The Minister started the service. I glanced up at Peter once and saw him looking very stern and serious, his jaw set in the determined way I know so well, but when the moment came for him to take my hand I felt his fingers grip mine and knew that he, too, was nervous.

But his voice was quite steady as he repeated his vows, while mine was low and rather tremulous.

Finally, the Minister blessed us and we went into the vestry to sign the register.

When old Jeannie came in I kissed her and introduced Peter. He was very sweet to her and she kept telling him how lovely my mother had been and how much they had all missed her.

Then we went out of the vestry, shook hands with the Munros, and the ceremony was over.

I kept feeling the ring on my finger as we walked back from the chapel. I was surprised that Peter had remembered or had time to bring one.

There seemed to be nothing to say and so I was silent, although I longed to know what Peter was thinking and if he was feeling the same as I was—excited, but isolated from reality as if one watched another person experiencing strange and unfamiliar emotions.

When we reached the sitting-room Grandfather called to Munro to bring in a bottle of port in which to drink our health.

Munro must have been expecting this, because he reappeared almost immediately with a tray containing whisky and a very old port which, Peter told me, would be quite unobtainable nowadays.

The Minister came in and he and my grandfather drank our health, and then we drank to each other, and when that little ceremony was over, we started to talk more naturally.

Peter was quite amusing about his trip to London, which having been made in the teeth of a gale had been most unpleasant for both him and the pilot.

Then at last I said I thought I'd go and change.

"I'm terrified of spoiling my veil, Grandfather," I said. "It's the loveliest thing I've ever seen. I've been very proud to wear it."

To my surprise, my grandfather put both his hands on my shoulders and said:

"You've done justice to it and I hope you will never fail those who have worn it before you."

Then he bent and kissed my forehead.

I felt the tears start in my eyes and without thinking I said:

"I only wish Mummy had been here."

To my surprise he replied:

"She ought to have been."

I felt that was a tremendous victory and, as I ran up-stairs to my bedroom, I was happy because I knew those words would give Mummy more pleasure than anything else.

I hadn't been in my bedroom more than a minute and was actually lifting the veil from my hair when there came a knock at the door.

"Come in," I said, thinking it was Jeannie—but it was Peter.

He came in, shutting the door after him.

"I've got a present for you, Mela, and I thought I'd like to give it to you now—at once."

"A present!" I exclaimed. "How exciting! What is it?"

In answer he put a small pink jewel case into my lap. I opened it and inside was the loveliest ring I have ever seen. A huge blue sapphire set with diamonds.

"Oh, Peter! How lovely of you!"

"An engagement ring—although our engagement didn't last very long."

I slipped the ring on my finger and held up my hand to admire the effect.

"Wait a minute!" Peter said. "That's my privilege."

"What is?"

"To put the ring on your finger."

Taking my hand he took the ring off.

"Have I done the wrong thing?" I asked, half jokingly.

"You have," he replied seriously.

Then he raised my hand to his lips, kissing the finger which already wore the wedding ring and then slipping the sapphire over it.

I was too surprised to say anything. Suddenly Peter put his arms round me and held me close.

"Have you any idea," he asked in a low voice, "how lovely you looked as you came down the staircase to marry me?"

"Did I? I'm glad."

143

My voice sounded small and ineffective. I was overwhelmed by Peter's encircling arms, by the closeness of him, by his face near to mine.

"Mela, do you realise you are my wife?"

I think I was going to answer him but the words were checked by the look in his eyes, by the knowledge that he was holding me even closer and that his lips were seeking mine.

I had a sudden moment of panic and then it was too late.

I was crushed in Peter's arms—I had no idea he was so strong. He kissed me, and I knew for the first time that Peter's imperturbable calm was only superficial. He held me fiercely, possessively . . . and in that moment I learnt that he loved me passionately.

There was nothing I could do. Nothing, indeed, that I wanted to do. I was overwhelmed by something immeasurably stronger than I was, I felt that I was being swept away by a triumphant, flaming desire which would not let me escape . . .

Suddenly Peter released me, so suddenly that I would have fallen had I not steadied myself against the dressing-table.

"I'm sorry, Mela," he said hoarsely, "I didn't mean to rush you like this. I meant to tell you gradually, but I couldn't help it. My dear, I love you so—I've always loved you ever since the first moment that I saw you."

"But Peter! . . ."

It was a cry of dismay.

"Yes, I know what you're going to say," Peter interrupted. "That this wasn't part of the bargain. But Mela —I'll be quite frank with you. When you offered to marry me, it was as if I saw the realisation of all my dreams. I've wanted you so, I've longed for you, and yet I knew that you never gave me a thought."

I tried to speak but he went on:

"Your heart was fixed on some other fellow and that was why I tried to refuse your generosity. But when you told me you'd never marry anyone else except me I felt that God had indeed answered my prayers. I love you, Mela—I'll teach you to love me—but if sometimes I go too fast for you, you must forgive me."

As he was speaking he had moved away from me but now he strode back towards me and swept me once again into his arms, kissing me hungrily, almost crazily, as if he could no longer control himself. I felt as if a tempest was sweeping over me.

He kissed my eyes and my hair, my neck and again my lips till at last he looked down triumphantly at my face, flushed and frightened, against his shoulder.

"Tell me you love me," he commanded. "Say it! I want to hear you say the words."

"I . . . can't . . . Peter . . ." I stammered.

As if I had dealt him a blow, the expression on his face changed. Abruptly he took his arms away from me.

"I'm sorry. I'm behaving badly and I've got no excuse."

He walked across the room as if he were fighting with himself, struggling for control.

"You're not angry with me, Mela?"

"No . . . of course I'm not . . . it just that it's . . . all rather . . . surprising . . . I didn't know . . ."

"No, of course you didn't, and I didn't have a chance to tell you until now."

I sat down on the chair in front of the dressing table and pressed my hair back from my forehead. I felt bewildered, out of my depth, and then Peter knelt beside me and put his arms gently round me.

"I'll be good to you, Mela," he said. "I'll do everything you want, but oh! my darling, try to love me a little bit."

It sounded to me like the cry of a child. The conquering male had gone and in his stead was a little boy who was lonely. Instinctively I put my arms round him.

"Of course I will."

"You promise?"

Again there was that wistful note.

"I promise."

I was conscious of his head, hard and heavy against my breast, of his arms round me. I had already learnt their strength even while for the moment they held me tenderly.

I knew his heart was beating fast, that his breath came quickly, and yet I was no longer afraid. We seemed to be bathed in a great peace.

How long we sat there I don't know, but at last Peter got up and putting his hand under my chin tipped back my head so that he could kiss me once again on the lips —an affectionate, loving kiss, very unlike the passionate ones which had seemed to take possession of my whole being.

"Change your clothes and come downstairs. Your grandfather will wonder what has happened to you."

"I shan't be long," I replied.

But when he had left the room I sat still, staring at myself in the glass! My thoughts were chaotic. I had never for one moment imagined that Peter might be in love with me. I thought he liked me and I, naturally, expected him to admire me, but this was something I had not anticipated even in my wildest dreams.

I couldn't but feel with dismay that I had married a strange man of whom I knew nothing.

The Peter who had held me in his arms, who had rained passionate kisses upon my face and mouth was not Peter the politician, Peter the friend, or, indeed, Peter the companion whom I had grown to like and to rely on these last days in Scotland.

This was a new Peter—someone who, if I was honest, frightened me.

I had thought I knew a lot about being made love to but now I felt absolutely inexperienced, and as if, unwittingly, I had released something too great for me to understand or to control.

But whatever my feelings I knew I couldn't sit there thinking about them. I must go downstairs again. Peter had already told me that it was impossible for us to leave until the next morning, for the only afternoon train left immediately after lunch.

When I thought of the night ahead of me I felt my cheeks burn. This whole marriage was turning out quite different from what I had anticipated.

I had believed, without putting it into words, that Peter intended our marriage to be in name only, at least, for the time being, that we would go on being friends, get to know each other gradually, and be good companions content with the same outside interests.

Now I was doubtful.

Hurriedly I changed my dress and went downstairs. It was dark and, as the passages of the Castle were dimly lit, I had almost to grope my way along them. I opened the door of the big sitting-room but there was no one there.

The fire was burning brightly and in front of it lay one of the retrievers who wagged his tail at my approach.

"Where's everyone gone to?" I asked, but of course he couldn't tell me.

Then I heard voices coming from the library and thought that my grandfather was very likely showing Peter some of the books and first editions which I had seen yesterday.

I sat in front of the fire patting the silky coat of the retriever and thinking about myself.

"How funny this is!" I thought. "Here you are, Pamela MacDonald, changed by a few words and a stroke of the pen into Pamela Flacton. You know very little about your husband and he knows less about you. What are you going to make of the future? What are you going to make of your life?"

I got up and walked across the room to where the pictures of my ancestors hung. I looked up at them with their calm, aloof faces, and I wondered if they had ever asked themselves the same questions and if they had found an answer.

"I suppose," I thought, "they'd tell me to do my duty. Well, I shall try to do that."

I felt as if they ought to give me a message more forcibly. Everything up to date had been so dramatic that now the ghost of my ancestors ought to appear before me to give me either a blessing or a curse—then I laughed at my own imagination.

"It's time I got away from here," I said to myself. "I'm getting quite ridiculous."

I walked back again to the hearth-rug but I was restless and yet still reluctant to go into the library. The truth was, that I was shy of seeing Peter again.

Those moments upstairs now seemed unreal, as if they had happened in a dream.

I could hardly believe that they were reality; that Peter—whom I'd thought so unemotional, and expected to find easy-going and complacent as a husband—should have left me bewildered and uncertain by the fire and passion of his lovemaking!

"I'll go and get a book," I thought. "I must have something to take my mind off myself."

I went out of the sitting-room and down the passage which led to the stairs. As I did so, I heard someone knocking on the big front door.

"They must pull the bell," I thought.

I knew that the kitchen was a long way off and that Munro wouldn't hear unless they rang, and then I remembered that the bell was an old-fashioned sort—a chain hanging beside the door—and difficult to distinguish in the dark.

I looked down the passages but there was no one in sight, and thinking I would be helpful I walked across the hall and lifted the heavy iron latch of the door. There was a man standing outside.

"Good evening," he said. "Can I see Sir Torquil MacFillan?"

I was just going to answer him, when, suddenly, it seemed as if my heart had stopped beating . . . I pulled the door open wider and the light from the lamp in the hall shone first on his Air Force uniform and then on his face . . .

"Tim!" I stammered, and, at the same moment, he recognised me.

Chapter Fourteen

"Mela!—by all that's holy!"

Tim stepped forward and seized hold of my hand. I shut the door behind him, then turned to face him in the dim light. I think both our faces must have been pale. He looked as astounded as if he had seen a ghost while I know I was trembling.

"Tim—oh, Tim, why are you here?" I asked.

"I can't believe you're real," he said, taking no notice of my question.

Then he came nearer and put his arm round my shoulders.

"I've missed you so, Mela. Did you get my letter?"

"What letter?" I asked.

"The letter I wrote you two or three days ago. No, I suppose it's impossible that you should have had it. I sent it to London."

"Of course I haven't had it. Do you suppose I should be so surprised to see you if I had?"

"Are you glad, too?"

I was just going to answer him and then I remembered—Peter! I moved away from him, trying to collect my thoughts, to think clearly above the thumping of my heart, which seemed as if it was going to leap out of my body.

"Wait a moment, Tim," I said. "Let's start at the beginning."

"All right, but oh, Mela, I've got such a lot to tell you. Let's go and sit down and get it all off our chests. But you are glad to see me, aren't you?"

"I'm surprised."

"That wasn't what I asked you. As you haven't had my letter you won't know what all this is about—but you aren't angry with me, are you?"

"Angry?" I asked. "I don't think I was ever that."

"Well, whatever you were," Tim insisted.

He spoke awkwardly, as if he was embarrassed.

"You see, Mela, all that stupidity at Winnipeg—well, that's finished and over."

"Are you referring to . . . Audrey Herman?" I asked.

My voice was cold and I found it difficult to say the girl's name.

"Of course I am! I made a fool of myself—I know that all right—and when I found you'd gone, when I got your telegram I could have kicked myself as far as San Francisco and back for being such an idiot. I love you, Mela, I've always loved you."

I stood staring at him. I could hardly take in what he was saying or believe that this wasn't some fantastic dream from which I should wake up at any moment.

Tim—saying such words to me!—words I'd longed to hear, that I'd prayed for night after night with the tears running down my cheeks.

It couldn't be true that I was hearing them now, hearing them when I'd been married to another man for exactly one hour!

I suppose really I ought to have felt that revenge was sweet—that now I could hurt Tim as he had hurt me that moment in Montreal when I had stood listening to him stammering out words which were to shake into ruins my happiness, my life and my whole future. Now it was my turn—and yet I couldn't force the truth from between my lips.

I could only stand there looking at his face, feeling stupid and incoherent like a child who's forgotten its piece at a school concert.

"So much has happened since we last met," Tim was saying. "So much, Mela, that now I can hardly realise that all this time you've been thinking that I didn't care about you—that I'd forsaken you. Oh, darling, you've got to forgive me for that! It was all a ridiculous mistake. And when I found out what a fool! It was too late. You had sailed—I, too, was embarking. But I've got to tell you all about it. Come on—where can we go and sit down in this gloomy place?"

He took my arm and then at last I was able to throw off the feeling of paralysis.

"Wait!—there's something I must tell you first."

"There's nothing you need tell me," Tim interrupted. "except the one thing I want to hear—that you still love me and that I'm forgiven. Oh, Mela, old girl! it was idiotic to think that anyone could come between us! Why, you and I have always been everything to each other—childhood sweetheart—that's what they call it, don't they?"

He put his arm round my shoulders again and pulled my head affectionately and in a half-rough manner against his shoulder. It was an old affectionate gesture which I used to tease him about, saying he was as clumsy as a bear. Sometimes we'd even fight about it when I'd just had my hair set and was ready to go out.

But now, instead of anger or laughter, the tears came to my eyes.

"Don't, Tim, don't!"

"What's the matter, honey?" he asked. "You aren't yourself. Don't look so miserable. This is the incredible, marvellous bit of luck, finding you here. I've been working out how soon I could get to London, chafing at the delay on the part of the Air Ministry—but I'll tell you about that in a minute. And then I find you here, on my very doorstep."

He stopped suddenly.

"But of course—what a half-wit I am! MacFillian was your uncle's name, wasn't it? This Castle must belong to him—or to your grandfather?"

"To my grandfather," I said.

The words came sobbingly from my throat.

"Well, really!" Tim exclaimed. "It's a small world, as they say. Of all the places in the whole of the British Isles to land up! Talk about the luck of the gods! And I

152

was thinking of you hundreds of miles away in London! It's 'all's well that ends well'—that's true, isn't it?"

He squeezed me affectionately as he spoke and then, at last, I was able to tell him.

"Tim, I'm married."

He didn't say a word but I felt him stiffen and, very slowly, his arm dropped from my shoulders. Hastily and hurriedly now the words poured from me. I couldn't look at him after a first glance which showed me his face, tense and stricken.

"How was I to know that I'd ever see you again?" I asked. "You were so positive, so sure. You broke my heart, Tim, that day in Montreal. I was desperate, almost crazy with unhappiness. That was why I came to England.

I gave a little sob.

"Mummy wanted me to get away—she wired my uncle and he asked me to come here. I sent you a wire. I believed then that if you cared for me at all you would stop me sailing—you would come and fetch me home. Oh, Tim, why didn't you?"

My voice broke and for a moment I could not speak. The tears were rolling down my cheeks but I made no effort to wipe them away.

"That was when I knew for certain how much I loved you—when I got that wire," Tim said. "It was handed to me just as we were going on board. I couldn't do anything about it then—you'd already gone. You had sent it to the camp and it was twenty-four hours before I received it."

"Well, it's too late now."

"Who is this man?" Tim asked, in a hard, abrupt voice. "How long have you known him and why should you rush off and marry him?"

"I . . . oh, there's lots of reasons," I replied. "Anyway, what's the point of talking about it?"

Tim walked across the hall and back again.

"Well, I suppose I deserve this. I can't say anything —how can I? It's my fault! I chucked away my happi-

153

ness and now I suppose I've got to behave decently and wish you luck."

I said nothing and then, suddenly, Tim gripped my arm so hard that it hurt.

"Do you love this man?" he asked. "Do you?"

I suppose he only had to look at my face to know the answer—to see the tears blinding my eyes—to read the misery in my heart.

"You don't!" he said triumphantly. "You don't! You still love me."

It was at that moment that I heard someone coming. I felt a sudden panic at being found like that and instinctively I sought somewhere to hide.

Quickly I turned and opened the door which led into the gunroom. I said nothing to Tim but he followed me. We shut the door after us and stood still in the dark, hearing footsteps pass through the hall and into the big sitting-room.

"What are we going to do?" Tim asked.

"I must talk to you," I said desperately.

Then, in the darkness, Tim put out his arm and drew me close to him. He held me very near and I felt his heart beating and his breath coming quickly against my cheek.

"Oh, Mela!" he whispered, and his voice was deep and shaken. "How can I let you go?"

I knew that I ought to resist him and yet I could not, and while I hesitated I felt his lips on mine. It was impossible to struggle. I could only know that I was happy again, that Tim was kissing me, and were I married to a hundred other men I should still love Tim.

"This is what I have been longing for," I thought.

But I was too overwrought to be elated and too bewildered to feel guilty. I only knew that this was inevitable—that Tim was here in my life again and I could not deny my own heart.

"Mela! Mela!"

He was murmuring my name over and over again beneath his breath as he kissed me; then we heard footsteps again and were both very still, his cheek against mine, until they had passed.

"We've got to talk about this," I said, as soon as I dared to speak.

"What's the point of talking?" Tim asked. "I want to forget everything except that I have found you and that you love me."

"It's no use talking like that." I replied, but even as I said the words, I wondered if there was any use in talking about anything.

Where would it lead us? I was married to Peter, married securely and absolutely, and nothing could undo that fact; not even Tim.

"We can't stand here," I said desperately, "someone will be looking for me."

I felt Tim sigh and knew that he passed his hand across his forehead. I made up my mind.

"Listen, Tim. We must keep it a secret that you and I know each other."

"Why?"

"Because I want to see you. Because . . . oh, I can't explain, but it will make things impossible if Peter—that's my husband—realises who you are. You see, I told him that I loved someone else. If he once knows that you are over here he will make it impossible for me to see you. We can't make plans, either for now or the future. If he realises . . ."

I broke off.

"Oh, this sounds terrible put into words—but I've got to see you, Tim, I've got to! And I can't begin to explain all this to someone else."

"I understand—of course I understand. Listen, darling. No one knows I'm here. I'll nip outside the front door and arrive again."

"You must ring the bell," I said. "No one can hear you when you knock. It's at the side—a long, hanging chain."

"All right. But look here—you'll have to make it easy for me to see you. Actually it oughtn't to be too hard. I've come here to ask for billeting accommodation."

"We're supposed to be leaving tomorrow, but I daresay I can manage to change the plans."

"You must. But if I go now I must see you alone—tonight—to tell you all that has happened."

"I'll try," I promised. "But Tim—do be careful when we meet. Remember we've never seen each other before."

"I'll remember. Good-bye, darling."

He caught me to him, but this time I only let him kiss my cheek. He held me tightly for a moment then softly he opened the door and peeped outside.

"All clear."

He tiptoed across the hall and let himself out through the front door. The heavy latch closed after him with a sharp click. Then there was a long silence while I guessed that he was groping for the bell. At last, far in the distance, I heard a tinkle.

Swiftly, I ran upstairs to my own bedroom. When I reached it I locked the door, as if someone was pursuing me, and flung myself face downwards on the bed.

I lay there panting till gradually my heartbeats became more normal, my breath came quietly.

"Tim! Tim!" I said to myself over and over again.

It seemed to me as if everything was turning dizzily round in a circle—Tim and Peter revolving endlessly with myself as the pivot on which they turned.

"This is madness!" I thought. "It's too incredible to be true!"

And yet I knew there was no escape and that I was facing a situation more frightening and more disturbing than anything I'd ever known in my whole life.

I was in love with Tim—I never doubted that for a moment—and yet I knew that I must consider Peter. He was my husband, and, what was more, it was I rather than he who was to blame for that.

"If only I could have known!" I raged. "If only I

could have looked ahead and foreseen that this might happen!"

I thought of how the Minister had told me yesterday of the Canadians who were at the aerodrome. Supposing I'd gone down then and met Tim, would I have refused to marry Peter today when he returned with the marriage licence? I didn't know the answer to that question. I wasn't certain what I'd have done.

My conscience and my honour felt bound to Peter, and yet my whole heart went out to Tim . . . the man I loved . . . the man I had always loved.

I sat up on the bed and then moved across the room to the looking-glass. I was horrified at my appearance. My hair was dishevelled, my eyes were swollen with tears, and I was very pale.

"What am I to do?" I asked my reflection.

I wondered whether it would be wiser to tell the truth, to go to Peter now, at once, to say that Tim was here and that I still loved him.

"Yesterday," I thought to myself, "I might have done that. Today—after what Peter told me just a short while ago—I can't do it."

The knowledge that he loved me made me afraid—afraid, too, in some curious way, of his contempt.

I couldn't quite explain that feeling even to myself except that I felt that neither Tim nor I was behaving in a way that was particularly noble or splendid. Somehow I knew that if Peter had been in Tim's place he would never have changed his mind, either over me or, again, about Audrey Herman.

But then, it was impossible to compare Tim and Peter. Tim was impulsive. He was like me, wildly enthusiastic over things one moment and bored with them the next. That's why we were bound to be happy, because we had so much in common.

Yes, Peter was different, but still, what did I know about Peter one way or another? Only one thing for certain—that this new and passionate man I'd married wasn't the sort of person to whom I could confide a love for someone else.

"No," I thought. "I've been wise. The only thing to do is to keep my relationship with Tim hidden—at least until I can find some way out of this mess."

I did my hair, made up my face to hide the traces of my tears, and then very slowly I walked downstairs. As I reached the hall, I could hear voices in the big sitting-room. Tim's voice—how well I knew the tones of it and of his high, boyish laugh.

Then came Peter's—low and quiet—I couldn't hear what he was saying. Lastly my grandfather's—deeper, more resonant tones. I opened the door.

For a moment I felt as if I was on a stage. For all three men turned to face me and I had to walk across the long expanse of floor to where they stood on the hearth-rug.

"Oh, here you are, my dear," Grandfather said. "This is Flying-Officer Grant—my granddaughter, Mrs. Flacton."

"How do you do?" Tim and I said simultaneously.

I felt his fingers squeeze mine.

"My granddaughter also comes from Canada. I wonder if you've met each other?"

"I don't think so," I said quickly, "but I'm sure we shall have a lot of friends in common."

"I'm sure we shall," Tim agreed, smiling at me.

"The Flying-Officer has asked me if he can billet six officers here," Grandfather explained, "and I've suggested that he come back and dine here with us. I'm sorry that I can't invite the others but we find food rationing rather difficult in this outlying district."

"I quite understand, sir," Tim said, "and it's very kind of you to ask me. I shall be delighted to accept. And now, if you will excuse me, I think I'd better get back and tell the C.O. of your kindness. He will be very grateful. We're frightfully overcrowded at the camp at the moment—they weren't expecting quite so many of us from across the Atlantic."

158

"Well, we're very glad to welcome you," Peter said. "You came across with one of the Air Training Units, I gather?"

"That's right," Tim answered, then looking at me he said; "I expect you'll find quite a lot of friends amongst our crowd, Mrs. Flacton. Whereabouts in Canada do you come from?"

His eyes were twinkling as he spoke and it was difficult not to laugh as I replied demurely:

"Montreal. And you?"

"How very strange! I come from Montreal too. I can't think why we haven't met."

"Perhaps you were one of those rough noisy boys whom I used to dislike so much at school. I've done my best to avoid them ever since."

"I'm sure they haven't allowed you to do that. What was your name before you married?"

"MacDonald. Pamela MacDonald."

"I seem to have heard that name somewhere," he said, wrinkling his forehead.

He was acting the part so well that I promised myself that somehow or other I'd get even with him for making me feel so silly while he asked these ridiculous questions.

"There are a lot of MacDonalds in the world," Peter suggested quietly.

I think his voice startled both of us as we realised that the game we were playing was serious. Tim hurriedly put out his hand.

"Well, good-bye, Mrs. Flacton. I shall look forward to reminiscing with you this evening."

"Good-bye," I said, in what I hoped was a polite but indifferent tone.

Tim shook hands with Grandfather and then he walked towards the door. He looked very handsome and attractive as he turned for a last good-bye. I felt his eye on me and longed to warn him once again to be careful.

159

I went towards the fire, holding out my hands to the blaze.

"A nice boy," Grandfather said. "'I'm glad to be able to put them up. They billeted some men on me here when the aerodrome was first started but otherwise I haven't been able to do much for them."

Peter came back in to the room. He had seen Tim out.

"It's freezing," he said as he joined us, and then slipped his arm affectionately through mine. "You look worried, Mela. Is anything the matter?"

I shook my head, but at the same time I was surprised that Peter should be so perceptive.

"Nothing. What's the time?"

"Time for a drink before dinner. May I ask Munro for some sherry, sir?" he inquired of Grandfather.

"Of course," was the reply.

Peter pulled at the bell

Grandfather walked off into the library and we were left alone. I suppose it was a guilty conscience but I felt awkward and ill at ease. Peter lit a cigarette.

"Nice looking young Canadian. Have you any idea who he is?"

I don't know why, but I felt as if the question spelt danger.

"There are lots of Grants in Montreal. I must remember to ask Daddy about him when I write."

"I wonder he didn't know you. Can't be so many girls as pretty as you are drifting about the city."

"Thank you for the compliment."

"I mean it."

At that moment, Munro, who had guessed what we wanted, came in with the sherry. He put it down on the table and Peter poured me out a glass.

"I like being here," I said suddenly. "Why must we leave tomorrow? Can't we stay another twenty-four hours?"

"I thought you were anxious to get back to London."

I turned towards the fire so that he should not see my face.

"You will think it very weak of me," I said, "but I am beginning to give up hope of you and I ever finding Uncle Edward's murderer. I know that I was the person who persuaded you into taking an active part in the chase, who made you believe that we might succeed where the police had failed, but now I'm not so sure. I've been shaken by our experiences up to date."

"The best thing that ever happened," Peter said softly.

"But why?" I asked unthinkingly.

"Because it has given me you."

His words annoyed me.

"I shouldn't be too sure of that," I said provocatively.

"Am I being presumptuous?" Peter asked. "You know I don't mean to be. I promised myself that I would be very gentle with you, that I would go slow, and wait for you to learn to love me. Now I'll promise you these things, and I'll try to keep my promise."

He spoke very solemnly and I felt awful at that moment to think that already I was deceiving him. Yet I couldn't tell him the truth—it was impossible! I was afraid—afraid not only of Peter but of being unable to see Tim again.

In that moment, I made up my mind that once and for all I must take command of the situation—that I must make Peter see what I wanted from our marriage, and not let myself be swept off my feet either from fear or from cowardice.

"I want to be friends, Peter," I said. "Real friends. And I think that where you and I are concerned that is the best foundation on which to build our marriage."

Peter knew what I meant. For a moment he hesitated and I knew he felt that in a way I was driving a hard bargain. Then he put out his hands and laid them on my shoulders.

161

"We will be friends, Mela," he said with a sigh.

He bent forward and kissed my forehead.

"Until I can make you love me," he added, and there was a note of determination in his voice.

Chapter Fifteen

I think mine must have been the strangest wedding night that anyone has ever passed.

To begin with, the more I thought about the situation in which I found myself the more I felt, not only bewildered and perturbed, but guilty.

I felt I wasn't playing the game in deceiving Peter, and yet, I had neither the strength of mind to tell him the truth nor the courage to give up seeing Tim.

I suppose if we had been great and noble people like the sort you read about in books I should have told Tim that we should have nothing more to do with each other; that he must on no account come to stay in the Castle; that it was my duty to leave as quickly as possible, and, now that I was married to another man, he must forget me.

But as I'm not a heroine in a novel, merely human and terribly unhappy, I did none of these things.

While I was dressing for dinner that night, I hated myself. I have always been a very straightforward person—at least, I've thought I was.

I suppose the truth is, it is very easy to be straightforward when one has nothing to hide. I always despised people who told lies, who were deceitful, and who intrigued just for the fun of it.

I've known girls who liked having clandestine love affairs just because they were exciting. It gave them a thrill to sneak out at night and meet a married man, or tell their mothers they were going to the cinema when really they were going to some pretty disreputable night-club.

I expect a lot of it was craving for adventure, but I have never wanted adventures of that sort. I've only desired that my love affairs should be simple and above board, yet nothing could be more involved than my present position!

"What am I to do?" I asked myself, and I went on repeating the words, "What am I to do? What AM I to do?"

There really didn't seem any easy way out of the maze, but, being a woman, however tense the situation, I had to try to look my best. I had brought with me a dinner frock of black velvet. It was cut on old-fashioned lines with a very full skirt and a funny little berthe of real lace over the shoulders.

I felt as I went downstairs that night that I might have been my own great-grandmother, but there was nothing old-fashioned about the look of approval both in Tim's eyes and in Peter's when they saw me.

Of course it was a dead secret that I had been married that afternoon, so Tim had no idea he made a fourth at my wedding dinner party. Peter had told me that he was sending an announcement to the newspapers that we had been married without putting any date.

"The day after tomorrow," he said, "is the first of April. It will give us a chance when People ask when we were married to say vaguely—'Oh, last month'. It will give the impression it was some time ago without us having to lie."

"You think of everything," I explained. "But what about Mr. Durbin? Won't he make inquiries?"

"He's going to find it difficult," Peter replied, "unless the Press track down the actual time and place of the ceremony. I don't think they'll do that if we are quite open with them. You must allow them to take some photographs of you and give a few nice, smug little interviews as to what you think about England."

I made a face at him.

"You sound as if you think I shall enjoy that sort of thing. Personally, I refuse firmly to be photographed or to express an opinion on any subject."

"That's right," I laughed. "Leave me to do all the dirty work."

"As I said," Peter replied, "you will enjoy it!"

This conversation had taken place before dinner and was interrupted only when Grandfather and Tim came back into the room. Tim had been taken to see the library which I have now discovered is my grandfather's special pride, and everyone has to inspect it sooner or later.

Peter tells me that the first editions are worth thousands of pounds. Quite innocently I suggested that it might be a good idea if some were sold and the money used to renovate the Castle, making it more up-to-date as regards lighting, heating and a water supply. Peter looked at me as if my suggestion was absolute sacrilege.

"I don't think you understand," he said patiently. "The MacFillan library is famous all over the world. It's unique, and to sell even a portion of it would, I think, break your grandfather's heart."

"I still think he'd be more comfortable if he had electric light here."

Peter sighed.

"It's going to take me a long time to give you the right English, or, rather, Scottish outlook regarding antiquity, family heirlooms and the pride of possession."

He was teasing me, but I knew there was a rebuke in his words, then, before I could reply, Tim came back from the library and I saw at once by his expression that he had been bored with looking at the books.

Tim doesn't read very much—in fact, I used to get very angry with him because he never would read the latest and most-talked-of novel until it was out of date. "I don't get time, Mela," he'd protest. "It's all very well for you, but when I get back from the office I don't want to sit down with a book, I want to go out, to dance, play games, and get some exercise. 'A paper a day' is quite enough literature as far as I'm concerned."

I saw his point of view, although at times it was annoying when one wanted to discuss some particular subject to find that Tim knew absolutely nothing about it and, what was more, had no intention of learning. Now Peter had read quite a lot—I discovered that when we were in Glasgow together—and he had also a considerable knowledge of foregin books.

When I was learning languages I discovered it was much more interesting to learn them through the literature of the country, so I read French novels, German philosophers, and Italian operas, and, in a way, I suppose I'm what is called quite "well-read", at any rate from a Canadian point of view.

Canadians are busy people and most of them have to work very hard to make money, so they don't get much time for reading. There was, therefore, every excuse for Tim's attitude. But I enjoyed discussing books and authors with Peter. I've never been able to voice my likes and dislikes in the literary world with a man before.

All the same, I haven't got such a passion for books that I want to give up my comforts for them, especially if I knew, like my grandfather, that I had thousands of pounds of potential luxuries lying there just waiting for me to cash in on them.

But judging by Peter's expression when I suggested selling the MacFillan library, such ideas label me an utter Philistine.

Poor Peter! I'm afraid he's going to get a great many shocks about me before we have been married very long, and yet he's so kind. I suppose that is why I feel so ashamed when I think of how I am deceiving him.

Once during dinner I caught his eye and he raised his glass so that I should know he was drinking my health. I smiled in response and then I saw Tim looking at me with a perfectly murderous expression and felt guilty about him.

Oh, dear! Why must my life be so complicated and so difficult? At times I almost felt as if the only thing for me to do was to disappear altogether—to run away from both men and start again somewhere under a new name. But, of course, that is impossible and so I've got to work out my own salvation as best I can.

When dinner was over we went into the big sitting-room again and Tim seized the opportunity, while Peter was putting a log on the fire, to say:

"I've got to see you, darling. Can't you meet me down here after everyone's gone to bed?"

I hadn't time to reply before Peter turned round and came and sat down beside me, and all the evening I kept catching Tim's eye with a note of interrogation in it.

He looked so miserable, that after a while I could bear it no longer and nodded my head just for the pleasure of seeing the relief come into his face, of knowing that he was pleased.

I imagined that I'd be able to manage it somehow, but it was risky for both of us. However, there was no possible opportunity of arguing or discussing the matter.

We all sat and talked in front of the fire until it was nearly eleven o'clock; then I got to my feet and said I thought it was bed-time. We all said good-night and Grandfather asked Peter if he would turn out the light on the stairs.

When I had been dressing for dinner, I had heard people moving about across the passage and I asked Jeannie, who was doing up my dress, what was happening. She told me that Munro was putting Peter's things into that room opposite mine.

"Why?" I asked, quite innocently.

When Jeannie told me that it was the dressing-room to the room I occupied I blushed. I realised then that my room was intended for a married couple. It was very large and had a great tapestry-hung four-poster bed.

I wondered now, as I went upstairs, how I was ever going to creep down to see Tim and what would happen if he waited there hour after hour and I didn't come.

"Poor Tim!" I thought, and knew that I must get to him somehow.

There was so much that we had to say to each other, so much to discuss, so much I longed to hear.

I had no intention of undressing but I decided that I'd take off my dinner frock and put on the hostess gown in which I had been married that afternoon. I had just done this and was putting my dress away in the wardrobe when there came a knock at the door.

"Peter!" I thought. "Now what shall I do about this?"

I stood still, hesitating, and then the knock was repeated and the handle of the door turned. Peter came in.

"May I come and say good-night?"

"Of course."

There was a big fire burning in my grate and I went across the room and sat down on the floor in front of it.

"Have you asked Grandfather if we can stay another night?" I asked.

Peter sat down in a comfortable chair, holding out his hands to the blaze.

"I think perhaps it would be better to keep to our original plan. I've got to get back to work."

I had meant to argue, to insist on staying because of Tim, but suddenly I felt perhaps it was wiser not to. Tim had talked of coming to London—I should see him again later. Just at the moment I felt I couldn't cope with the present difficulties of having both Tim and Peter together under the same roof.

"It will be easy to come back here," I thought. "I can always make the excuse of wanting to see Grandfather and perhaps I shall be able to come alone."

"All right," I said aloud, "if you think it best."

"It isn't much of a honeymoon, is it?" Peter said softly. "Perhaps we shall be able to have one later on— a real one."

He said the last two words meaningly and I knew what he meant. I put out my hand towards him.

"I still want us to be friends—first."

Peter took my hand and held it between both of his.

168

"I want to be friends too, Mela, but you won't forget that I love you?"

"Of course I won't forget that."

There was silence for a moment.

"I'm afraid I am going to be rather a jealous husband."

I felt myself stiffen but I tried to make my voice light as I asked:

"Why do you think that?"

Peter's fingers tightened round mine.

"Because I'm jealous already. I hate to see other people looking at you. You're so lovely I know they can't help it, but you're mine—and I want to make sure that neither you nor anyone else forgets it."

I felt afraid. There was something deep and primitive in the tones of Peter's voice.

"You're moving too quickly for me," I said. "I thought you were the person who was always telling me not to be in a hurry. Now it seems the boot's on the other foot."

"And yet you told me that you wanted to 'make haste passionately'. Do you remember saying that, Mela, as we were driving back to Glasgow?"

"I didn't mean—this," I prevaricated.

"But I do," Peter said. "I mean just—this."

He bent forward and, putting his arms round me, pulled me nearer to him so that I was kneeling beside his chair.

"Mela," he whispered, "have I got to wait very long?"

"Oh, please . . . Peter!"

Instantly he released me. He got to his feet and stood with his back to me looking down at the fire.

"I'd better go to bed. Good-night."

He walked towards the door. Without thinking of the consequences, I gave a little cry.

"Don't go like that!"

"If I don't go now I shall never go," Peter replied.

Then striding back across the room he lifted me to my feet, holding me very tightly in his arms.

"Don't tease me, Mela. If you do I warn you that you're playing with fire. I love you . . . I want you madly. I want to be gentle, to be sweet with you, but if you try me too far I shall lose control. I shall do things which we both might regret later on. Good-night."

He bent his head and kissed me. It was a kiss of flaming, searing passion. Despite everything I was feeling, despite my thoughts of Tim, it thrilled me. Something within me, something which I couldn't restrain, responded to it.

For a moment I clung to Peter, returning his kiss, and then abruptly, almost roughly, he walked away from me and, without looking back, left the room.

I stood where he had left me, my fingers against my lips, my cheeks burning. Once again I told myself that the man I had married was not the man I had known and liked. Deep down within myself I felt that it was not a question of liking this Peter—this man who was my husband—one would either love or hate him, there could be no half-measures.

Resolutely I forced myself to think, not of Peter, but of Tim. Tim, the boy I had loved for so long—who had meant everything to me and who, I told myself fiercely, still did mean everything.

I thought of the years we had spent together, of those happy times when every available moment had been spent in each other's company; of the summers when we had bathed at Dorval and gone down to St. Andrew's to swim, sail and play tennis; of the years when we had found endless enjoyment in light-hearted gaiety and endless happiness in just being together.

"How can anybody or anything," I asked myself, "alter my feelings for Tim?"

Tim was part of me. Life without him was impossible. Hadn't I found that when I'd left home because everything reminded me too vividly of his presence—when I'd come across the Atlantic longing to die?

I thought of all the fun we'd had together; of the little home we'd planned so often—a cosy apartment on Sherbrook Street, or perhaps, if we could afford it, a house on the Côte de Neige where one could look out over that exquisite view and breakfast on a balcony high above the tops of the trees.

"A room with a view"—how often had I thought the words of that song especially applicable to Tim and me.

Yes, Tim was part of me as Peter could never be. I felt that he was mine and I was his, even as one might say that parents and children are indivisible one from the other.

Dear Tim! I remembered his surprise at seeing me, how his face had gone white and then pink, how he had kissed me in the darkness of the gun-room . . . and yet now, standing in my bedroom alone, I felt as if Peter's kiss stood between Tim and me.

I had never been kissed like that before. I was afraid of something it had done to me—something it had awakened within me.

The clock on the mantelpiece struck the half-hour.

"I've got a long time to wait," I thought, and I moved restlessly up and down my room.

I wondered how soon it would be before Peter was asleep. Supposing he couldn't sleep—supposing he heard me and followed me downstairs? The house was old, the boards of the floor creaked as one moved across them—at the same time, the walls were thick.

I was frightened and nervous, and yet nothing at that moment would have altered my resolution to go to Tim, to see him and talk to him.

It wasn't only because I wanted to so much, it was also a sense of obligation. I felt that I owed it to him. Why I should feel that I don't know, because, after all, Tim had treated me badly, but at last I understood what had happened.

That girl, Audrey Herman, whoever she might be, had fascinated him. He was living under new conditions, he was working hard, and it would be like Tim to

171

play hard too. Unlike Peter, he never could do things cautiously, look before he leapt, count ten before he spoke, or any of those ridiculous things which one was told to do as a child.

Tim is impulsive. On an impulse he had thought that the attraction Audrey Herman had for him was more important than anything else. Impulsively he decided to tell me at once to break off our engagement.

Now I could understand how desperate he had felt when the awakening had come—when he had realised that his real feelings were not involved and that he still loved me.

I felt that I was being rather wise in seeing all that, but still, however much I understood Tim's dilemma and what had happened, that didn't help the present situation. As I walked up and down my bedroom the difficulties of my position seemed to increase rather than to diminish.

At last the clock struck twelve, slowly the hand crept round to quarter past. I turned out the lamp which stood on my dressing-table, picked up an electric torch, and very, very cautiously opened my bedroom door.

Once it creaked and I held my breath, hardly moving, then I saw there was no light showing beneath the door across the passage.

Quietly and on tiptoe I started to creep towards the stairs.

Chapter Sixteen

I don't think I shall ever forget how long the distance seemed between my bedroom and the big sitting-room of the Castle.

Every creak of the stairs, every footfall, sounded like a pistol shot, and by the time I finally reached the door I felt as though I must be grey-haired with strain and fright.

I turned the handle gently and saw that Tim was waiting for me. Grandfather had, of course, turned out all the lights when he went to bed as was his habit, but the flames licking the huge logs piled on the fire cast a circle of glowing light on to the hearth.

The high roof and the rest of the room were in darkness so that it looked as if Tim stood waiting for me on a golden island.

"You darling!" he exclaimed as I walked across the room. "I was afraid you wouldn't come."

"Hush!" I cautioned.

Although he had spoken in a low tone the sound of his voice alarmed me.

"No one can hear us here," he replied, and added, as he touched my hand: "Why—you're shivering! It's unlike you to be nervous, Mela."

"I'm terrified," I admitted. "After all, it's all very well for you. I don't really know how you had the impertinence to ask me to meet you—seeing that I'm a married woman."

Tim grinned at me in the impish way which I knew meant he felt particularly pleased with himself.

"I took a chance on it."

"Chance on what?"

"On your not sleeping with your husband. After all, the English are always supposed to be pretty cold lovers, and what's more—there's something 'phoney' about this marriage of yours."

"I don't know why you say that?" I said.

I felt that my reply was feeble and not even a rebuke. I ought to be angry with Tim for his remark, but I just couldn't be.

"Well, isn't it?" Tim insisted.

"Let's hear your story first," I suggested. "We've both got a lot to tell each other."

"Oh, no, 'ladies first', " Tim said—then his tone changed.

"Mela, old girl, what does it mean?" he asked. "We're joking about this but don't you realise it's got me on the chin? When you told me you were married I thought I must be mad or dreaming—even now I can't realise it. Besides, it isn't possible that you fell in love again—you haven't been in England long enough. There must be something behind it all."

"There's a lot," I answered. "In fact, there's so much that I don't know where to begin, not only to tell you but to think about it myself. But Tim—let's start at the beginning. Tell me what you did from that moment when you walked out of the house. Heavens!—how long ago it seems."

While we had been talking to each other we had been standing, but now Tim pulled a couple of cushions off the sofa and put them on the floor in front of the fire.

"Let's be cosy," he suggested, then added: "I say, Mela, you do look stunning in that get-up."

Although I didn't say them aloud the words "my wedding-dress" trembled on my lips. They stabbed me with a pang of pain. Strange wedding-dress, indeed!— and still stranger wedding! But I said nothing and eagerly Tim began to talk.

He told me how he had gone back to Winnipeg after he had seen me, and that he had tried to think he had done the right thing, but the memory of my stricken face and the memory, too, of all the happy times we'd

174

had together seemed to stand like a barrier between him and his interest in Audrey Herman.

"She suddenly seemed a bit cheap," he confessed. "I suppose it was because I'd seen you again. You always did stand head and shoulders above any other girl."

But he hadn't got much time to consider Audrey Herman or his changed feelings because, almost immediately on his return, he was told that he was to be amongst the next contingent of airmen to embark for England.

Tim hadn't really finished his training, so this was unexpected, but during the months he had been in Winnipeg he had invented a small improvement on the bomber sight which was being used on their practice aeroplanes. This idea of his had been sent to the Air Ministry in London and they had cabled to Tim's commanding officer to send him over as soon as possible as they thought very highly indeed of his improvement.

Of course, Tim was thrilled, and, knowing him, I could quite understand that for a day or so he hardly had time to think of me or any other girl.

He was just absorbed in his work and in the idea of going overseas, and then—as he had already told me —when they were actually on board the ship at Halifax, he received my telegram.

"It was at that moment," Tim said, "that I realised, Mela, just how much you meant to me. I knew then that Audrey Herman had just been a stupid flirtation, one of those damned silly things a man gets involved in when he's bored."

He stopped but I didn't speak and he went on:

"I wanted to wire you to tell you everything was all right, but of course I couldn't do that. You were at sea and we were not allowed ashore before we sailed, and so I could only plan the things I'd say when we met— how I'd tell you I was sorry and knew what an idiot I'd made of myself."

"And then you wrote to me?"

"I wrote to you as soon as I got a moment. We were

a long time at sea—those convoys are slow, as you know. When we got to Liverpool we were sent first to an aerodrome in Lancashire before we were finally posted here. I have been expecting every moment to get to London. I knew I should find you once I got there."

I sat still, staring into the flames. I wondered what would have happened if Tim had arrived before I had come north with Peter.

I suppose that I should have promised to marry him there and then, that I should have stayed in England a little while, to see as much of him as possible, and then perhaps I should have gone back to Canada to wait until the war was over and we could pick up the threads of our lives where we had dropped them.

But now there was nothing to say. Here I was—a married woman; and although I wanted to tell Tim everything I felt that the reason for my marriage was not only my secret but Peter's too.

Yet I had to say something. Tim was right in thinking mine was a "phoney" marriage. It would be impossible for anyone who knew me as well as he did to be deceived—though I hoped to deceive the rest of the world.

"Now it's your turn," Tim said as he finished speaking. "Tell me, Mela—tell me exactly what's happened."

"I don't think I can," I replied, "it's all too complicated. Surely it's sufficient for you to know that when you left me nothing else in my life seemed to matter. I came over here because Mummy planned it. When I found that my uncle had been killed, I was too miserable to go back to Canada right away and so I stayed on and married Peter."

"For which I must blame myself, I suppose," Tim said bitterly. "Oh, Mela!—why couldn't you have waited? Why couldn't you have guessed that I'd come back to you?"

I felt relieved when Tim jumped to the conclusion that he was to blame for my marriage.

After all, it was fundamentally the truth for if it

hadn't been for Tim I'd never have come to England, and if it hadn't been that I felt so utterly lost and miserable without him I would never have thought of employing such a drastic method to save Peter's reputation.

So I made no effort to enlighten him further as to the truth but merely replied to his question.

"How could I ever imagine you would change? I thought you were engaged to Audrey Herman—I thought you meant to marry her!"

"I was a crazy loon! But oh, Mela! I love you—I do really. You can't put me out of your life like this."

"What else can I do?"

"Go on seeing me and loving me. You do love me—you know that, Mela. You daren't deny it."

"But Peter?"

"What does he matter? These Englishmen are all alike. I've only got to look at him to see he isn't your sort. Cold and reserved—you'll never be happy with a chap like that."

"If you only knew!" I thought to myself, remembering those scaring fiery kisses of Peter's when I had gone up to change my wedding-dress, and how, only an hour ago, he had held me fiercely in his arms, then left me because he feared he would lose his self-control.

No, Peter was not cold when one knew him, and yet I too had been deceived by his reserve; I to had been taken in by that imperturbable calm.

"How are you going to stick it?" Tim was saying. "You won't like the life over here, Mela—lah-di-dahing about and being a society hostess to the snobs. They aren't like us, these people—they're stuck up and so convinced of their own superiority that you wonder at times if they are human."

"How do you know all this?" I asked. "You haven't been here long."

"Oh, I know them all right," Tim replied. "You remember I never thought much of the English. Your mother, of course, is different; but you used to find a lot of them as boring as I did."

"I know," I answered, "but being here in their own country makes a difference. You wait till you see London! When you see what they've stood up to in the way of bombing—well, one has to admire them for that—and a lot of them are as homely and as human as we are."

"Shut up about them!" Tim said suddenly. "I'm jealous, Mela. I'm jealous of you being here, of you having an English husband, of you belonging to any man but me!"

"Well, there it is," I said with a sigh. "All the jealousy and all the talk in the world won't change things from what they are."

"There must be some way out."

"Well, what?"

"I don't know. I suppose if there wasn't a war on you and I could run away together. We can't even do that now or I should be hoicked back and shot as a deserter."

"Well, what do you suggest?"

"We'll think of some way," Tim replied soothingly. "When we get to London we can manage to see something of each other."

"And suppose we can't?"

"But damn it!—we must. Don't you worry, Mela, things will come right—they've got to."

I couldn't help smiling at Tim's easy philosophy. He was always the same; he always believed that things would work out all right; that unpleasant facts, if shelved long enough, would somehow be changed by magic into pleasant ones.

Tim was a person who was always ready to believe that "all is for the best in the best of all possible worlds". He found it hard to be unhappy, perturbed or miserable for more than a few moments.

Convincingly as he had told his story, I couldn't miss seeing that there was a time lag. There was a week or so, for instance, between the time he discovered that he didn't care so much for Audrey Herman and the time he received my telegram.

Surely he could have written to me, at least sent me one word of encouragement and hope? Then again, he had been in England for two or three days before he had written to me.

Had he written on the ship crossing the Atlantic and posted it the moment he docked, I might have got that letter before I married Peter. But still, it was no use thinking of what might have been; we had got to try to find some solution for the future.

I looked at Tim and it made my heart ache. He was so young, so eager, and so attractive. As we sat there before the fire I suddenly felt immeasurably older.

I felt as if the emotion and the misery which I had been through this past month had aged me considerably while it had left Tim just the same, just as lovable and —though I hated to admit it—just as irresponsible.

I saw now that way back in the past I had always been the practical one; I had done the planning about our marriage, about our home, about all the things we were going to do. Tim had lived in the moment, happy to be with me, wanting only to "do things" and have fun.

Now it was up to me again and I could see Tim was going to be little or no help. And yet, I asked myself, what was there I could do? I was married to Peter and, for the moment at any rate, I couldn't contemplate letting him down. Besides, as Tim said, even if I wanted to run away with him it was impossible.

"Tim," I said suddenly, "we ought really to be honourable about this—we ought to make up our minds not to see each other."

Tim grinned.

"Sounds all right, but I don't mind betting you're not going to do it."

"I ought to," I said severely.

"There's a lot of things we ought to do which we
179

don't, and this is one of them. Don't be high-minded, Mela, it doesn't suit you! Besides, we love each other. No amount of words can talk us out of that."

"And no amount of words can talk me out of being married to another man," I replied sharply.

"Damn him! I still can't think how you could have been so silly, Mela."

"Well, I have been," I answered wearily, "and it's no use arguing about it. I'd better be going to bed now—it's getting late."

In answer, Tim reached out his arms and drew me close to him.

"Don't go. We've been talking all this time—I haven't had a chance to tell you how much I've missed you, how much I've wanted to kiss you."

"You'd better not tell me now."

My words weren't really a protest—I felt myself go weak and limp as Tim touched me—I let my head fall back against his shoulder. I loved the feeling of his cheek warm against mine, of his arms, firm and strong, holding me close.

"Oh, Tim!" I whispered. "If only we could put the clock back—if only there was no war and just you and I, happy as we used to be."

"Going off to dance at the Normandy Roof. They were fun, those nights weren't they? I wonder who is there this evening? Not many of the usual crowd, I expect."

"Didn't you ever think of the little home we were going to have, when you were in Winnipeg?" I asked, "or were you busy planning one with Audrey Herman?"

"Oh, she never used to talk about things like that. She was a good sort, jolly, kept you laughing all the time. Sometimes her tales were a bit on the risky side —not exactly fit for the village sewing-bee—but otherwise she was a really nice girl. You'd have liked her, Mela."

"I'm sure I should," I said sarcastically.

Tim laughed and tightened his arms about me.

"I love making you jealous."

"I'm not jealous—not now. Audrey Herman has done all the harm she can possibly do to my life. The best thing we can both do is to forget about her."

"But you couldn't forget about me?"

"You know I couldn't and I don't see how I ever can. Oh, Tim darling, it's hell, but I do love you so."

"Oh honey!"

He started kissing me then and I felt as if I'd never known such happiness, and yet beneath it was that discord of misery, that nagging, incessant pain which nothing could soothe or relieve. Finally, I drew away from him and there were tears in my eyes.

"Good-night, Tim," I whispered, "and good-bye for the present."

"You're upsetting yourself. Don't be a silly. You aren't to worry about things. They'll come right somehow and some time."

"I'd like to believe that," I said through my tears.

"You've got to believe it," Tim insisted. He put his arms round me again and hugged me. "You're too lovely to be miserable. Besides, I like you smiling."

"I'll try to remember that," I said, and then I pulled his dear face down to mine again. "Take care of yourself, Tim."

"You bet I will," he answered, and then holding me still closer he said suddenly: "Don't go, Mela, don't leave me yet."

"But I must," I replied, and looked at the clock above the mantelpiece. "It's half-past two. You've got to be up at six. I heard you tell Grandfather."

"I'm not tired," Tim protested, "and if I were it wouldn't matter. We may not see each other again for some time. Oh, Mela! don't go."

He kissed me again and then suddenly lifted me high in his arms and carried me back towards the fire. He crossed the wide hearth-rug and put me down among the sofa cushions on the big damask-covered sofa.

The light from the flames did not reach it and it was in a warm velvety darkness that I looked up to see him bending over me.

"I must go," I said feebly.

Then as I felt Tim's arms round me and his mouth against mine I was still.

"I love you, Mela, I love you! I can't let you go!"

There was something urgent in his voice; something, too, in the fierceness of his kisses that I had never known before. I felt suddenly afraid, not of Tim, but of ourselves.

I felt his hand at the loose neck of my dress and I knew then that there was a new strength within me, a strength both to resist temptation and to save a love that was too precious to be spoiled.

"Please, Tim," I said, "please! . . . please! . . ."

I pushed him away from me and struggled to my feet. My breath was coming quickly as I faced him, my hands pressed against my breasts.

"No, Tim," I whispered.

Without another word I turned and fled from him. As I reached the door, I saw him standing very straight and still in the light of the fire.

Then I was in the cool darkness of the hall, groping my way up the ancient staircase.

Chapter Seventeen

"You look as if you are sorry to say good-bye," Peter said as the train steamed slowly out of the small wayside station.

"I am," I confessed, looking back over the moors shrouded in a grey Scotch mist.

It seemed strange that I should mind leaving the Castle which, all my life, I had thought of with contempt and something approaching disgust; nevertheless, I was speaking the truth.

In the short time that I had dwelt under my grandfather's roof I had come to love and admire, not only the building itself, but all that it had stood for in the lives of my ancestors and what it meant even now to the austere old man still living there.

I couldn't put it into words, but it seemed to me as though it was symbolic of all that was proud, staunch and true in the older generation.

I had grown, too, to have an affection for my grandfather. I could understand now why Mummy's eyes had so often clouded over when she spoke of her own country. There was a tie there—a tie of flesh and blood which could not be ignored.

I admired my grandfather and, in a way, I revered him. He might have stepped straight out of an old history book, and although one might say that he was often narrow and prejudiced in his ideas, one could not but acknowledge his integrity and the strength of character which had kept him true to his creed and to his standards.

Before I said good-bye to my grandfather, I had kissed Jeannie Ross and she had said to me:

"Tell yer mither to come hame. The Laird hasna many years ahead of him and though he's too proud to ask her, there's a grand welcome awaiting her the day that she crosses the threshold."

"I'll tell Mummy," I promised.

Then Jeannie, holding my hand between both of her old, wrinkled ones, said in a low voice:

"Bless ye, dear lass, and may God one day give ye the happiness ye seek."

I was too surprised to have any answer to this, but afterwards I wondered how Jeannie knew that I wasn't happy. How could she have seen that that quiet, and, in some ways, romantic marriage of Peter's and mine was not the ideal love match which every woman hopes will be hers?

Jeannie had sensed the truth, and she was the only person in the Castle who had any idea how unhappy I was or how I had spent the night before sobbing bitterly until the pale dawn crept over the moors and mountains.

I suppose really it was not only unhappiness caused by saying good-bye to Tim, but also reaction after all the excitements and drama of the past days.

Whatever it was, when I got back to bed I couldn't stop crying—I just howled like a schoolgirl hearing my own sobs going on and on monotonously.

After what seemed hours, I had got up to bathe my face with cold water, to rub my forehead with eau-de-cologne, and to draw back the curtains to see the dawn.

There was a strange stillness over the land, a hush as if the world held its breath and waited—and then as the sky lightened, as the earth seemed to stir, yawn, and waken to a new day, I felt a new strength enter into me.

The tiredness and misery of the night passed away and I heard, as clearly as the song of a bird, a singing within my own heart. I was alive . . . I was young. . . there was so much to do . . . so much to be experienced What was the point of regrets and unhappiness?

Yesterday was past—whatever I felt, whatever had

happened, nothing could be altered or undone. I must go forward.

Slowly and yet perceptibly the glow deepened in the sky. I heard the cluck-cluck of a grouse winging its way down the valley; I heard the chatter of the starlings as they woke in the bushes beneath my window; there was the wailing mew of a gull as it came inland from the shore; far away in the distance I heard a cock crow.

"I'm happy!" I suddenly said to myself and was amazed at my own statement.

But it was true—I was happy. Underneath all the difficulties and problems which confronted me was a fundamental happiness in living which nothing could change or destroy.

"Things will come right," I thought joyously.

Going back to bed I slept soundly and without dreaming until Jeannie wakened me, bringing an early morning cup of tea.

When I dressed and went down to breakfast it was difficult to recapture the mood I had experienced at dawn, and yet deep inside me it was there—a little spot of contentment which even the thought of leaving Tim behind could not entirely disperse.

I had known it was impossible to see him again and yet, stupidly, I half hoped that he would appear before I left or that a note would come from him—that he'd send me a message, just one little token to tell me that he was still thinking of me and still loved me.

But there was nothing—only Peter, helping me into the train, being as kind and attentive as usual and quite unaware that I was longing desperately for another man.

The journey to Glasgow was dull and uneventful. We talked a little but I have always disliked talking in a train, and I think I slept for a while after we had luncheon and Peter had suggested that I put my feet up on the seat and tucked a rug round me.

We got to Glasgow about tea-time. We took our luggage to the hotel and Peter said he would go back to the station and see about our sleepers on the night train.

"I'll wait for you in the lounge," I told him.

"All right," he said, "I won't be long. There's nothing you want, is there, darling?"

I shook my head and he hurried off.

When he had gone, I thought that I'd go and wash my hands in the cloakroom of the hotel. I picked up my handbag but left my coat and rugs and various papers in the lounge.

The ladies cloakroom was down a flight of stairs, at the bottom of which were a row of telephone boxes. As I walked slowly down I glanced—I suppose idly—at the boxes and saw that only one was being used. There was a man inside. I did not recognise him immediately but his features were vaguely familiar.

Then I remembered.

When one has really to do something very quickly in life it is difficult to say—"I thought of this and then I did that"—it is almost as if the thought and action are simultaneous. I can't remember thinking.

I only know that I ran swiftly down the last two or three steps, opened the door of the box next to the one which was engaged, and was inside with the door shut almost as quickly as it takes to speak of it.

I could hear quite distinctly what "the Reverend" was saying.

Automatically, I picked up the telephone book and started turning over the pages. If anyone saw me they would think I was looking for a number, but all the time I was listening . . . listening to the sound of that slow, sarcastic voice.

"Yes, he'll do his best . . ." he was saying. "I told him that you needed nearly a quarter of a ton for these new pamphlets . . . He says they've tightened up the regulations . . . Oh, that's good . . . it will tide us over for this month, at any rate . . . You will have to pay cash, of course—I'll bring it down to you in notes . . . Yes . . . yes, I've got it with me . . . I'll come along now . . . tell him the corner of Silver Street . . . we can't be too careful . . . Right away . . . Good-bye."

I heard him put down the receiver and then open the door of the box. As he came out I took my receiver off its hook, my back towards the glass door; then, very cautiously, I turned just a fraction so that I could see what happened to him out of the corner of my eye. He was going upstairs.

As he reached the top, I put down the receiver and hurried after him.

"The Reverend" was wearing an overcoat and carrying his hat. He walked straight across the hall and through the big revolving doors which led into the street. I had no time to consider what I should do—I had to follow him at once or lose sight of him.

I followed him. I was thankful for two reasons that I was wearing a fox tie round my shoulders; the first reason was that it was very cold outside and I had left my fur coat in the lounge. The second reason was more important—it half hid my face and therefore made it less likely that I should be recognised.

I followed "the Reverend" into the busy street and kept him well in sight as he walked along, wending his way through the workers coming off a shift, and the shoppers hurring home before the black-out.

Very soon he turned off the main road down one of the side streets. Here I was in more danger of being seen, so I kept some way behind him, but was careful not to let him out of my sight.

I wondered vaguely what Peter would say when he got back to the lounge and found I had gone; and yet I felt I was doing good work.

It was obvious that "the Reverend" was meeting someone—perhaps the man they were looking for, the head of the organisation.

After a while, the street got narrower and more

187

dingy; there were slum houses now on each side, grey and forbidding, many of the windows cracked and broken from recent raids and patched with pieces of cardboard or brown paper.

Then, at the far end of the street, where "the Reverend" must turn either to right or to left, I saw a man standing. I jumped to the conclusion that he was waiting for "the Reverend".

The latter made no sign of recognition until he was right on top of him. As they met, "the Reverend" spoke only two or three words as one might casually inquire the way of a stranger, but—as I drew nearer— I saw him take a package from his pocket and give it quickly into the other man's hand.

Unexpectedly, he turned and started walking towards me.

I had a moment of sheer panic—a moment when I longed only to turn and run—then, resolutely pulling myself together, I walked steadily on.

With an effort which was almost superhuman, I avoided looking at "the Reverend". I looked ahead until, as we drew nearer to each other, I opened my bag as if I was searching for a handkerchief. My head was bent, my face half hidden in my fox tie.

We passed so close that our shoulders almost touched and, incredible though it seemed, all was well— he didn't notice me! I reached the end of the street.

In the distance, I could see the man to whom "the Reverend" had given the package hurrying along. He was tall and I imagined quite young, wearing a cap and a heavy tweed overcoat. I glanced back the way I had come.

"The Reverend" was walking up the street, but more slowly now, as if his errand was completed.

I made up my mind and started hurrying after the man with the package. It took me a little time to catch up with him. I didn't want to run in case I attracted attention to myself, but soon I was only thirty yards behind him and I knew that it would be difficult for him to escape me.

We walked on and on, twisting in and out of mean narrow streets where dirty children played on the doorsteps, we crossed thoroughfares where I must dodge between trams and be careful not to lose my quarry amongst a throng of bicycles and lorries.

Once or twice I wondered if it were wise to go on, or whether it would not be better to go back to tell Peter what I had seen and let him notify the police; but now I had undertaken the hunt, I hated to give up. I felt there was definitely a chance of learning something important.

Why, I wondered, had "the Reverend" handed over the package in the middle of a street? Was this the man to whom he had been talking on the telephone? What was on the pamphlets to which he referred? If they were ordinary pacifist propaganda why should there be so much mystery about them?

Suddenly, the man ahead of me turned swiftly to the right and disappeared. I hurried quickly after him.

There were no turnings in the road, there was only a dark and narrow passage leading to a courtyard surrounded by grim, dirty houses. I looked about me, bewildered, and then at the far end I saw that a door was open, but every house in the courtyard was empty; the few panes of glass left in the windows were dark and unseeing, like sightless eyes. Some of the doors were boarded up, one or two were padlocked; the whole place was desolate.

I moved quietly towards the open door at the end of the courtyard . . . I reached it . . . and, as I did so, a man shot out and confronted me.

"What d'ye want?" he asked in a menacing tone.

For a moment I was too scared to answer. His appearance was enough to intimidate the bravest. He was tall, with a coarse, brutal, unshaven face, he had a greasy handkerchief knotted round his throat and a cap pulled low over one eye.

"Well?" he insisted as I did not speak. "Have ye lost yer tongue?"

"Does . . . does Mr. Brown live here?" I asked.

To my horror, the man stepped forward and seized me by the wrist.

"Let's have the truth," he said roughly. "Who are ye? One of they new polis-women?"

"Let me go," I said. "I have told you—I am looking for a Mr. Brown who I understood lived round here."

The young man who had taken the package came up the basement steps.

"What's a—happening, Christy?" he inquired.

When he saw me he added in a frightened voice: "What's her want?"

"That's what I want to know," the man who was called Christy replied. "I'm thinking she's been following ye."

The young man started.

"Will you kindly let me go," I interjected, pulling at my wrist which was hurting under the pressure of Christy's dirty fingers.

"Not so fast—not so fast," Christy said. "We'll be after inquiring into this."

"If you don't let me go at once," I said, "I shall fetch a policeman."

"Oh, ye will, will ye?" Christy replied. "Well, I'd like to know how ye'd be doing that."

Then, in an aside to the young man, he said:

"Ask the guv'nor to come up."

The young man clattered away and I stood there, feeling, I must confess, absolutely terrified. I didn't like the look of Christy and there was something eerie about this quiet, deserted courtyard with its blank, sightless windows and the twilight creeping over it.

"Let me go," I pleaded again.

And then I did what, I suppose, was an incredibly stupid thing—I screamed.

Instantly, Christy's great hand was clamped over my mouth. It half suffocated me and I had a moment of sheer convulsive panic when I struggled and fought with all my strength against his other arm which was enfolding me. But it was no use.

Brutally and roughly he held me, my arms clamped to my sides.

Then he lifted me bodily off my feet and carried me down the dark stone steps into the blackness which yawned beneath us.

Chapter Eighteen

I was still struggling, though not so violently, when we reached the bottom of the steps.

While fighting to get free, I was half afraid of being dropped down into the darkness below, and also Christy's hand across my mouth was almost suffocating. He was swearing and cursing when the door at the foot of the steps opened and a man stood there.

"What the hell is all this?" he asked.

"Polis-girl," Christy said briefly. "They've rumbled us, Guv'nor."

He stood still, holding me so that I could see the man who was speaking. He was short and dark, with a swarthy, un-English complexion and I thought there was also a suspicion of a foreign accent when he spoke, although it was difficult to be certain.

Christy and the man with the package both spoke what seemed to me a mixture of Scotch and Irish, but this man was better educated than either of them.

"If she is," he said angrily, "what the devil do you want to bring her down here for?"

"She wer screaming."

The bullying manner Christy had adopted towards me was gone and now he was speaking in a whining, subservient way.

His grip on me relaxed and, as his hand over my mouth slackened, I bit it as hard and savagely as I could. He let out a yelp of pain and I managed to release myself from his encircling arm.

Standing firmly on my own feet once again, I said to the man in the doorway:

"Will you kindly explain the meaning of this outrage?"

He stared at me as if puzzled, but when Christy

made a sudden movement as if to seize me again, he said:

"Leave her alone."

Then, turning abruptly to me, he added:

"What are you doing here?"

"I was looking for a man called Brown."

I could see that he didn't believe me.

"Well, it's very unfortunate for you," he said in a quiet, sinister voice, "that he doesn't happen to reside here. I'm afraid you'll have to give us the pleasure of your company for a few hours."

"What do you mean?"

"You'll find out."

He walked across the passage to open another door. As he moved, I glanced into the room from which he had come. It was lit by artificial light and I could see various machines and great stacks of paper.

I hadn't time for more than a cursory glance before "the guv'nor" said with an ironical politeness:

"Kindly step this way."

He held open a door, and I walked past him into a small, almost dark room. I turned to see if he was following me and, as I did so, the door was slammed to and I heard the sound of a key turning in the lock.

"What are you doing?" I shouted. "Let me out."

I rushed to the door and started rattling the handle but of course it was no use; it was quite a heavy door and any effort I could make against it was quite ineffective. Then I heard "the guv'nor" speaking.

"Go up to Charlie's right away and get his van," he ordered somebody. "Tell him it's urgent and bring the big car along as well. We shall need it. Get a move on."

I heard someone go running up the steps and then there was the sound of tremendous activity.

"I know what they are doing," I thought to myself. "They're moving out—that's why I've got to stay here."

I looked round the room in which I was imprisoned. When the house had originally been built, I imagine it had been a store room or larder; now it was empty, save for a row of filthy dirty shelves along one wall.

There was a small window high up against the ceiling which, so far as I could see, looked on to a shaft. Very little light came through it and I guessed it was some feet below ground level. The floor was covered with dirt, old pieces of straw and paper.

Damp, oozing through the walls, had run in dark dank streams down what had once been whitewashed plaster. The place smelt, and I felt that if I was imprisoned there long enough I should be suffocated by the atmosphere.

I felt for my handkerchief to wipe my face. It was sore and I felt dirty from contact with Christy's hand. Then I realised that I had dropped my bag and my gloves; they must have fallen away from me in the struggle.

I regretted that I hadn't got a powder puff with me or some lipstick—it would have been good for my morale if I could have made up my face again.

However, I straightened my clothes and pulled my hat down on my head. I was dishevelled and badly scared by what had occurred and I wondered frantically how long they would keep me here and what Peter would do when he got back to the hotel and found I had vanished.

I could hear men moving about and every few minutes someone went up the steps and I could tell by the slow weighty way in which they ascended, the lightness of their tread as they returned, that they were carrying heavy loads. Everything movable in the lighted room, I presumed, was being taken up above ready for the lorry.

It was when I had been in my dark cell for nearly half an hour that I began to be really frightened.

"Supposing," I thought, "that they just go away and leave me! Supposing that they turn nasty and decide to get rid of me!"

I tried to comfort myself by remembering that they

were pacifists and therefore the idea of doing anyone physical harm should be repulsive to them.

At the same time, there was a ruthlessness about
"the guv'nor" which made me feel that it was unlikely
he would be too particular as to what he did, either
to me or to anyone else.

"Peter's right," I thought. "I believe there's more in
this than just pacifist propaganda. Sabotage would come
easy to these men."

A little while later, I heard the sound of a lorry
backing into the yard. I wondered how it had got in
because the little alleyway down which I had approached was certainly not wide enough for a car—in
fact it would have been difficult to get a full-sized
perambulator down it with any ease.

Then there was tremendous activity up and down
the steps. I could hear "the guv'nor's" voice giving
orders—men breathing hard and muttering "Over to
ye"—"Easy does it."

"They must be taking the machines upstairs," I
thought. "No wonder they are annoyed with me!
They've got to move out all these big things just because I've discovered them."

I was beginning to get tired of standing and yet I
couldn't bring myself to sit down on the filthy floor
or even to lean against the damp, stained walls.

Once or twice I thought of banging and asking for
a chair, but I did nothing—not only because I thought
it more dignified to stay silent, but also because I shrank
from seeing those men again. I was bruised where
Christy had held me so tightly and my lower lip had
been cut by my teeth.

"Supposing they leave me here!" I kept thinking.
"Supposing they don't let me out."

Over and over again the idea presented itself to
my mind until, almost like watching the emotions of
another person, I realised I was becoming more and
more terrified, getting a kind of claustrophobia, feel-

ing that I couldn't breathe—that the narrow walls were closing in on me.

It was dark, the last glimmer of light had faded and I was bitterly cold. Suddenly, I could bear it no longer. I rushed towards the door and battering against it with my fists cried:

"Let me out! Let me out!"

I heard a man's voice growl:

"Tell that bitch to shut up!"

Then someone made a remark which brought a guffaw of coarse laughter.

Then I was absolutely terrified, with a fear which was uncontrollable and overwhelming. I was desperate, like a trapped animal, mad with panic which possessed me like an evil spirit.

"Let me out!" I screamed, and at that moment I heard another voice.

"Now then—what's going on here?"

My heart leapt with relief. Someone else had arrived! I screamed again—

"Help, help! Let me out!"

A perfect babel of voices arose. I could hear men's voices, some steady and calm, others half-hysterical—then the door was flung open, so suddenly that it almost knocked me over for I was standing close to it.

The light streamed in from the passage and for a moment I could only blink, being unable, after the darkness, to distinguish anything.

Then—most welcome sight!—I saw a policeman and two other men in ordinary clothes who were obviously police, too, for they were putting handcuffs on "the guv'nor," Christy, and the man who had carried the package.

"Oh, I am glad you've come!" I exclaimed.

One of the plain-clothes men came up to me.

"Mrs. Flacton, isn't it?"

"Yes, I'm Mrs. Flacton," I replied, "but how did you know?"

"I'm sorry you've had rather a bad time, ma'am,

but we couldn't get here any quicker. We had to get help, you see. Now then," he said sharply to the men, who were staring at me, "upstairs with them. The van's outside."

I looked on wonderingly as "the guv'nor," Christy and the other man were marched off, and the plain-clothes man turned to me with a smile.

"You've done us a really good turn this evening, Mrs. Flacton."

"I don't understand."

The detective's smile broadened.

"I don't suppose you do," he said. "But you see, when you followed 'the Reverend' out of the hotel, the man we had watching him was not far behind you. We've been following him ever since you and Mr. Flacton told us who he was, but we had learnt nothing.

"Luckily, the man we had on the job this evening had seen you with Mr. Flacton and knew who you were; and, when 'the Reverend' turned back from Silver Street, he had the sense to leave him and see where you were going. He guessed you must be on to something that he didn't know about and so he kept you in sight.

"It was pretty plucky of you, Mrs. Flacton, to go down those streets by yourself. I'm not saying that you would have come to any harm—but you might."

"I wish I'd known he was following me," I said. "It would have saved me some bad moments when I got here."

"It must have been very unpleasant, but when he saw you'd got yourself into trouble he, very wisely, made no attempt to tackle things on his own, but came haring back to the station and we got here as quickly as we could."

"Well, I'm more than thankful to see you. And now I think I ought to go back to the hotel—I'm afraid my husband will be rather worried about me."

"The Chief will have rung him up," the plain-clothes

man said. "We thought perhaps he was in ignorance of what was happening when our man told us that you'd come out alone."

I explained then how I'd overheard "the Reverend" in the telephone box.

"It was very plucky of you indeed," I was told in an admiring voice.

I began to feel quite a heroine.

But, heroine or no heroine, I knew what I must look like after my struggle with Christy and being shut up in that awful cell, and I was thankful to see my bag lying underneath the stairs. Everything was intact except my small looking-glass, which was smashed.

"That looks like seven years' bad luck," I said to the plain-clothes man and he laughed.

"Not for you, Mrs. Flacton, but I should think that's about what these men will get."

"Why—have you discovered something definitely incriminating?" I asked.

"I should think we have," he replied. "Look at this."

He took me into the room where I had seen the machines. They had gone but a policeman was sorting and stacking large piles of pamphlets. He gave me one to read. It started:

"Don't shoot! The German soldier is your brother. You should not take his life any more than you would deliberately kill one of your own family."

"To be distributed amongst the armed forces," the plain-clothes man said grimly. "There's a pretty big penalty for that alone; but there's more in this than meets the eye."

He patted a large collection of ledgers lying on the table.

"This is what we've been hoping to get hold of— the names and addresses of the people who are actively concerned with this crowd."

"Who's the man they call 'the guv'nor'?" I asked.

"I'm not quite certain of that yet, but he's a nasty bit of work. If I had my way I'd put him up against a wall."

"That's too clean a death for some of them," the policeman who was sorting out the pamphlets interposed.

I shuddered to think I had been at the mercy of such men and was remembering my sensations of horror when I heard someone coming down the stairs and, a second later, Peter came into the room followed by another man.

"Mela!" he exclaimed. "Are you all right, darling?"

He hurried across to me and, taking no notice of the plain-clothes man and the policeman, put his arm round my shoulders. I was surprised to see that for once Peter's expression was really registering emotion. He looked harassed and desperately anxious.

"I'm all right now."

"I'm afraid Mrs. Flacton has had rather an unpleasant time, sir," the plain-clothes man said. "I was just telling her what very good work she has done for us."

"Good work be damned!" Peter replied. "Are you quite certain that you're not hurt?"

"Not seriously," I answered. "I'm only bruised and—to be honest—I was very frightened."

Peter took both my hands and held them tightly in his.

"You're never to do such a thing again. Never—never! You must have been crazy!"

"At any rate, I've really pulled off a coup, haven't I?"

I turned to the plain-clothes man who was smiling, but standing respectfully to one side, and I guessed that the man who had arrived with Peter was the Chief Inspector. He was reading one of the pamphlets. Then he held it out to Peter, but he spoke to me.

"You have indeed pulled off a coup, Mrs. Flacton, and I think the whole country will owe you a deep debt of gratitude. This is exactly what we suspected.

If these people aren't responsible for the sabotage that's been going on, I shall be very much surprised."

Peter barely glanced at the pamphlet. Instead, he looked down at me. I felt almost embarrassed by the intensity of his gaze. I moved away from him.

"We'd better be getting back, hadn't we?" I suggested. "I don't know what time our train goes."

"Oh, we've plenty of time," Peter replied, "but I think it would be a good idea if we went back to the hotel. Is there anything else you want, Chief?"

"I'm afraid there is," was the reply. "I'd like Mrs. Flacton to make a statement of what occurred. Would you mind coming to the police station on your way back to the hotel?"

"Does she have to be involved in this?"

"Not if we can help it," the Chief Inspector replied, "but I must have a statement. If we get enough evidence from what we find here—which seems very likely—I see no reason why Mrs. Flacton's name should be dragged into the case."

"I'd be very grateful if she could be spared that," Peter said. "After all, it's not been a pleasant experience for her."

His hand tightened on my arm as he spoke.

"It's been beastly!" I exclaimed. "Come and see where they locked me up."

I showed Peter the dirty little room in which I had been imprisoned and then we went up the stairs and out into the fresh air.

The police car was waiting at the corner of the street, surrounded now by a large crowd of people who had gathered hoping to see the fun. I felt certain they thought I had been arrested, but Peter laughed when I told him I felt like a criminal.

"What's happened to the men?" I asked.

"Oh, they've gone off in a Black Maria," Peter said. "By this time, they are all safely behind bars."

The Chief gave a few orders before we left, and I

saw they were packing the pamphlets and everything else from the room downstairs into another car.

As soon as we drove off, Peter slipped his arm through mine and drew me close to him.

"Thank God you are all right!" he said.

He spoke in a quiet voice, so that the Chief, who was sitting in front with the driver, couldn't hear what he said.

"Were you worried?"

"I couldn't think what had happened at first. I found your coat on the chair where I'd left you and I thought you had gone to wash, but then as the time went on and you didn't return I began to get anxious. I made inquiries in the hall, but no one had seen you go out."

"Just as I was beginning to wonder what I ought to do, the Chief telephoned me. He told me what had been reported and that they had already sent off a party of police to rescue you. You can imagine what I felt, Mela. I wondered what had happened to you—if you'd been hurt; if those devils had injured you."

He drew me closer. "I drove down to the police station and we came on here, but I don't think I've ever passed through a more miserable time. I was frantic."

It was funny to hear Peter's voice quite agitated, to realise that he was really upset. I was so used to him speaking calmly, to his being controlled and reserved, however peculiar the situation. I laughed—I couldn't help it.

"Oh, Peter!" I exclaimed. "I love you when you are really agitated about me."

"And I love you," he answered, and his hand gripped mine so hard that it hurt.

It didn't take me long to make a statement once we got to the police station, and when I had signed it and shaken hands all round and everyone had congratulated me on being so clever, we went back to the hotel.

Peter and I had an early dinner in the restaurant. He was very sweet and attentive to me and I began to feel that I had really done something wonderful.

I wondered what Tim would think when I told him. I wondered, too, if he would have been as perturbed as Peter was. I couldn't imagine him being agitated in quite the same way.

Tim seems to court danger because he never realises that things are dangerous; it never strikes him that anything is likely to go wrong and injure him physically; and I think that sense of immunity for himself affects him in the same way about things that concern me.

I remember once when we capsized in a sailing boat and were nearly drowned. We had to swim in a very dangerous current to the shore. I knew how dangerous it was because two people we both knew had been drowned only the week before, but Tim was quite unconcerned.

He laughed and talked and I knew him well enough to realise he wasn't doing it to cheer me up, to keep me confident or anything like that, but because it never for one moment entered his head that we mightn't get back—that our lives might be lost.

I can imagine Tim in the same position as Peter after this adventure of mine just saying: "Good for you, old girl", and starting to talk something else.

But it really was rather nice to have Peter proud of me and so pleased, and still terribly agitated at the mere idea that things might have gone wrong or that I might have been hurt.

When we got on the train at nine o'oclock, Peter opened the communicating door between our carriages and asked me if there was anything he could do for me.

"I think I'll go straight to bed. I feel tired now and there's not much to sit up for."

I pulled off my hat as I spoke and ran my fingers through my hair.

"You must be tired," he said sympathetically.

"You're quite certain you're all right?"

"Of course I am," I replied, reassuring him for perhaps the hundredth time.

Then he put his arms round me and drew me close to him.

"If anything happened to you now," he said. "I think it would kill me. I love you, Mela—I love you so desperately. And I don't think I realised how much until this evening."

Chapter Nineteen

As we drove down the street to Peter's house—or rather, to what I must now think of as our home—I suddenly felt ashamed and horrified while passing the blackened, crumbling walls of the house in which Uncle Edward had been killed.

All my affection for him flooded back into my mind, to remain there accusingly, making me see how utterly selfish I had been and how unfaithful to his memory.

I had loved Uncle Edward very dearly and was humiliated to think how, with my marriage to Peter and the complications over finding that Tim still loved me, I had been able to put all that affection to one side and concentrate only on my own small interests.

I remembered that I had sworn to myself I would find his murderers; I had been impatient to Peter's cautious and less emotional tackling of the problem; and yet, despite all that impatience I had been the first to give up, to let the fire of enthusiasm die down.

There wasn't time to tell Peter what I had been thinking before we drew up outside his green front door. How long ago it seemed since I had first crossed the threshold escorted by the inspector! How different I felt in myself.

But this wasn't a moment to be introspective for, ahead of us, was the somewhat embarrassing difficulty of breaking the news to Sybil and Vilie that we were married.

It was still too early in the morning for either of them to be up. Our train had got into London at seven o'clock and it was now only about half-past.

We went into Peter's study, where a fire was burning brightly on the hearth, and Bates, the butler, told us that breakfast would be ready in just a few minutes.

"I'm hungry," I said.

"Did you sleep well?" Peter asked.

"Absolutely perfectly. I feel that really I ought to have lain awake racked with agitation by the events of the evening, but instead, the moment my head touched the pillow I was asleep. I don't remember anything until the attendant woke me up at half past six."

"I wish I could say the same. I was worrying about you most of the night, thinking of all the awful things that might have happened to you."

"Well, they didn't, so why worry? Peter, do you think that 'the guv'nor' and those men who worked with him really had anything to do with the killing of Uncle Edward?"

"I don't know," Peter answered. "I feel that it is unlikely. Of course we may discover the papers that were taken from your uncle's safe, in which case we shall know certainly that they were his murderers, but I think that while they would sabotage machinery, they would stop at taking life."

"Then we are no further forward than we were before," I said with a sigh.

"We shall know in a few days. The Chief promised to get in touch with me if anything of importance was discovered."

I held out my hands to the fire.

"I'm feeling rather guilty."

"Why?"

I explained in a few words what I had felt as we passed Uncle Edward's house.

Peter put his arm round me.

"No one could have done more than you have. You mustn't be disappointed if it takes time to bring these criminals to justice. They'll be found in the long run."

"Do you really think so?" I said.

"I'm certain of it."

At that moment, Bates told us that breakfast was ready and we went into the dining-room. When we had finished, Peter said he had a lot of work to see to so I went upstairs to superintend my unpacking.

I hadn't been in my room more than a few minutes when he opened the door and walked in.

"Hello," I said in surprise. "Is anything the matter?"

"Why should there be?" Peter asked with a smile. "Don't look so astounded at seeing me—it isn't very complimentary."

"Sorry," I smiled.

"I'll tell you what I came to see you about," he went on. "How exactly do you want us to word the explanation of our marriage to Sybil?"

"I was leaving that to you."

"I don't want . . ." Peter began.

But what he was going to say I never knew for, at that moment, a gay voice called out:

"Can I come in?"

Without waiting for my reply, Sybil entered, clad in her dressing-gown.

"How are you, dear child?" she said, and then she saw Peter. "Peter dear, welcome home. I'm so sorry I wasn't down but I had no idea your train would be so early."

While she was kissing us rather effusively, I heard another voice at the door. It was Vilie. She was looking entrancing, I had to admit that even to myself, in a négligée of pale pink satin trimmed with masses of swansdown.

"I thought all this noise and excitement must be over Pe-taire's return," she exclaimed. "Pe-taire dear, it is so lovely to have you home again."

She kissed him effusively on both cheeks and turned to me.

"And Mela, too. We've missed you so much. We have been so lonely, haven't we, Sybil?"

"We have indeed," Sybil replied. "And what have you been up to? Tell us all the news and excitements from the North."

"We have 'been up to' rather a lot," Peter replied.

206

Although his voice was calm, with a hint of humour in it, I knew that he was nervous.

"As a matter of fact, Mela and I have got some rather exciting news for you."

"What is it?" Sybil asked, looking from one to the other of us, while Vilie darted a quick look of suspicion at me.

"Mela and I are married."

For a moment there was absolute silence—so complete that I could hear myself draw a deep breath—then Sybil gave a little cry.

"My dears, I had no idea! When did this happen? I . . ."

Her voice trailed away into incoherence, and Peter laughed.

"I was afraid it would be a bit of a shock; at the same time, I hope you will congratulate us."

"Of course I do," Sybil said, "and I hope you will both be very happy."

There were tears in her eyes as she kissed Peter and me again. Although I was interested in what Sybil felt and thought, most of my attention was riveted on Vilie. I have never seen anyone's face register more emotions in the space of a few seconds.

She was angry, suspicious, resentful, spiteful, all within a minute—before, with quite an admirable effort at self-control, she exclaimed:

"But it is too exciting! How wonderful for you both and how happy you must be!"

"Tell us all about it," Sybil commanded. "Where were you married?—and why did you have to be so secretive about it?"

Peter was ready for her questions.

"Mela wanted the ceremony to take place in Scotland so that her grandfather could be present," he said, "and I'm afraid we both wanted to avoid publicity and all the usual chatter that goes with a fashionable wedding."

"It's very unkind of you to keep all the fun to yourselves," Sybil exclaimed in a facetious manner.

I could see that underneath a surface animation she was worried, and I guessed that already she was wondering about the future and how much this new development would affect herself.

We talked for some time, and then Peter said he really must do some work and Sybil said she'd finish dressing. They wandered off and I was left alone with Vilie. She walked across the room and took a cigarette out of the glass box which stood on the writing table.

As she lit it, she looked at me piercingly from under her dark eyelashes, then she sat down on the bed, wrapping her dressing-gown over her legs.

"How clever you've been, Mela," she said in her sweetest voice, but I glimpsed the naked steel under the smooth surface.

"Clever?" I asked, raising my eyebrows.

"Brilliant! You've certainly wasted no time in getting what you wanted."

"Are you referring to Peter by any chance?"

"Of course. And are you so very, very happy?"

I thought swiftly of how Tim had sensed that my marriage was what he called "phoney" and I was determined, if it was humanly possible, to keep Vilie from thinking the same thing.

"Very, very happy," I said with exaggerated emphasis.

"You are lucky!" Vilie ejaculated, and then she got up from the bed and walked across to the fireplace.

"All the same," she said in a low voice, "I think Pe-taire has treated me very badly."

"Why?"

"It is so difficult for me to tell you. I am sure Pe-taire has said nothing. After all, Englishmen don't talk about the women of whom they are fond, but Pe-taire and I . . . well . . . how can I put it into words? We meant so much to each other—and now . . ."

She shrugged her shoulders and made one of her expressive gestures.

"Are you trying to tell me," I asked brutally, "that you and Peter were lovers?"

Vilie looked at me with wide, dark eyes.

"How did you guess?" she asked in a voice hardly above a whisper.

"Well, I don't believe it."

"Of course you wouldn't care to hear such a thing," Vilie started.

"It doesn't matter whether I care about it or not," I retorted. "I know Peter well enough to know that he would not have an affair with a girl who was under his protection and living under his roof. What you expect to gain by telling me such a story I don't know, but I'd take a pretty big bet that there isn't a word of truth in it."

If ever one woman wanted to murder another, Vilie wanted to kill me at that moment—in fact, had she had a weapon of any sort near her hand I think I should have been frightened.

As it was, she seemed inarticulate with anger as, without another word, she walked out of the room.

When she had gone, I wonder what had made me so sure that she was lying and I came to the conclusion that it was because Peter had a fine character.

One had only to be with him to discover his integrity. I knew instinctively that he would never have demeaned himself by being Vilie's lover surreptitiously while she was living in his house and chaperoned by Sybil.

I didn't get much time to think about what had happened for there came another knock at the door. I called out "Come in", and there stood Max!

"Peter has just told me!" he exclaimed. "I am furious with you!"

"Furious with me?" I repeated stupidly.

He smiled as he raised both my hands to his lips.

"For not keeping yourself for me. You know I loved you first, long before Peter thought about it."

"How ridiculous you are!" I said laughing.

There was a natural, spontaneous gaiety about Max which was infectious.

"You are not to laugh," he said reproachfully. "I am very serious. I am quite devastated to think I have lost you."

"I shouldn't worry too much."

"You mean there's still hope for me?"

"I mean nothing of the sort," I said, pretending to be severe but not succeeding very well.

Max was so ridiculous and he looked very handsome with his dark hair and white teeth—like the hero of some fairy story.

"I hardly expected to find you still here," I said a moment later.

"I shall not be in uniform for another week so I still have a chance to win you away from the impetuous Peter."

"You'd better not let Peter hear you say that," I retorted, and at that moment Peter walked into the room.

"What am I not to hear?" he asked in a quiet voice and I knew at once that he was furious at finding Max in my bedroom.

"We were only joking," I said hastily; but the frown between Peter's eyes did not lighten.

"I wanted to speak to you alone, Mela," he said in a pointed manner and Max quickly walked towards the door.

As he shut it behind him, Peter turned to me and in quite a savage voice asked:

"What's he been saying to you and what is he doing in here?"

"He came in to congraulate me," I answered, "and we were only joking."

"I don't care for those sort of jokes," Peter said.

I realised that this was not a moment to laugh at his jealousy or to treat it lightly.

"I'm sorry," I said humbly, "but it's only Max."

"What do you mean—'it's only Max'?" Peter demanded. "That young man seems to take a great many liberties with you."

A spirit of rebellion entered into me at that moment. It rather annoyed me that Peter, who was my husband only in name, should be laying down the law in this manner. Besides, I liked Max and I felt it was ridiculous for Peter to be making such a fuss about him.

"I shouldn't make a mountain out of a molehill," I said quietly. "Max is an amusing boy, and I don't think my behaviour with him or his with me need trouble you unduly."

"But it does trouble me a good deal," Peter retorted. "You forget that I saw him kissing you when you'd only been in this house a few hours. It is not the mode of behaviour I expect of my wife."

"And what do you expect of your wife?"

"That she should behave like a lady," Peter replied, and I knew then that he was really angry.

I was angry, too. I felt that he was belittling me, suggesting that I was undignified and common, and I felt also that he was unjust. Max was only a young boy—it was absurd that Peter should take him seriously.

"I always had a suspicion that the English were old-fashioned," I said slowly, and in my most sarcastic voice, "but now I am certain of it. In Canada we are far too emancipated to consider that a woman is a chattel of her husband and therefore has no feelings or independence apart from him."

"You know I don't expect that," Peter said. "But there is one thing I won't have, and that is, other men making love to my wife. Let me make that quite clear."

I wondered what he would say if he knew about Tim and, for the first time, I realised that I was rather frightened of Peter. Something warned me that it would be wise not to drive him too far. I stopped being angry, walked across the room and put my hand on his arm.

211

"Don't be cross, Peter," I said. "There's honestly nothing to be angry about and this is not a very good way to start our homecoming."

I felt him relax and, taking my hand, he kissed it.

"I'm sorry, Mela, but I warned you that I was jealous about you."

"You warned me, but I did expect you to be reasonable."

"I'm sorry," Peter said again and put his arms round me and kissed me. "Thank goodness, that young monkey will be out of the house in a week! And I must have a talk to Sybil later in the day and suggest she make other arrangements. Perhaps I can persuade her to take Vilie with her."

"So we are to be 'alone in our glory'?"

"Do you mind that? I want you to myself—I want to be alone with my wife."

Although he didn't ask a question I knew that he was waiting for my reply, yet somehow I couldn't say the words that I knew he wanted to hear. I couldn't pretend that I wished to be alone with him when in reality I was hoping to see Tim, longing for his arrival in London.

There was a silence between us—an awkward silence—then Peter sighed.

"I came upstairs to tell you," he said, "that I have had a call from Glasgow. It was the Chief. He tells me that they have been through all the papers which were found and taken statements from all those concerned, but, so far as he can see, they cannot in any way be connected with your uncle's death."

"Then we are back where we started," I said sadly. "All this has happened and it has got us no further."

"I'm afraid that's true," Peter answered.

But I knew he was thinking that we ourselves had gone a great deal further. I walked away from him towards the window.

"What do we do now?"

"I shall be going round to Scotland Yard later in the

day. We can but hope that they have found some clue which might be of assistance, and if they haven't, then we must just wait and hope that something will come to light in time."

"I would like to avenge Uncle Edward," I said softly, looking up the street.

"So would I. You might go and see Rosy Hewlett some time and see if she can suggest anything else."

"She's already helped us into rather a lot of trouble," I said with emphasis.

"It has been worth while," Peter replied confidently. Then he opened the door.

"Good-bye, Mela, for the moment."

"Good-bye."

He hesitated.

"You aren't angry with me?"

"Would you care if I was?"

Peter shut the door again with a sudden slam. Then he walked across the room and, putting his hand under my chin, tilted back my head.

"You're having a very bad effect on me," he said accusingly. "I'm going to find it difficult to concentrate on my work. Whatever I am doing, I find myself thinking of you. I think you have bewitched me. If we lived in the Middle Ages I'd have you burnt at the stake!"

I laughed, but I felt slightly at a disadvantage with my head tipped back and yet, at the same time, I rather liked the feel of his strong fingers on my neck.

"I must be the right sort of politician's wife and keep your ambition clearly before you. Go and work, Peter."

In reply he pressed his lips against mine, kissing me long and lingeringly. There was no fierceness in his kiss but only possessiveness which seemed to draw me to him, sapping my will, making me limp and pliable in his hands.

Then, when my head was against his shoulder, my eyes half shut, he let me go. He said nothing, merely walked in his jerky, limping manner across the room and out through the door, leaving me alone.

"What do I think and what do I feel?" I asked myself, and could find no answer.

I liked Peter kissing me, I wasn't going to deny that, though I felt that I was being in some way dishonest to Tim. Is it possible to love two men? I wondered and laughed at my own question.

I didn't love Peter, there was no likelihood of that, but I was fond of him. He was a nice person and one wouldn't be ashamed of anything he did or of belonging to him.

I still found it hard to remember that I was no longer Pamela MacDonald. There had been two cablegrams waiting for me at the house and Bates had brought them to me while we were having breakfast.

One was from Mummy, the other from Daddy. For a moment, when I saw my new name on the envelope, I felt they could not be for me. "Mrs. Peter Flacton."

How strange it seemed! And still stranger to read Mummy's and Daddy's congratulations on my marriage.

I wondered now what they would think of Peter and I knew with absolute certainty that they would like him—Mummy especially. I suppose he is the sort of person that everyone would like for a son-in-law—steady, reliable, conscientious, and rich.

What more could any father and mother ask for their daughter?

When I had been so unhappy about Tim, I had realised that Mummy and Daddy had not been half so enthusiastic about my marrying him as I had always believed. They had thought him too reckless and, although they had been certain he would steady down with marriage, they would have preferred an older man.

"Well, Peter is older," I thought now, "he is certainly steady enough."

I wondered if the thought of what would compensate them for knowing that I must live in England and far away from them.

Sitting in my bedroom after Peter had gone, a sudden

214

wave of home-sickness swept over me. I wanted to be in Montreal, to be with Mummy and Daddy. I did not really care if Tim was there or not, I just wanted to be at home—to be surrounded by people who loved me, who had always cared for and appreciated me.

I felt young and vulnerable and "stranger in a strange land". Everything had become very complicated—Tim and Peter, and now Vilie and Max, all mixed together like pieces of a puzzle which would not fit in and reveal the pattern.

"What shall I do now?" I thought, and knew for the first time there was nothing I could do.

I was caught! Married to a man who loved me and whom I did not love—a part of his household, bearing his name. I felt afraid of the future and my confidence seemed to ooze from me and I longed with an almost unbearable longing to be able to run home to Mummy.

"Don't be such a little fool!" I told my reflection in the glass, but the feeling was there all the same.

Restlessly I powdered my nose and changed my dress, then I went downstairs to the drawing-room to find Sybil and Vilie sitting on the sofa in front of the fire.

As I entered, they stopped speaking and I knew instinctively that they had been talking about me. Sybil got up and linking her arm through mine said gushingly:

"We have just been talking, Vilie and I, and wondering what arrangements you would like us to make about leaving here."

"You must talk to Peter about that," I suggested guardedly.

"I'm sure Peter will do anything you suggest," Sybil said.

"I'd rather leave him to manage his own affairs, Peter understands these things far better than I do."

"What a model wife you are, Mela," Vilie exclaimed.

"But of course," I answered suavely. "Why shouldn't I be?"

What we said was simple enough, and yet there was

215

an edge on the words and an atmosphere of antagonism between us which even Sybil sensed. She looked from Vilie to me unhappily, and then said soothingly:

"I'm sure Mela is right—we must talk to Peter. Shall we go and see him now?"

"He has gone out," Vilie said. "He told me he had an appointment."

She gave me an inscrutable glance as she spoke and, although I knew she was purposely trying to arouse my curiosity, I could not help wondering when she had seen Peter and what they had said to each other.

Chapter Twenty

As I came down the stairs Peter called me into his study.

"I don't want to worry you, darling, but you may notice when you go out that there is a plain-clothes man watching the house."

"What for?"

"It's ridiculous really, but Scotland Yard thinks there might be an attempt at burglary here."

"Burglary!" I echoed. "Why?"

"Well, they had the idea that the men who opened your Uncle Edward's safe haven't found all that they expected to although why they should want more is beyond me!

"It's just an idea of the Chief Inspector's and I think he may be wrong; but while we were away, some suspicious-looking individuals were caught hanging about the house, and the Chief Inspector has therefore insisted that they put a man on guard both at the front entrance and at the back."

I could see Peter was minimising the whole affair so that I should not worry.

"What else can they want?" I asked. "Surely, if they got all those papers there's nothing more they need?"

Peter shrugged his shoulders.

"One can never tell. If there's Nazi influence at work, they are certain to be insatiable. There were, of course, a lot of important papers and records which luckily were not at that time in your uncle's safe but were at his office."

"Why should they think you have them?"

"I can't think, because actually I have nothing here of any importance. I expect the men they saw were perfectly ordinary burglars or maybe quite harmless

217

individuals who had no interest in me or in any other politician."

"Well, I don't like it," I said nervously.

I don't know why but I felt nervous at the idea of men watching the house.

Peter looked worried.

"Look here, Mela, would you rather go away? I know your grandfather would be glad to have you, or else there are some relations of mine in the country who would welcome you with open arms."

"Don't be such an idiot! You don't think I'm worrying about myself, do you? I'm thinking of you."

I have never seen Peter looking so pleased or so happy.

"That's the nicest thing you've ever said! Sometimes I feel that you wouldn't care a damn what happened to me, even if I was blown up by a bomb this very moment."

"Of course I'd care. How can you be so stupid! And if there's any danger, I'm glad they've got policemen watching the house—I'm only sorry we can't have a whole regiment to protect us."

"I'm not as important as that yet, but if you are going to be nice to me, Mela, I'm quite certain I shall be one day."

I picked up my bag which I had put down on the table, put it under my arm and started to button my gloves.

"You'd better hurry up. I'd like to be the wife of an eminent statesman."

Peter got up from his desk and stood beside me. He waited a moment, then he asked:

"Won't you kiss me good-bye?"

"I'm only going out for an hour," I replied. "Is it really necessary?"

I was teasing him, but for a moment he thought I was serious; then, as I smiled at him mischievously, he put out his arms and drew me close.

"You're looking lovely. Whom are you going to dazzle?"

"Only a house agent. I'm going with Sybil to find a little flat where she can set up house at your expense."

"Who said I was paying?" Peter asked quickly.

"Nobody," I replied. "But I don't have to be intuitive to guess that. When Sybil first talked of moving it was to be one room in Battersea or Hampstead—now we are searching Mayfair for a flat with at least six rooms facing south."

"Don't let her know that you know I'm helping her," Peter cautioned.

"Why not?"

"She feels self-conscious about it."

"Nonsense!" I retorted. "The trouble with you, Peter, is that you are too kind-hearted. I think Sybil and Vilie are imposing on your good nature. If I'm not careful there will be nothing left for me."

"You shall have everything in the world you want, if it is possible for me to give it to you."

"Thank you. I shall keep you up to that one day. Now I must go."

I turned my cheek towards him, but deliberately he sought my lips. I felt a little tingling thrill because he was so masterful.

"Good-bye, my darling, and take care of yourself," he said as he released me.

"I am the person who should say that!" I replied.

I went out of the study and shut the door. Sybil was coming down the stairs.

"Are you ready, Pamela?" she asked. "If we don't hurry we'll get nothing done before lunch time."

"I'm quite ready."

Bates hurried across the hall to open the front door for us. As he did so, I heard the bell ring in the servants' quarters. He opened the door. Tim was standing on the doorstep.

"Tim!" I exclaimed. "What a surprise!"

"I arrived this morning. How are you, Mela?"

I introduced him to Sybil and then we stood talking awkwardly on the doorstep until I suggested he should come with us.

"We are going to a house agent in Hanover Square," I told him. We all got into the car and the conversation was rather difficult. I could see that Sybil was curious about Tim. When we got to the house agent's office she got out first and Tim murmured something about leaving us. Seizing the opportunity, I said:

"I shall just walk a little way up the street with Flying-Officer Grant. I won't be a moment, Sybil—you go in and see if they've got anything on their books."

She did as I suggested and at last Tim and I were alone.

"I've got to see you," he said. "Can't you get rid of the old trout?"

I laughed because I knew that such a description would annoy Sybil who had been coy and girlish in the car.

"I've got to see you," he repeated. "I have been to the Air Ministry this morning and I'm due back there again this afternoon. I'm not certain how long I shall be in London but I'm here for at least a day or two."

"I don't know quite what to suggest," I said. "It's so difficult. Why don't you come to dinner this evening?"

"I don't mind doing that, but I want to see you alone. What are you doing tomorrow?"

"Nothing as far as I know."

"Well, lunch with me. You must just make an excuse to get out on your own."

"I'll try, but it won't be easy. Peter knows that I have no friends in London."

"Why not tell him the truth? I'm a friend, if you like to put it that way."

"You don't understand," I said unhappily. "Peter is jealous of me."

"Damn it all!—so am I," Tim replied. "Come on, Mela, it isn't like you to make difficulties."

220

"All right, I'll arrange it somehow. Come to dinner tonight, anyway."

"Can't we go off and dance somewhere together when dinner's over?"

"Don't be so ridiculous, Tim," I said. "You talk as if Peter is an old man of eighty who's content to let his young wife dance about with men of her own age. Peter has no intention of letting me do anything of the sort, I can promise you that."

"Blast the fellow! Oh, Mela, why on earth did you get married?"

I turned away from him.

"I've got to go. Sybil will think it queer if I hang about here much longer."

"Well, I'll see you this evening then," Tim said, somewhat ungraciously. "What time do you dine?"

"Half-past eight."

"Well, I'll be there at eight. Get down early and there'll be a chance for a talk before dinner."

I promised to do that and hurried into the house agent's.

But our plans did not work out right. Peter kept me talking before dinner and then, when I was completely dressed and putting a last finishing touch to what I imagined was a glamorous appearence, I upset a bottle of nail varnish all down the front of my dress.

Of course, that meant changing and it was nearly twenty minutes past eight when I hurried down to the drawing-room. To my surprise, I heard voices, and when I opened the door there was Tim, and, sitting by his side on the sofa, chatting away inconsequently, was Vilie . . .

It is extraordinary how irritating Vilie can be. I couldn't dislike a woman more. She was wearing a soft white dinner gown of shadowy lace and it made her look very fragile and attractive.

I was not so stupid or conceited that I couldn't see Tim had not worried unduly about my being late. What was more, I guessed that Vilie had been trying to flirt with him, for he jumped to his feet exclaiming, "Hello, Mela dear," with a heartiness which told me at once that he was feeling guilty.

"Hello," I said coldly, and then to Vilie: "How nice of you to entertain Flying-Officer Grant for me."

"It has not been a very difficult task," Vilie replied, quite unabashed by my sarcasm. "He is so, so interesting."

Tim smiled at her and I could have slapped them both, although by the end of the evening my feelings called for far more drastic action. I can't even think of that dinner without feeling hot with anger.

Vilie behaved outrageously and there was no doubt about it that Tim encouraged her. Of course, he always was an idiot where women were concerned—nobody should know that better than me—at the same time, you'd have thought that any decent young man with Tim's upbringing would have been disgusted by Vilie's ostentatious and affected manner of behaviour.

But Tim seemed to like it, and, what was more, Peter kept encouraging them. He took up the attitude that he and I, as two old married people, should be only too glad to encourage "love's young dream"—and by the time we left the dining-room to have coffee upstairs I was almost speechless with rage.

Then came the crowning insult of all. Vilie, in that soft, cooing voice of hers which always makes me think of taking a surfeit of maple syrup, said:

"Oh, dear!—how gloomy the war news is. How I wish we could forget about it for a little while—just dance and be happy and pretend such terrible things weren't happening all over the world."

Tim fell for that.

"Why shouldn't we? I'm sure you can tell me what are the most amusing places in London."

Peter looked at me.

"Would you like to go and dance somewhere, Mela?" he suggested.

"No, I wouldn't," I replied snappily. "We'd much better sit here and talk."

I had no intention of letting Tim and Vilie dance together if I could help it. But I had not counted on Vilie's cleverness.

"But of course!" she said, clasping her hands. "I'd forgotten! How tactless we are being! Mela and Peter are a honeymoon couple and here we are being very '*de trop*'! We must be kind and leave them alone."

She raised her eyes to Tim and he was just ensnared like a stupid little rabbit. Almost before I realised what was happening, Vilie and Tim had gone off in a taxi together to some night-club and I was sitting alone with Peter.

Sybil was out to dinner and I could see, as Peter came back into the room having seen the other two off, that he was fancying us as a kind of Darby and Joan sitting each side of the hearth, me with my knitting and he with *The Times*.

It was with the greatest difficulty that I prevented myself from either screaming or bursting into tears.

"Vilie seems to have made quite a conquest," he said, and then, as I didn't answer, he went on: "Perhaps that is one solution to the problem of what I am to do with my ward, although I can't imagine Vilie settling down in Canada when the war is over."

"I'm sure you wouldn't like her to go so far away," I said nastily.

"I don't mind where she goes as long as she is happy and safe."

"You can hardly expect me to believe that you are so disinterested, especially when Vilie tells a very different story."

"What do you mean by that?" Peter asked sharply.

"How long had Vilie been here before I came?"

"You haven't answered my question," Peter said sternly. "What did you mean by that remark, Mela?"

I had made up my mind that I wouldn't repeat what Vilie had said to me in my bedroom, but now I was

223

so angry about Tim that I threw all discretion to the winds.

"Vilie tells me that you and she were lovers," I replied. "You can hardly expect me to welcome the knowledge."

Peter walked across to me and stood very near.

"It is a lie," he said quietly.

"Of course I couldn't expect you to give away another woman's secrets," I said, more or less echoing Vilie's own words.

"I have told the truth," Peter insisted in a steady voice. "It is a lie and you know it is."

"How should I know?" I asked, wide-eyed.

Peter put out both his hands and gripped my shoulders so hard that it hurt.

"I am telling you the truth and I expect you to believe me."

"In that case, am I to tell your guest that she is a liar?"

"Anyone who tells you a story of that sort is a liar and you can tell them so. But I can't believe that Vilie said anything of the sort."

"So you prefer to think that I am the liar?" I said bitterly. "Vilie's perfect as far as men are concerned, I quite realise that. She's so pretty, so young, so innocent and so ill-treated by fate! Personally, I'm quite sure she's none of those things, and if you weren't such a simpleton you'd realise it."

I had spoken both violently and aggressively. Peter, who was still holding my shoulders, gave me a little shake.

"Don't Mela. I hate to hear you talk like that and about another woman. Vilie's been through a very tough time—we've always got to remember that. Think what it would mean to you if you'd lost your home, your father and mother, and everyone you held dear."

"That's just about what I have lost," I said, "by marrying you. I certainly can realise what Vilie is feeling far better than you can imagine, and what's more—I wish to God I'd never married you!"

I saw Peter's face as I turned away and rushed out of the room—slamming the door behind me—and ran upstairs to my bedroom.

Only when I was alone lying on my bed, feeling the hot waves of anger ebb away from me to be replaced by an abject misery, did I admit to myself that I had been unfair and unjust. I had vented my rage against Tim and Vilie on Peter, I had hurt him unbearably, and I hated myself for being so uncontrolled.

Yet when I thought of Tim and Vilie I felt that almost any action of mine was justified. Of course, I blamed her—who wouldn't? Tim was only a silly boy being led away by a pretty face and a fascinating foreign manner.

"Damn them! Damn them!" I said into my pillow, kicking my heels up and down on the bed as I used to do when I was a little girl and got into what Mummy called "my tantrums."

I had been there about half-an-hour when I heard a knock at the door. I didn't say anything; the knock came again and then Peter's voice said:

"Let me in, Mela."

"Go away," I replied. "I'm tired—I'm going to sleep."

There was a moment's pause, then he asked:

"Mayn't I come in and say good-night to you?"

"No. I want to be alone."

I heard him sigh and then he went away. When he had gone I felt lonely, sorry for myself and yet in some ridiculous manner resentful that Peter had obeyed me. I wished that he had broken down the door and forced himself upon me.

I wanted to be comforted and yet I felt prickly, ready to snarl and repulse anyone who tried to be kind. I thought of all the horrible things I could do to Vilie, I even imagined that I might denounce her as a spy, as being in some way responsible for Uncle Edward's death.

I hated her enough to do her any injury . . . then I began to feel ashamed.

I am a very quick-tempered person but the reaction comes almost as quickly. I got up from my bed and looked at myself in the glass.

My face was tear-stained, my hair untidy, my dress crumpled where I had lain on it. I slipped it off and put on the house coat in which I had been married, then I powdered my nose and tidied my hair and went downstairs.

The drawing-room was empty and I guessed that Peter would be in his study. Very quietly, I opened the door, intending to surprise him, but the room was in darkness save for a glow from the fire. I went in, switched on the lights and rang the bell. When Bates came I asked:

"Has Mr. Flacton gone out?"

"Yes, ma'am, he went out a few minutes ago."

"Do you know where he has gone?"

"I have no idea, ma'am."

I felt deflated and mortified. This was an anti-climax, both to my rage and to my hopes of reconciliation.

"Peter won't be long," I told myself as I fetched a book from one of the shelves and sat down in a big leather armchair by the fire.

I suppose emotion is exhausting; anyway, after a little while my head began to nod and then I knew nothing more until I opened my eyes to see Peter standing over me.

"Hello," I said sleepily.

"You've been asleep, Mela."

"I came down to say I was sorry and . . . you had gone out."

Although I was still drowsy, I saw the gladness in Peter's face and the sudden light in his eyes.

"You darling!" he murmured.

He knelt down beside me and lifted my head on to his shoulder.

"I was a pig and I'm sorry," I whispered.

He kissed me and I felt cosy, secure and comfortable. What did anything matter as long as Peter was there to look after me—to keep me safe—to go on loving me whatever happened?

"I love you, Mela," he kept saying, as he kissed my forehead . . . my hair . . . my lips . . .

Chapter Twenty-One

The telephone rang beside my bed before I was properly awake. The maid had called me and the sunshine coming in through the window dazzled my eyes as I opened them. I picked up the receiver and held it to my ear.

"Hello," I said.

It was Tim.

"Good-morning, Mela darling, are you alone?"

"Yes, of course I am, I've only just been called."

"Good heavens!" he ejaculated. "I've been up for hours. How lazy you're getting. Have you forgotten the days when we used to bathe before breakfast?"

"You're not suggesting I should take a dip in the Serpentine, are you?" I asked.

"No, I've got a much better plan than that. Listen."

His voice sounded gay and excited. I shut my eyes and momentarily recaptured the old thrill of the days before the war when Tim would ring me up and begin "Say, listen, Mela . . ." and go on to suggest some plan by which we could amuse ourselves.

"I've had a car lent me," he was saying now. "Chap in the Air Ministry who says I ought to see a bit of the English countryside. He's told me all sorts of jolly places to go to. I'll come round and fetch you in about an hour's time."

"Don't be silly!" I replied. "I can't rush off with you just like that.

"Why not?" Tim enquired. "If your husband isn't busy he ought to be. There's enough bad news in the paper this morning to give any politician a headache."

"But what can I say to him?"

"Tell him the truth. Good gracious, the man's not a

228

Turk, is he? I thought they believed in the emancipation of women over here."

I wanted to reply that I thought all men who were in love would like to keep their women veiled and unseen by other men, but I knew that Tim was hardly likely to appreciate such an idea, so instead I said:

"We've got to think about this. Don't be in such a hurry."

"Oh, I can't waste all the morning arguing!" he replied impatiently. "I'm in a call box. Be a sport, Mela, and think up some lie—that is, if you're afraid to tell the truth."

His gibe didn't sting me into rebellion as doubtless he thought it would, instead I hesitated.

"I don't know what to do."

"Come on, Mela," Tim pleaded, "you know what fun we'd have, and after all, I may have to be going back north very shortly—in fact, this may be our last chance of seeing each other."

After that, of course I couldn't resist. Tim was clever enough to use the one argument to which he knew I'd have no answer—that I might not see him again.

"All right, I'll come, but don't meet me here. I'll be outside Westminster Abbey in an hour and a half."

"Well, don't be late, and bring a thick coat with you. I've planned a perfectly marvellous tour all round Sussex and Surrey."

"In that case I'd better bring a suitcase," I laughed.

"It's an idea," he replied.

After we had said good-bye and rung off, I jumped out of bed; as I was having my bath, I wondered how I was going to tell Peter my plans for the day. Actually, when I got down to breakfast things weren't too difficult, Peter was preoccupied by a large post and the news in the papers.

"What are you going to do today, Mela?" he asked, and, before I could say anything, added: "I'm afraid I shall be out to lunch. There's a meeting of the 1939 Committee and a luncheon afterwards. Then the House is sitting this afternoon. I'm sorry, darling, it will be very dull for you, but we will find out what Sybil and Vilie are doing when they come down."

"Don't worry," I said hastily, "I'll fix something up."

I was thankful that both Sybil and Vilie were late for breakfast. Peter was actually going out of the room as they came in and he did not stop to discuss their plans for the day. Peter's engagements gave me the excuse for which I was looking.

I ran upstairs, hurried into my outdoor clothes, then went in to say good-by to Peter.

"Where are you going so early?" he asked.

"I thought I'd see if Rosy Hewlett was at home."

Peter nodded. "A good idea, but if you'd waited I could have dropped you there in the car."

"Oh, I'd like to walk," I replied hastily. "Good-bye Peter. I suppose you'll have gone by the time I get back?"

"I'm afraid so. Take care of yourself, dear."

"I'll try," I smiled, but I felt guilty as I turned towards the door.

Whether it was the haste in which I was leaving the room or just fate I don't know, but I caught my arm in the high back of a chair and it knocked the brown bag I was carrying out of my hand.

It opened, and the contents scattered all over the floor, a lipstick rolled under a chair, my powder box upset, handkerchief, pencil, and money flew in every direction.

"Bother!" I exclaimed.

Both Peter and I got down on our hands and knees to start picking them up. It was then that the clock on the mantel piece chimed the hour and I knew that Tim would be waiting for me.

Hastily, I stuffed the things back into my bag and clipped it shut. Peter opened a little silver box which he found underneath the sofa.

"Rouge!" he exclaimed. "You don't need that, Mela,

230

you're quite beautiful enough without 'painting the lily'."

"That's what you think. You should see my face unadorned in the morning."

"I hope to one day," Peter replied seriously, as I took the little silver box out of his hand.

"Good-bye," I said as I reached the door, and slipped away leaving Peter standing in the centre of his study looking after me.

I ran all the way to Westminster Abbey but when I arrived Tim was looking impatient.

"I thought you were never coming," he said reproachfully.

"I've been as quick as I could," I panted, as I got into a small blue two-seater car, "but you don't know how difficult it is."

"You should start as you mean to go on. Assert your independence in the first few weeks of married life and it's yours for eternity."

"What do you know about it?" I asked scornfully. "You've never been married."

"That's not my fault," Tim replied complacently.

He was driving carefully through the traffic and quite slowly for him because, he said, it was darned difficult to remember to drive on the left-hand side. Soon we began to leave the crowded streets and houses behind.

There were wide motor roads down which Tim could speed to his heart's content; there were green fields and tiny old villages with thatched cottages which made me exclaim as we passed them.

It was a lovely day. I think there was an English poet who wrote about the joy of being in England when it was April—there certainly seemed to me a kind of magic in the air, the sun was golden and dazzling, the trees and hedges were beginning to bud, and once, when we were passing a wood, we saw that it was carpeted with breathtakingly vivid bluebells.

Before we left the city behind I made Tim stop while

231

I went to a call box and rang up the house. Bates answered the telephone.

"Oh, is that you, Bates? It is Mrs. Flacton speaking. I shall not be back for lunch."

"Very good, ma'am. Shall I put you through to Mr. Flacton?"

"No thank you," I said hastily, "I won't worry him."

I rang off before Bates could say any more and hurried back to Tim.

"I'm not going to worry about the consequences of this," I told him, "I'm just going to enjoy myself."

"Good," he replied. "Think about me and forget yourself for a bit."

I wanted to retort that I was not thinking of myself but Peter, but of course that sort of remark wouldn't have gone down well. As we drove along, Tim took his left hand off the wheel and laid it on my knee, palm upwards.

I knew what he meant—it was an old gesture and one which recalled many lovely times together. I slipped my hand into his and his fingers tightened over mine.

"Happy?" he asked.

"Terribly."

That question and reply were almost a password between us.

We drove on, but we turned off the main roads and explored narrow lanes, we found hills covered with pine trees and a lake with its silver water dancing in the sunshine, and once, far in the distance, over undulating hill and dale, I caught a glimpse of the sea.

"I understand now," I said, "why people can never forget England, why poets call her a garden, why people like Mummy hold her memory unrivalled in their hearts after years and years of exile."

"It's not a bad dump," Tim said grudgingly, but I knew that he was almost as thrilled as I was.

We lunched in a tiny village where nearly all the houses were thatched and had diamond-paned windows which an old man told us had been there

232

since Elizabeth's reign. He may have been exaggerating, but anyway the whole village was amazingly old and there were even ancient wooden stocks on the village green.

The luncheon in the local pub was good—roast chicken, apple tart, and cheese. Tim drank beer but I had cider which really tasted of apples.

"I'm loving this," I exclaimed as we had our coffee after lunch sitting on high oak chimney seats before a log fire.

"So am I."

"Wouldn't it be fun if this was our honeymoon—if we could go wandering over England together in a car, staying in quaint little places like this, exploring the countryside and being utterly happy together?"

"Would you like that?" Tim asked.

"You know I would."

Tim said nothing but I knew by his face that he was regretting as much as I was the misfortune which had parted us, and had resulted in my marrying another man. But it wasn't like Tim to be unhappy or morbid for long; very soon we were laughing again and we set off in the car to see more.

We drove on and on. We had tea in another village, not such an attractive one, and although the tea-house called itself "Ye Olde Grey Gables Tea Roome" it was quite obvious that the whole thing was a fake and very expensive. Comparing it with our good luncheon we felt resentful and soon went on again.

It was six o'clock when I looked at my watch and said:

"We must be getting back to London, Tim."

"Oh, not yet," he said. "You're going to have dinner with me."

I shook my head.

"I can't do that. As it is, I am going to have great difficulty in explaining where I have been all day Besides, Peter will be home for dinner; the House rises early these days."

233

"I'm not going to spoil the day by taking you back before dinner," Tim insisted obstinately.

"But you must."

"I refuse. Besides, do you know how far we are from London?"

"I haven't the slightest idea."

"About eighty miles."

"Oh, Tim! How could you be so inconsiderate? This will get me into terrible trouble."

"Rubbish! Besides, as I told you on the telephone this morning this may be our last chance of being together."

"What do you mean by that?"

"Well, it's a secret, but there's talk of us going out East."

"Oh, Tim!"

I couldn't express what I felt at that moment. Tim going into danger . . . Tim going to some strange foreign country from which he might never return . . .

"So you will have dinner with me, won't you?" he asked.

"Yes, all right, I will."

Tim smiled at me and I knew him well enough to know that he was triumphant at having got his own way.

"Tim!" I said severely, "are you really going abroad or was that a bit just put in to make sure that I would insist on going home?"

Tim didn't meet my eyes, he looked ahead and there was just a fraction of hesitation before he said:

"Well there is talk of it."

"Oh, Tim," I expostulated. "you are unscrupulous! You'd really do anything to get your own way."

"Why not?" he asked complacently.

I had to laugh, I couldn't help it. It was so like Tim—his whole attitude to life has always been any-thing for expediency, anything so long as he is not disappointed or unsatisfied.

"You can't go back on your promise now," he said.

"I suppose not, but I'd better telephone again, otherwise Peter will be anxious."

About half-an-hour later, we found the most delightful old inn in a tiny village at the foot of the Downs. It was all oak beams and the bar had sawdust on the floor just as it must have had for hundreds of years.

There was no one else there to dinner and we had the tiny dining-room all to ourselves. There was a big fire burning in the grate and funny old sporting prints hung round the walls of men steeple-chasing in night-shirts. They made me laugh and I examined them one by one as I was waiting for my telephone call to come through.

At last the bell rang and it was with a beating heart that I lifted off the receiver. It was answered by Bates.

"Is Mr. Flacton in?" I asked.

"Oh, is that you ma'am? Mr. Flacton came in about an hour ago. He was rather worried about you."

"Is he there now?"

"I think he has gone round to a Mrs. Hewlett's," Bates replied. "I heard him saying something about it to Lady Flacton."

"Well, when he comes back, Bates, tell him that I am quite all right and that I shan't be back for dinner. I am with friends in the country."

"I'll tell him, ma'am. I'm certain he will be very relieved."

"Thank you, Bates."

"I've been caught out in Lie Number One," I said to Tim. "The only thing to do now is to make a clean breast of it. I shall say I met you in the street and that you persuaded me to come with you."

"My back's broad enough to take it," Tim laughed. "Don't look so worried—it doesn't suit your style of beauty."

"Bother my style of beauty!" I said crossly. "I'm going to have a terrible job explaining this.

235

Tim looked at me and then he put his hands on my shoulders.

"Do you know, Mela, I believe you're in love with this husband of yours."

"Of course I'm not," I replied quickly.

"Well, if you aren't why are you so frightened of worrying and troubling him?"

"Oh, just because he's been decent and nice to me. There's no point in upsetting people, is there?"

"No point at all, but it's better than being upset yourself. Mela, you haven't really changed towards me, have you?"

"You know I haven't."

"I want you to love me—I want you to go on loving me."

"Do you really care what I think or feel?" I asked; and then, despite everything my pride did to prevent it, the question which I had been holding back all day came to my lips. "Why did you go out with Vilie last night?"

"I couldn't very well help it, could I?" Tim replied, but he dropped his hands from my shoulders and took his cigarette case out of his pocket.

"I don't know. It seemed to me you weren't offering much active resistance."

Tim grinned.

"The enemy onslaught was terrific."

"She's like that with everyone," I said scornfully. "The very first night I arrived in England I was absolutely horrified at the way she was throwing herself at Peter's head. But men seem to like it."

"A little flattery goes a long way. You didn't mind, did you?"

I wasn't going to admit the truth—that I had minded, and minded terribly. Instead, I answered his question with another.

"What time did you get back last night?"

"Oh, in the small hours of the morning. We went to two or three places—jolly good fun they were, too, but expensive! Why, I hadn't a cent left by the time the dawn came."

"I'm glad you enjoyed yourself."

Tim laughed.

"Go on being jealous. I like to have beautiful women scrapping over my charms."

I was silent and he saw that I was hurt.

"Mela, dear. I didn't mean that, but, after all, I couldn't refuse to go out with her last night and you wouldn't come. It's a bit lonely for a fellow being in a city where he knows nobody and has no friends."

"Of course it is, I said compassionately, feeling I had been unkind, "But Tim, I don't like Vilie. She's horrid, and I can't think why you don't see it."

"Oh, she's amusing. And she's pretty, too—no one can deny that."

"And so everything else must be forgiven her, I suppose?"

"Well, why not?" Tim asked, almost truculently. "She's good to look at, amusing to talk to, a perfect dancer. Good heavens! what else does one ask for an evening's amusement? One isn't planning to spend the rest of one's life with the girl. Besides, if you want to know, she spent half the time we were out talking about your husband."

He laughed.

"You'll have to look to your laurels there, old girl, if you don't want to lose him."

I suddenly felt fed up with the whole conversation. Although the thought of Tim and Vilie together had been nagging at the back of my mind all through the happiness of the day, now we were talking about her the whole atmosphere was changed and overcast.

"I'll go and wash," I said. "I feel rather dusty and dirty."

I went upstairs to find a modern bathroom, although it had oak beams across the ceiling and only a tiny lattice window looking out over the courtyard and garden. While I was there, I peered into one of the

237

bedrooms and saw quaint old wooden beds and a dressing table with frilled skirts of white muslin.

I washed my hands, combed my hair, and felt better.

"We must get back to London immediately after dinner," I thought.

And I decided that the only thing to do was to tell Peter the whole truth of what had happened.

"He won't like it, but after all, there's no real harm in what I am doing."

When I got downstairs I found that Tim had ordered two glasses of sherry. We sipped them, sitting comfortably in front of the fire. I don't know why, but something made me ask Tim:

"What exactly did Vilie say about Peter?"

"Oh, she extolled his virtues all right. You'd have thought from all she said that the man was almost superhuman. I couldn't help thinking there was a catch somewhere."

"I hope you said equally nice things about me?"

"Of course I did! As a matter of fact, although you've got such a down on her, she was jolly nice about you and most sympathetic about all our misunderstandings."

"Tim!" I exclaimed in horror. "You don't mean to say you told Vilie that I had known you before we met over here?"

Tim looked shamefaced.

"Well, I didn't tell her exactly, she just sort of guessed it from something that was said. Oh, I don't know how it happened, we'd both had a lot to drink by that time and to tell you the truth, Mela, I don't know what I did say."

"But Tim, you must be crazy! Don't you understand?—she'll go straight and tell Peter and then he will never forgive me for having lied, for having decieved him when we met at the Castle."

"Now she won't do anything of the sort," Tim said soothingly. "I told her it was a secret, told her not to breathe a word to a soul—and she promised me."

"Vilie's promises won't count for much. How could you have been so mad, Tim? You must have known the harm it could do me."

Tim began to look sulky. It always infuriated him to be put in the wrong.

"I never liked the idea of all this pretence from the beginning," he said unjustly. "We ought to have said straight out that we knew each other and were friends."

"I quite agree with you, but we didn't, and nothing is more infuriating than being caught out in a lie."

"Don't you worry. Vilie won't let you down."

What was the point of arguing? I wondered. All the men seemed to have this trust and affection for Vilie, while I wouldn't have trusted her with anything, least of all my reputation.

"I suppose it's no use discussing it," I said wearily. "But we do seem to have made a mess of things. Let's have dinner quickly and get back to London."

"That doesn't sound very complimentary. I thought you liked being with me? After all, Mela, I'm the one who's really been injured over all this."

My heart melted towards him despite the fact that I knew it was entirely his fault it had happened at all.

"If only you hadn't told Vilie," I said unhappily.

"Well, it's done now. Don't let's spoil our last hours together, Mela. Here, we'll both have another glass of sherry."

He called the waiter and gave the order and at the same time asked for the wine list. To change the subject, I talked about the inn, telling Tim how charming it was upstairs and how clever they had been to combine modernity with old age. When the waiter came back with the sherry and the wine list, Tim turned over the pages and gave an exclamation.

"We're in luck! They've actually got some champagne left. Bring us a bottle of No. 21, waiter."

"I'll drink your health, Tim," I said.

"I'll drink to something much more interesting than that," he replied. "Besides, I've an idea."

"What is it?"

"I'm not going to tell you until after dinner," he said mysteriously, "but I promise you that it is something very nice."

Chapter Twenty-Two

We had a simple but well-cooked dinner.

Tim was in tremendous form, making jokes, teasing me, and altogether being his most charming self. Although I tried to respond at the back of my mind there was a little nagging voice which told me that I ought not to be there. I ought to have gone home, back to Peter.

I had also a very vivid idea how unpleasant my return was going to be.

I suppose there is nothing more disconcerting than to be caught out in a lie. How I wished I had never said that I was going to see Rosy Hewlett! But the deed was done and I wondered what Peter would think.

It was funny how much I wanted to establish myself in his eyes and make him think me a fine person. I suppose if any man loves a woman she always wants to appear at her best before him.

I like Tim to admire me yet I wouldn't have minded confessing a fault to him in anything like the same degree as I did to Peter. Perhaps it was because I have such a clear idea of Tim's faults, while Peter seems to have so few.

Barring his smugness and his complacency—which I suppose are, in reality, only an English kind of veneer developed by environment, rather than the clue of his own personality— he seems to me to be almost too perfect.

It is ridiculous, of course, and I expect in time I shall find he has all sorts of annoying habits, but for the moment they are well hidden—from me at any rate.

And so all through dinner I kept thinking of mis-

241

deeds and dreading the moment when I must face Peter and give him an explanation.

After all, I owed him one, he was my husband and he had always been very considerate and sweet to me.

It was all very well for Tim to say—"What does it matter?" and tell me laughingly that I should have to start another "Boston Tea Party" on my own. I just didn't feel like throwing Peter overboard—not even for Tim.

It was a funny thing, but more than once that evening I kept thinking that Tim was not the marrying sort really. However easily he could explain away his behaviour the night before with Vilie the fact remained—and I was wise enough to see it—that he had enjoyed himself.

It had been what he called "a bit of fun." There was no reason in the world why he shouldn't have his fun and everything else he wanted; but at the same time it was very likely, if he went on in that way, that he would break the heart of any woman who married him.

I wondered once or twice whether Audrey Herman had been really fond of him, and if he had broken her heart very nearly as completely as he had mine, when he came away from Winnipeg without saying good-bye to her.

But when one is with Tim it is very difficult to find fault with him. He is like a child, enjoying every second of the present, pouring all his vitality and energy into the pleasure of the moment. Such high spirits are infectious and it is hard not to respond and be as irresponsible as he is himself.

I admit that after a few glasses of champagne I found it easier than ever to find Tim amusing. He has the kind of humour that tickles mine. I suppose that if our conversation had been written down or recorded we shouldn't have thought it at all funny, but at the time it struck me as being exceedingly humorous.

The time sped past and, suddenly, I looked at the clock and gave an exclamation.

"Tim! It's nearly nine o'clock!"

"What about it?" he asked. "Do you want to hear the news?"

"Don't be so ridiculous!" I replied. "It will take us nearly three hours to get back to London. We must go at once!"

I got up from the table and started to collect my things which I had left by the fire.

"Wait a minute," Tim said, "let me finish this cigarette."

The old waiter, who had been attending to us, took our empty coffee cups and left the room. When he had gone, Tim threw his cigarette into the fire and standing beside me, said in a low voice:

"Have we got to go, Mela?"

"Of course we have," I answered impatiently, "and at once. Put your coat on, Tim. It's bad enough being out to dinner, but what Peter will think if we get back after midnight I can't think."

"Then why go back?"

"What do you mean?" I turned and looked at him with surprised eyes.

"You know what I mean. Don't go back, Mela— stay here with me tonight."

"You must be crazy!"

"I'm not. I'm merely being sensible and very much in love. What's the use of all these heroics? You don't love this husband of yours, you never have—you love me. Why shouldn't we find happiness here together?"

"You can't know what you're saying, Tim!"

"I do. I've thought about it for a long time. We're young, but life is very uncertain for everyone these days. Why shouldn't we take what happiness we can when we can get it?"

"You mustn't talk like that—really."

"But I am talking like it. Listen, sweetheart. I'm in the Air Force. I love the life, but you know and I know that it is a pretty precarious thing. At this moment they are very likely saying on the wireless—'Two of our aircraft failed to return.' Supposing I was in one of them?"

"Don't, Tim!" I exclaimed. "That isn't a fair argument and you know it."

"'All's fair in love and war'," Tim said, and he smiled.

It was his smile that broke the spell which had seemed to bind me while I listened to his words. With an uncertain laugh, I picked up my coat.

"Really, Tim, you are too ridiculous! For a moment I thought you were serious."

"I am serious. I mean every word of it. You're not such a child as to believe that a man doesn't suggest such things to a decent girl unless she has his wedding ring on her finger. All that sort of bunk went out with the Victorian era."

His voice deepened.

"I love you and I want you. I'd prefer you to be my wife but, as you've chosen to belong to another man, well—too bad! I still want you, although the ring on your finger wasn't put there by me."

"There's no question of arguing about this," I said. "Come on, let's go."

"I quite agree with you, there's no point in arguing. Therefore, Mela my sweet, I'm not going."

"What do you mean?"

"What I say," Tim replied, sitting down before the fire. "I'm going to stay here tonight and you are going to stay, too, and we are going to be very happy."

"How can you be so ridiculous!"

"I'm not—I'm merely being honest for once. I'm considering our own inclinations and our own desires, rather than those ridiculous copybook standards which were given us by old people who had forgotten how to live and love."

I stood staring at him, irresolute and uncertain. I

felt that he must be joking, and yet something within myself warned me that he was serious.

"Well, how do you think we are going to explain our presence here?"

"That's quite easy. In another hour or so I am going to ring up your husband and tell him that we have broken down. I shall say that, as luck would have it, we are not far away from some friends of mine and we are going to walk over and spend the night with them. He'll believe it."

"You seem to have thought of everything," I said sarcastically.

"I have. In fact, there's nothing for you to do but to sit down and be nice to me. This is our honeymoon night—yours and mine."

"I've never had a honeymoon yet," I said, "but if you think I am going to snatch one clandestinely and surreptitiously, fabricating a collection of lies which nobody but a child of five would believe, you're much mistaken! I'm going back to London now whether you take me or whether I have to walk."

Tim laughed.

"You'll soon get tired of walking, even if you knew the way—which you don't. No, darling, you can't go. Be sensible and give in with a good grace."

I put my coat down and walked across to his chair.

"Listen, Tim," I said in my most coaxing voice. "This joke's gone far enough. I'm late as it is. Stop teasing me and let's start for home."

He took hold of my hand and pulled me forward so that I was sitting on the arm of his chair.

"Listen, sweet, I know you feel in honour bound to protest and all that sort of thing, but it doesn't cut any ice with me. I want you and you want me—that's all that matters."

"But it isn't, Tim. Can't you see that there are much more important things than that? If we did, in any conceivable circumstances, behave as you want us to, we should feel not only disloyal but unspeakably mean. We

245

should have done a thing which—well . . . which isn't cricket."

"My goodness!—how English we are getting," Tim teased, and then, his voice serious again, he asked: "Don't you love me, Mela?"

"You know I do," I answered. "I love you and I've always loved you, but I shouldn't love you if we behaved in such a manner as to lose our self-respect."

"That's pure cant and nonsense. If I possessed you you'd love me with your whole being. At the moment you don't understand the meaning of the word love. Why should you?"

"If love means being dishonourable, cruel and despicable," I replied, "then I don't want to know the meaning of it. I'm sorry, Tim, but you know what you ask is an impossibility."

"It's not only a possibility but a certainty," Tim said.

He set his jaw in the way which I knew of old meant that he was going to be particularly obstinate, however unreasonable his idea might be.

"Please, Tim," I pleaded. "Please don't spoil our lovely day together."

"That's just why I'm not going to take you home. Can you imagine more of an anticlimax than handing over the woman you love to the man to whom she's married?"

"Well, that's what you've got to do. Come on. If you don't, I shall drive the car away myself and leave you here."

Tim got up from the chair.

"All right. Wait here till I bring the car round to the front door."

He put on his overcoat and went out of the room.

When he had gone, I realised that I was shaking with the strain of the past few minutes. I put on my coat and gloves and looked apprehensively at the clock. Would it be wise to telephone again? I thought I would.

Then I was afraid to in case Peter answered the telephone. I went out into the hall. There didn't seem to be many people about, although I could hear voices coming from the bar. I opened the front door.

It was a clear, starry night but there was no moon; it was also quite chilly. I listened, but there was no sound of the car, and, after a moment, I shut the door and paced slowly up and down the hall.

I must have been there over five minutes before the bar door opened, and there was the sound of laughter as Tim came into the hall.

"What a long time you've been," I said, "And where's the car?"

"The car's all right."

"Where is it?" I asked sharply. "I thought you were bringing it round to the front door."

"Don't be silly," he replied. "I only went to make certain that you wouldn't drive it away. Now it's completely immobilised."

For a moment I thought he had been drinking whisky in the bar. Tim has never had a strong head; unlike most of my countrymen who like whisky, it always disagrees with Tim. But my fears were unfounded, Tim was being difficult without any artificial aid. The only thing was to be pleasant—anger wouldn't get us anywhere.

"Don't tease me, Tim dear," I pleaded in my sweetest way. "What have you done to the car? Tell me and let's go home. We can talk about things as we go."

"You're not going to trick me that way. Come here."

He took my arm and half dragged me back into the dining-room and then putting his arms round me he started to kiss me. I suddenly felt furious with him. All my tact and diplomacy disappeared and I struggled to free myself from his arms. It wasn't easy, for Tim is very strong.

"Stop it!" I cried. "You aren't to kiss me. We've got to go back home at once. Do you hear me?"

247

"We're going to do nothing of the sort. I want to kiss you. Kiss me, darling."

I wrenched myself free and, running out of the room, I slammed the door behind me; then I found my way into the yard behind the hotel where I knew Tim had put the car. It was standing in a corner. I tried to open the door, but it was locked. I knew it was impossible for me to drive the car away.

What parts of the engine he had tampered with I didn't know but at least the car was completed immobilised as far as I was concerned. I was wondering what to do when a man came out of the hotel and started to crank up a lorry. He saw me standing there and asked:

"Anything wrong, miss? Can I give you a hand?"

"I was just wondering," I said slowly, "whether you are going towards London?"

"Yes, I am," he answered, "but not into the city. I've got a load here to be delivered at Putney."

"Would you be kind enough," I said quickly, "to wait just a few moments? I might ask you to give me a lift, but would you wait while I find out if it is necessary?"

I felt that was rather garbled—at the same time, it was difficult to know what to say.

"That's all right, miss," the driver said. "I'll hang on for a minute or two."

I ran back into the hotel and into the dining-room. Tim was still there sitting in a chair, his legs outstretched before him.

"Listen, Tim," I said. "This is an ultimatum. Either you take me back in the car right away or I'm going on a lorry which is starting now."

Tim looked at me steadily for a moment, then he rose to his feet.

"Oh all right," he answered, "have it your own way. Women are all the same—they'll always cheat if they get the chance."

I made no answer to that remark but as he came slowly across the room towards me I walked on ahead, thankful that I could hear him following me. The lorry was still waiting in the yard.

"Thank you very much," I said to the driver, "but I have managed to make other arrangements for getting through to London. It was so nice of you to have waited."

"That's all right, miss."

I got into the car. Tim had started the engine.

"If you don't know the way," I said, "you can follow the lorry. He's going as far as Putney."

Tim didn't answer and I knew he was sulking. We drove in silence, keeping the lorry in sight until he got onto the great concrete motor road, then Tim put his foot down on the accelerator and we shot ahead.

Tim is like me, he gets over his moods quickly. We hadn't been going for more than an hour when I felt his hand on my knee, palm upwards. I slipped mine into his.

"Happy?"

I did not respond with the password.

"Not very."

"I'm sorry, Mela, but it's all your fault."

"It would be," I murmured.

"You shouldn't be so damned attractive, and you shouldn't be married to another man."

"That's no excuse for you behaving badly," I said evenly.

"I know," Tim grinned, "but I don't really need an excuse."

I tried to be angry with him but I couldn't. In a few moments we were laughing. We joked and chattered until we were right into London and very nearly home, then suddenly Tim stopped the car in a quiet street.

"I want to kiss you good-bye, Mela. May I?"

"Of course."

He put his arms round me and drew me close.

249

"I'm damned sorry we didn't stay. Aren't you?"
I shook my head.

"We shouldn't have enjoyed it really, we should have been ashamed of ourselves."

"Don't you believe it!"

He kissed me passionately and lingeringly and yet, somehow, I couldn't respond. The arguments of the evening had spoilt something between us. I felt so immeasurably older and wiser than Tim.

I could quite genuinely believe that he couldn't see why I wouldn't stay with him—why I wouldn't throw all responsibility and morality overboard and just enjoy myself whatever the consequences either to ourselves or to others. Tim was a child—I was grown-up.

I sighed as Tim kissed me once more and the clock struck one.

It was only when I was actually on the doorstep that I felt almost too terrified to go in. I was trembling as I searched in my bag for the latchkey.

"Good-by, sweetheart," Tim called to me as I opened the door. "And good luck."

I smiled at him automatically and waved my hand. It was so like Tim, I thought resentfully, having got me into this mess to go gaily off, quite unperturbed, while I shrank in anticipation from the explanations which lay before me.

Tim hadn't offered to come in with me and, although I should have refused to allow him, I rather wished that he had been a little more considerate of my feelings. And yet, I told myself, why should I care?

Surely I was taking up rather a Victorian attitude—the shrinking little Englishwoman, frightened of her lord and master!

I could quite understand how my grandmother might have felt, for instance, had she to go back and make explanations to Grandfather after some youthful escapade, but Peter!—well, Peter need not worry me unduly.

I looked at myself in the mirror in the hall and noted

that I was looking very attractive, and then, jauntily, with a spring in my step, I crossed the hall and opened the study door.

As I expected, Peter was waiting there for me. He was waiting at his desk, and as soon as I entered he put down his pen and rose from his chair.

"Here I am," I said cheerily. "I hope you haven't been worried about me."

"I got your message," Peter answered, "but I didn't expect you to be as late as this."

"I was in the country, and you know how the black-out delays one."

"Who have you been with?"

I told the truth.

"Flying-Officer Grant."

"An old friend—how nice for you!"

There was something in his voice which made me nervous.

"I ran into him this morning when I went out and he asked me to go for a drive. He had been lent a car by someone in the Air Ministry. We didn't mean to be so late but you know how it is, motoring—especially in a strange country."

"What an extraordinary coincidence, meeting him like that," Peter said. "Almost as extraordinary as finding him at your grandfather's."

I felt myself stiffen at the implication.

"What do you mean?"

"Only that I hope, in future, you will not think it necessary to lie to me."

Peter took something out of his pocket and held it towards me.

"I found this on the floor this afternoon. It must have fallen out of your bag, and when Vilie saw it she told me that you and Grant are very old friends. It may seem strange to you but I have a rooted dislike to my wife carrying on an intrigue behind my back."

His voice, although it was low and quiet, flicked me like the lash of a whip.

I looked at the photograph. It was one I had always carried of Tim since we had been first engaged, and across it was written:

"To my sweetheart, from Tim."

Chapter Twenty-Three

I think I am the most miserable girl in the world. Everything seems to have gone wrong and I can't even begin to think how it will ever come right again.

Vilie has certainly managed to get her revenge—I don't think she could have thought out a more subtle one, not even if she had put poison in my food—for my whole life is poisoned right enough—at least, my life here in this house.

It is awful to notice the difference in the atmosphere—to feel stung and frozen by Peter's cool politeness, by his cruelty. And gives a polish to a hardness which amounts almost to cruelty. And yet there is nothing concrete that I can complain about.

He is just damnably polite to me and as distant as if I were a stranger he had met for the very first time. In actual fact, he is far more formal; I never realised that Peter could be like this; that I could find him so unapproachable—so utterly aloof.

I don't think I shall ever forget the humiliation of that moment when he handed me Tim's photograph.

Wildly I sought for some explanation but all power of expression deserted me and all I could do was to stare at the inscription, and looked in a dazed manner at Tim's handsome face staring at me from the piece of cardboard on which it had been printed.

I struggled to speak, to force some words from between my lips, but it was Peter who first broke the silence between us.

"There is nothing you need say," he said calmly and in that deadly quiet voice which I know so well by now.

"But I can explain, Peter," I said quickly. "I will tell you exactly what has happened."

"I assure you there is no need," he replied.

Then, before I could say another word, he walked to the door and opened it.

"I am sure you are tired after your long day in the country. Good-night, Mela."

I was mesmerised into doing what he wished. I walked through the open door and heard it shut behind me. Only as I got outside did I take a deep breath and feel as if someone had thrown a bucket of cold water over me. I turned to go back but somehow—it seemed ridiculous now—I just couldn't.

I had no idea that Peter could be like that, so strong, so ruthless. I think perhaps it would have been better if I had it out with him there and then; instead, I crept upstairs to my own bedroom, humiliated and ashamed.

When I got there, the first thing I saw was a vase of orchids on my dressing-table. Peter had given them to me the day before and as I looked at them I realised— perhaps for the first time—that I had been a fool.

Peter's affection and, indeed, Peter's love for me had begun to mean quite a lot these past days and not I had antagonised him. I did not realise then how wide was the gulf between us, but I was upset enough to tear Tim's photograph into tiny shreds and throw them into the fire.

I was ashamed of my behaviour that day, and also of Tim's. I knew neither of us had behaved well.

Suddenly I felt—as I suppose thousands of people must have felt before—that I had got into such a muddle in my life the only thing was to start again, and I had wild ideas of running away, of escaping.

How I longed then for Mummy and Daddy—for Canada where I had my friends—for all the dear familiar things I had known since I was a child! But even while I longed for them, something deep down within told me they would not be so satisfying now.

I wanted more than the past, I wanted to be admired and even loved by the people I knew here, by Peter and my grandfather. I thought then how shocked and horrified the latter would have been by my behaviour, and I felt a worm.

It hadn't been worth it—that day in the country with Tim—not worth all this trouble I had brought upon myself.

And how much trouble it was going to be I had no idea until the next day. It took me nearly twenty-four hours to realise to the full extent the barrier Peter had erected between us—then I began to understand his intentions. We were never alone.

Somehow he contrived, but in the most unostentatious manner, to be with me only when Sybil, Vilie or Max was there.

Then he was polite, with that damnable, icy politeness which seems to me as chilling and as devastating as a wind blowing over the snows of Siberia. He did it well, I must admit; in fact, I am not certain that Sybil realised what was going on.

Vilie knew, and I saw the satisfaction in her eyes, but I was wise enough not to give her the pleasure of letting her think I was upset. I chattered away in public; I talked to Peter; and yet all the time I knew by a dozen signs exactly what he was thinking of me.

His eyes never met mine, he never looked at me save in direct conversation, and then his eyes were grey and steely. Sometimes I fancied there was disgust and contempt in them, and once or twice I found myself choking back a sob.

Peter was punishing me all right, and at last I could bear it no longer.

Tim rang me up early to say that his invention had definitely been accepted by the Air Ministry. He was as excited as a schoolboy and bubbling over with plans.

Of course, I congratulated him—I was really very pleased. It was brilliant of Tim and I was glad for his sake that things had turned out so right for him.

"Oh, boy!" he was saying. "Wait till I get over Berlin, then I'll show those blasted Huns something!"

I could quite believe it. I shouldn't be a bit surprised if Tim won the D.F.C. or even the V.C. He's tremendously brave, he has no fear of any sort, neither of things nor of people.

That is why I suppose he couldn't understand what I was experiencing. Actually, I didn't attempt to tell him. What was the use? He was no more to blame than I was. I shouldn't have gone in the first place; and Tim is spoiled—he has always had his own way and he always expects to get it.

Looking back over what he had said that evening, I am quite certain he was genuine when he said he would love me no less, and maybe more, if we became lovers without being married. The ceremony would mean nothing to Tim.

He wanted me and that was all there was to it. And yet I could but ask myself the question as to whether, once we were married, would he still go on wanting me? After some years when he had grown used to me and the excitement of love had become a little dimmer?

Anyway, such a question did not matter particularly—not now. What must concern me was Peter.

After Tim had told me about his bomb-sight, he said he was leaving for the north that morning. He had got to finish his training and if the Air Ministry wanted him again they would send for him.

"I'm afraid I shan't have a chance of seeing you before I go, old girl," he added.

Actually, I sighed with relief. I couldn't quite imagine what would have happened if Tim had come to the house and met Peter.

"Good-bye, then," I said, "and God bless you."

"Oh, I'll be seeing you," Tim replied. "I'm certain to be coming south again. I don't believe those blighters at the Air Ministry can put the thing together without my expert help."

After a few more words, we rang off and I felt, as I hung up the receiver, that it was the end of an episode in my life. I faced the fact in that moment that I really did not love Tim half as much as I thought I did.

The change had come over me gradually but inevitably and I was sensible enough to admit it. Tim who had once meant everything in my life, was no longer the pivot round which I revolved. I saw him for what he was—lovable, charming, and utterly irresponsible.

I was doubtful, even if there had never been a war, whether we should have been happy together; whether he would ever have settled down in that little apartment in Montreal which I had planned with such care. I had been so sure we were made for each other—now I doubted it.

Perhaps we should have drifted on for some years and then an Audrey Herman would have occurred in our lives and I should have lost Tim just as I had when he went to Winnipeg.

The only thing I regretted were those tears I had shed, the misery which I had been through and the way I had let myself be swept away into an uncontrollable unhappiness.

How stupid it seemed now!—and still more stupid to have made such a mess of my future by lying and subterfuge which had all been quite unnecessary.

"I'll tell Peter the whole truth," I thought. "After all, he loves me—his love can't have died overnight."

But even as I reasured myself with those words I wondered if it had. After all, that's what had happened to my love for Tim. That had died—why not Peter's for me?

I went downstairs to breakfast determined that somehow I'd force an issue with Peter, but he wasn't there. Bates told me that he had gone to breakfast with the Foreign Secretary. Politicians in England, it appears, often ask each other to breakfast—an uncomfortable meal, I should have thought, for intellectual conversation.

So I breakfasted with Vilie who took pleasure in exclaiming how tired I looked, which I always feel is a woman's way of saying one looks plain. I wasn't going to admit to her I had been awake half the night worrying and feeling miserable, so I said that I felt ill and thought it must be the enervating climate of London.

"I wonder you don't go home," Vilie said.

"Home?" I questioned with a puzzled look, as if I wasn't quite certain what she meant.

"To Canada."

"Why should I? My home is here now—with my husband."

"Oh, but you may not have him for long."

I stared at her, a feeling of horror creeping over me.

"What do you mean?"

The question burst from between my lips. Wildly I thought of all the things that Peter might mean to do— to divorce me . . . to run away with Vilie . . . It was stupid, of course, to let her frighten me like that but her remark was so unexpected.

"Hasn't Pe-taire told you?" Vilie asked.

With an intonation in her voice and an expression on her face which said that she knew very well that he hadn't.

"He may be sent East. The Government is considering sending a representative overseas and Pe-taire thinks there is a chance of him being nominated for the post."

I sat very still. I didn't want Vilie to see how deeply I was affected by what she had told me. Peter going away! That meant there would be only two courses open to me—to go home, or stay here in this land where I was a stranger and had no friends.

"It sounds a most important position," I said lightly. "I'm sure Peter will be delighted if he gets it."

I pushed my plate away as I spoke and rose from the table. It was impossible for me to eat any more. Vilie was not deceived with what, I felt, was a gallant effort to hide my real feelings.

"Poor Mela!" she cooed. "You will have to kiss and make friends before he goes."

"Perhaps there would be a better chance of that if you were not here," I retorted.

Vilie clasped her hands together.

"Oh, Mela!" she said in a broken voice. "How can you be so cruel to me? I quite realise that you don't want me in your home but alas! I have nowhere to go. I am alone in the world, orphaned and destitute!"

She was acting, I knew that, but I knew too that I had been fool enough to put myself in the wrong. She would repeat what I had said to Peter and I could well imagine what construction he would put on it.

"I think it would be far more sensible for me to leave," I said, perhaps unwisely.

Bitterly I noted the gleam in Vilie's eyes, the suggestion of a smile on her lips.

I went out of the room and slammed the door. That, of course, was undignified, but I didn't care.

"I hate Vilie," I told myself; "I hate the whole household and all the things which have antagonised Peter and me."

I went upstairs, put on my outdoor things, and then walked in the spring sunshine round to see Rosy Hewlett.

It was when she came bustling into that fantastically overcrowded little sitting-room with a welcoming smile on her face, wearing a frilly georgette blouse that was too young for her and those monstrous rows of artificial pearls round her neck, that I felt she was the only friend I had this side of the Atlantic.

"I've been longing to see you, dearie," she said. "I was hoping you'd be coming round or else I should have written you a note. When I heard about your marriage, I was as pleased as if it were a daughter of my own. Your uncle thought the world of young Flacton. Many a time he's said to me:

" 'Rosy, you mark my words, that boy will go far.'

"Of course, I'd never seen him until the other even-

259

ing when he came round asking for you. When he told me who he was, I didn't half give him a welcome and then he tells me that you'd got married up at the Castle.

" 'Mr. Flacton,' I says to him. 'if poor Edward was here it would be the happiest day of his life.'

"You should have seen how pleased he looked, but he was worried about you."

"I've been meaning to come and see you ever since we got back to London," I said; "but . . ."

"You've had a lot to do, of course," Rosy interposed. "It's to be expected—besides, you're still on your honeymoon—no time for an old woman like me. I'm always here. You come when you have the time and don't worry if you have something better to do."

"I haven't anything better to do," I said.

My voice choked.

"What's the matter?" Rosy asked. "You don't look too well, dearie, now I come to think of it. Here, we'll have a glass of port—it'll do you good."

"No, I don't want any—really," I replied. "I'm just a bit upset. Things have gone wrong."

"There!—don't say you've quarrelled already," Rosy ejaculated. "And if you have, don't let it worry you too much. Thre's not a woman—or for that matter a man—living that doesn't find it a bit upsetting to be married at first. You have to make adjustments, you've got to settle into new ways and to new methods. I expect you and young Peter have been having a bit of a tiff and now . . ."

"Oh, it isn't a bit of a tiff," I interrupted. "I must tell you . . . I must talk to someone. You're the only friend I have here, the only person who I feel might understand and give me advice, just as Uncle Edward would have done if he had been here."

"That's true enough," Rosy said. "He never failed those as turned to him; so believe me, dearie, I know what you mean when you say you'd have turned to him if he had been here."

"If he had been, " I said miserably, "the whole trouble would never have arisen."

Then I told Rosy what had happened; I told her everything, except what had really caused Uncle Edward's death, from that morning in Montreal when Tim had told me he was in love with someone else, right up to Vilie's information that Peter might be going abroad.

Rosy didn't interrupt—she sat looking at me as I talked, her face set in an expression of kindly sympathy. We were sitting in the full light of the window and I could see in the parting of her hair where the fantastic bronze colour ended and the new, undyed hair had begun to grow.

Her face was powdered nearly as badly as it had been when I first saw her and on her podgy hands she wore no less than five rings—yet none of these things mattered in the slightest.

Her personality shone through them, her kindliness and her understanding were completely undimmed by her taste in ornamentation.

I think I loved Rosy Hewlett at that moment almost more than I have ever cared for anyone outside my own family, and I understood exactly why Uncle Edward had loved her and why she had been worth more to him than all the other well-bred, well-dressed and important women in the whole world.

As I finished speaking, Rosy said:

"I'd like to slap that Vilie! She sounds a proper 'young miss' to me. The sooner you have her out of the house, dearie, the better. Don't you put up with it for a moment. If she can't destroy your happiness one way, she'll try another. I know the type."

She snorted.

"Let your husband give her as much money as he can spare—he's got plenty of it—but get rid of her. They're no use, that sort. They're what your uncle and I used to call 'man-eaters.' You'll find them on board ship; you'll find them in every country in the world as far as I can see, and they're all the same."

She snorted again.

"Show them a pair of trousers and they are after it like rats after aniseed."

"But it's too late," I moaned. "Vilie's done the damage now."

"Oh, don't you worry about that," Rosy said. "I can quite see as how young Peter's feeling hurt and a bit sore with you. Men are like children—hurt their pride and they are that touchy that you have to coax them back to your side again. You go back to your man and put your arms round his neck and give him a kiss and tell him you love him. It will be all right after that."

"I can't do that," I said wearily.

"Why not?"

"Because it wouldn't be true. As I told you, I don't think I love Tim any more but I don't love Peter either. I don't love anybody—I'm just miserable, fed up and homesick."

Rosy Hewlett looked at me in a funny way and I felt somehow she was debating with herself as to whether to say something or not; then it seemed she decided not to. She got up in silence, walked across to the sideboard and produced a decanter of port.

"Just half a glass," she said persuasively. "If there's anything more exhausting than telling the story of one's life, I don't know it."

To please her I took the half glass she poured out for me, and then she went away to the kitchen and came back with a slice of fresh home-made cake.

"Put that inside you," she commanded, "and then we'll begin to make plans."

I did as I was told, simply because it was less trouble than to argue and besides, I didn't want to disappoint Rosy.

"Now, listen to me dearie," she said, when she was sitting down beside me and had had a sip of her own port. "Girls like you have a responsibility towards the men they meet. You're a very pretty young woman and it is to be expected that at least half the men you meet will fall in love with you and if they don't want marriage then they will want something else, and why not? It's 'the nature of the beast,' so to speak."

She paused.

"But you can't just go about the world taking all the cream off the top of the milk and putting nothing back into the bottle.

"You married young Peter because you thought you were doing him a good turn, but if you are quite honest with yourself, do you think you would have done it in other circumstances—if he hadn't been such a nice, presentable young man, if he hadn't had any money at all, and if it had meant any real sacrifice on your part?"

"No, I suppose you are right there," I admitted. "I suppose I wouldn't."

"Well, then," Rosy went on, "you've got to look after him. He's only young; he's not had any more experience of marriage than you have, and I am as sure as I am sitting here that he worships the ground you walk on."

She smiled and patted my hand.

"Englishmen are idealistic, you know, I suppose it is because they've all got a bit of a mother complex. That's what your uncle used to say. What women does the average English boy see and learn about? His mother and his nannie, and perhaps a sister or so—then he's shut up with other boys until he's a man."

"I don't quite see what you are trying to say," I said.

"I'm not surprised, dearie, I find it a bit hard to put into words, but it's just this—I expect young Peter's shy of you."

"Shy!" I ejaculated. "If you saw how he's behaving to me!"

"Well, shyness takes people funny ways. I expect he's shy and I expect he's hurt, and he's not going to let you know about either if he can help it—especially about being hurt. He'll hide that under all the dignity and reserve that he can command."

"If what you say is true, he's certainly a good actor," I said bitterly.

"Make it hard for him to act, be sweet, tender and affectionate—and as for his jealousy, well, if you can't handle a man when he's jealous you've got a lot to learn. It's the strongest weapon that we women have put into our hands."

"I think it would be far better if I went back to Canada. I've been a failure and I might as well admit it."

"If I thought you meant that I'd wash my hands of you, but I know that's only talk. You're not going to admit failure, you've got too much guts for that. Your uncle always got what he wanted and I daresay you will too."

She looked at me shrewdly.

"What exactly do you want?"

"I don't know," I murmured. "Peter to be nice, to admire me, to . . ."

"To love you, I suppose? Well, there's one thing in this world which makes a man say that he loves you quicker than anything else."

"What's that?" I asked curiously.

"Letting him know that you love him," Rosy replied.

Chapter Twenty-Four

I walked back from Rosy's flat very slowly. I was thinking. I can't quite explain my emotions, except that I felt as if the top had been lifted off them to reveal a flaming volcano within.

It was a lovely day; the sunshine was glittering on the water in St. James's Park where the ducks were swimming and preening themselves on the grass; there was that faint blue mist in the distance which I had grown to associate with London and—although I wouldn't admit it—to love; the spires and towers of Whitehall were silhouetted against a translucent sky.

Everywhere there were signs of spring. Flowers, yellow and crimson, in the park, chestnuts beginning to bud, a flight of pigeons, grey and white, wheeling round the flag over Buckingham Palace.

"This is London!" I thought, and I knew that already it meant something personal and real to me—something it had meant to Mummy all those years when she had looked out over the wide, unpopulated prairies and had watched the brave new cities rising brick by brick.

There was much that was wrong in England, I thought, much that could be improved, and yet it was impossible not to admire her for what she was and to venerate her for the tradition and customs which had remained unchanged through the centuries, a part of every English man and woman's daily life.

I remembered how I had come to London full of fire and energy, ready to sweep everything on one side as long as I gained what I wanted myself and could get my own way; but now I was content to take things slowly and to know, with something of that strange fatalistic serenity of the English, that all would come right in the end.

Perhaps that is the greatest thing that the English peoples have inherited—the complete and absolute conviction that in great things and in small, right will always triumph, that they themselves will never be defeated.

I suppose part of the new emotion I was feeling was that of humility, for, by the time I had reached home, I was prepared to humble myself before Peter, beg his forgiveness and ask that we should be friends again.

But, as so often happens in real life, the moment of resolution comes and then one has to wait before putting it into effect. Peter was out and no one seemed to know when he was likely to return.

I wandered rather disconsolately up the stairs and heard my name called from Vilie's bedroom.

"Quick, Mela, quick! Come and help me."

"Help you do what?" I asked, then stared in amazement from the doorway. Vilie was packing—there were two suitcases open on the floor and the bed was covered with dresses.

"Where are you going?" I asked.

"It is too wonderful!" she replied. "My cousin—he has just arrived in England. We hadn't heard from him for so long we thought that he must be dead, but no!—he is safe and he is staying in Hampshire with an old friend. I can't remember his name—Lord Somebody—but he has asked Max and me to go down there at once and be with our cousin. Oh, Mela, I am so happy!"

Impulsively, Vilie jumped to her feet and kissed my cheek. I was so surprised at this demonstration of affection that I rudely made no attempt to return the gesture; instead I sat down on the arm of a chair and asked:

"Is your cousin young?"

Vilie laughed.

"Young and handsome!"

Of course I might have guessed it!—Vilie wouldn't have been as excited as that over any ordinary relation.

"I wish I had a photograph to show you," she went on, "then you would see how good-looking my country-men can be. One day, perhaps, I will bring him here, but not yet—not until he has renewed his promises to me."

"You were engaged?"

"We were betrothed long ago," Vilie said with a dignified little gesture as though she deprecated any ordinary word to describe such an alliance. "My cousin is very important. Here I suppose he will be poor but in our own country he was a very rich man and the position he held was of extreme importance."

"And now I suppose you will get married," I said. "I shouldn't worry about the money, Vilie, the great thing is that he is alive and you can be with him."

"I feel that too," Vilie said simply.

"And you love him?"

Vilie sat back on her heels before the open box and clasped her hands together.

"But so much!"

My curiosity prevented me from being conventional.

"Then why . . ." I asked, then hesitated. It was difficult to put into words. Vilie looked at me under her eyelashes.

"Why did I make love to Pe-taire?" she questioned.

"Yes, that's what I wanted to know."

Vilie paused for a moment; then she smiled in that mischievous, provocative manner which men find so irresistible.

"It is always wise to be prepared for any eventuality," she said.

I had to laugh. It was quite impossible not to relish Vilie's frankness—to have a sneaking admiration for the unscrupulous way in which she behaved badly and admitted it.

"I'll help you pack," I volunteered.

Soon, I too was on my knees, folding dresses, putting shoes into quaint little check bags, and emptying the contents of drawers into the boxes. Vilie had managed to accumulate a lot of things in the short time she had been in England. When we had finished, we both gave a sigh of relief.

"Thank you, Mela," Vilie said, then added: "How glad you will be to see me go!"

I didn't attempt to deny it, I just smiled.

"I don't blame you," she continued. "I have behaved very badly to you, but you can imagine how annoying it was for me to have another girl—and such a pretty one—arriving here just as I thought Pe-taire was beginning to be interested in me."

"I'm sorry," I said, half facetiously.

"Oh, it doesn't matter now," Vilie replied, quite seriously, "but at the time I thought it very inconvenient. I was planning, of course, to take Pe-taire away from you, but my dear—to tell you the truth, I never had a chance. He is crazy about you, that man."

"I think you are mistaken."

"I am never mistaken about men. Pe-taire loves you—loves you so much that I expect he will go away to the East and break his heart just because he thinks you don't love him."

"I'm sure he won't be so silly," I said lightly.

I couldn't bear to discuss Peter with Vilie, even now when I knew she was no longer an enemy, no longer a discordant element in my life.

"You are so proud," Vilie exclaimed unexpectedly. "Well, I am sure you will find happiness your own way, Mela, but it seems to me that you deliberately choose the thorny path."

I wondered what she meant by that, for she was unusually serious; but before I could even begin to guess what she meant, her mood had changed.

She was chattering gaily again, asking my advice on her appearance, and, finally, about a quarter of an hour later, swept out of the house looking entrancingly pretty and so radiantly happy that I felt it was inevitable that her cousin would fall in love with her all over again the moment he saw her.

When Vilie had gone, Bates told me that Sybil had gone to the country and would not be back until very late.

The house felt very empty and very quiet. I began to wonder how I would enjoy living there alone with Peter without any of the others bustling in and out. I knew that it would be lovely to be alone with him; but if he remained as he had been lately, the house would then be a hell and quite unbearable.

Slowly the time passed and then, from where I was listening in the drawing room, I heard Peter come in and go into his study.

It took a certain amount of resolution on my part to walk slowly down the stairs—to beard him in his den. I opened the door. Peter was standing with his back to the room looking out of the french window which faces on to the courtyard.

There were pink tulips planted round a tiny sundial; however, it was not them but something else which preoccupied his thoughts, for he did not hear me come into the room until I spoke his name.

Then he turned round quickly.

"Oh, hello, Mela," he remarked casually.

I knew that all feeling and warmth had been deliberately erased from his voice and the expression on his face changed.

"Vilie's gone," I said, playing for time, wondering how I could approach the subject I had come to discuss.

"Yes, I know," he replied. "Her cousin rang me up at the House. A charming man and an extremely clever one. I am delighted he has got here safely."

"And Sybil is out to dinner," I went on. "It looks as if we shall have a tête-à-tête."

"I am afraid that will not be possible. I have the Foreign Secretary, an old friend of mine, coming here to see me at nine-thirty and I have already arranged to dine early at the Carlton Club."

I don't think I let the disappointment I felt show in my face.

269

"Why are you seeing the Foreign Secretary?" I asked.

"I have various matters to discuss with him, one of them being a proposal from the Prime Minister that I should accept the post of Minister in the Near East."

"Have you decided to accept it?"

"Not yet," Peter replied. "That is what I am going to discuss with my friend tonight, but I think there is no reason why I should refuse."

He said the last words deliberately and I knew what he meant. I was not a reason, for I was not really his wife, only a woman who bore his name and who had deceived him after only a few days of marriage. I felt then it was hopeless.

Peter was like a wall of ice and I hadn't the power to melt him. What, indeed, could I say? Although I had come prepared to plead and beg for his forgiveness, the last tattered remnant of my pride held me back.

"Well, I'm glad I know your plans," I said.

Then quickly, in case he should see the tears which, despite all my resolutions, had started to my eyes, I left the room. I thought I heard him call my name but I couldn't be sure. I ran upstairs and locked myself in my bedroom.

How long I lay crying on my bed I don't know. Finally there came a knock on the door. For one moment I thought it might be Peter, then Bates's voice asked me what I would like for dinner.

"I shall be out," I said firmly.

I had no idea what I was going to do or where I was going. I felt I couldn't sit alone in the dining-room, go through the farce of eating with Bates waiting on me and be conscious all the time he must be thinking this was a queer marriage and a still stranger honeymoon for the master he had served so long.

I got up from the bed and put on a coat, then I walked downstairs and let myself into the street. I wandered on until I saw a funny little restaurant tucked away between two large buildings. I went in and ordered myself a kind of snack meal which tasted far better than it looked.

There were all sorts of queer-looking people seated at the small tables and I gathered after a time that most of them were artists and that I had found my way to Chelsea. If I hadn't been so miserable I think I would have been interested; but, as it was, I felt too unhappy to be conscious of anything but my own dull despair.

What was going to happen to me? What, indeed, could happen in my life? I sat as long as I could in that little restaurant, anxious to pass the time; longing for the day to end so that I could go to bed and forget, at least for a little while, all the muddle and trouble I was in.

Finally, nearly all the customers began to wander off, the laughter and the chatter ceased, and I had to get up, pay for my meal of which I had eaten very little, and go out into the streets again.

It took me some time to get a taxi, but, finally, one came along and I jumped into it and directed the driver to go home.

When I opened the front door, I saw a strange hat and coat on a chair in the hall and knew that the Foreign Secretary must be with Peter. I could also hear voices in the study and I crept past the door and upstairs.

The top of the house was in darkness. As I went towards my own room I saw a faint light coming through the open door of Peter's. I crossed the landing Peter's room looked out over the back of the house. He had shown it to me but I had never been in it save that once.

Now, as I stood in the doorway, I saw that the curtains were undrawn, the windows wide open to the light. Peter had told me that he hated sleeping in a closed room and now the open windows seemed to me symbolic of his freedom, of his escape from all the darkness and misery which waited for me.

271

Standing there alone in the room, I smelt the fragrance of tobacco, the lavender soap which Peter always used, the sweet tang of his hair lotion. It was also reminiscent of those moments when he had held me in his arms—when I had felt his lips on mine—when his kisses had compelled an acquiescence and a surrender against my own will.

Then I knew! In that moment it came to me blindingly, as vivid and as searing as a flash of lightening. I loved Peter! Of course I loved him!

I had loved him almost from the beginning—almost as soon as he had begun to love me. That was why I ceased to be unhappy about Uncle Edward; why, when Tim came into my life again, I had found him childish, irresponsible; why I had hated Vilie, and why I had been so utterly miserable now Peter was angry with me.

Fool! Fool that I had been not to realise it sooner, not to have responded when Peter was waiting for me, not to have discovered this love within myself before it was too late.

For it was too late now; I couldn't help but realise that.

I walked across the room and touched Peter's things—the pillow on which he laid his head, the books by his bed, his hair brushes, the ornaments he had on his mantelpiece. It was too dark to see them, but my hands could feel them and I found some strange, wistful comfort in the contact.

"Oh, Peter!" I cried within my heart. "If only I hadn't been such a fool!"

"How can I tell him?" I wondered. "How can I make him see and understand that I have altered—that now I love him?

At that moment I heard the air-raid warning go. Its prolonged wail like some wild banshee seemed to symbolise in its rise and fall all my own misery and distress. I listened to it, making myself almost a part of its hideous shrieking.

Far away in the distance I heard a bomb fall, and then the guns went into action.

I moved forward towards the window and leant out. I knew this was strictly against all regulations but that didn't worry me. I wanted to watch what was happening, to take my thoughts off my own troubles.

Then I heard a movement down below. It was a tiny sound but it made me peer down into the shadows and wonder what it was. Below me there was the courtyard. I could just distinguish the sundial, the beds of tulips, and the walk of crazy paving which led to a door opening on to the street. That, I knew, was always kept locked.

The garden was still and empty, but again I heard a slight sound and realised it came from the garden next door. Something was moving there amongst some old shrubs whose dry leaves, fallen during the winter, were rustling.

At first, I though it might be a cat and vaguely remembered that the house next door was empty.

Then I thought it was a burglar and recalled how Peter had said that the people had gone away leaving valuable possessions without even a fire-watcher to guard them.

The rustling noise came again and my heart began to beat fast as I saw that a man was hoisting himself over the wall which divided the two houses. I stood watching as he scrambled down into the courtyard . . . then—and only then—did I realise the danger.

It must have been how Uncle Edward's murderer had approached him when he was sitting in his study. In the room below facing on to the courtyard were Peter and the Foreign Secretary.

It was Peter of whom I thought—Peter who I knew was in danger.

I started to scream. I screamed at the very top of my lungs and, even as I did so, some critical faculty warned me that Peter would hear the sound coming from the garden and would go towards the window—perhaps towards his death.

Still screaming, I rushed across the bedroom . . . I upset a chair and heard it thud to the floor . . . I reached the top of the stairs, shouting Peter's name over and over again.

I recollected that there were detectives both at the front and at the back of the house. My scream would have alarmed those at the back—but would those at the front hear me?

But—more important still—would Peter come away from the window?

I started to run downstairs. I was still calling him. As I reached the landing there was a tremendous explosion, deafening and reverberating . . . I felt the house shake.

For a moment my terror was so intense that I thought I must be hurt.

Then I knew that I was quite unscathed and that it was my voice, broken and sharp with agony, calling: "Peter! Peter!"

Chapter Twenty-Five

"Mrs. Flacton, we owe you a deep debt of gratitude," the Home Secretary said, "and I have just been telling your husband how much I admire your courage."

I glanced across at Peter who was sitting the other side of the room, but he didn't meet my eyes and, with a stab of pain, I realised how pale he looked. There was a bandage round his head which I knew hid a wound that had required six stitches.

I longed to run across to him, to put my arms round him, but instead, I must go on listening to what the Home Secretary was saying.

"The man we have caught has already made a full confession," he went on. "He was actually instrumental in causing your uncle's death, but most of the responsibility rests with those who directed him."

"Is he a German?" I asked.

"No, he's an Irishman, a member of the I.R.A., but it was Nazi brains that instigated the crime and Nazi money that paid for it. By the way, Flacton," he said, turning to Peter, "the German Consul in Dublin is deeply implicated in this and I think the Irish Government will have to ask for his recall."

"Have you recovered the papers which were in my uncle's safe?" I asked.

The Home Secretary shook his head.

"So far they have not come to light, but we are hoping, Mrs. Flacton, hoping very much indeed that they will be discovered in the near future."

"Are you quite sure you have got the whole gang?" Peter inquired.

"If the man we caught — thanks to your wife — is to be believed, we have already brought in every member at present in this country. It would be stupid, of course, not to anticipate that their places will very likely be taken again by other malcontents who have become tools in German hands."

"Naturally," Peter agreed, and the Home Secretary continued:

"But the swiftness with which we have been able to move and the penalties which these people will pay for their crimes will undoubtedly be a strong deterrent, at any rate, for the time being."

"They will be shot?" I asked.

"I see no possible recommendation to mercy," the Home Secretary replied. "Your uncle was foully murdered and, but for your presence of mind, this recent incident might have had the same fatal results."

"You mean . . ."

"That had you not seen the man and given the alarm your husband, and undoubtedly the Foreign Secretary too, would have paid the supreme price for being public men."

I shuddered.

"You see," the Home Secretary continued, "when you screamed the man became flustered, detonated the bomb he carried, and threw it.

"He had intended to shoot the occupants of your husband's study even as he shot your uncle—we found a silencer on the gun in his pocket—and then to set a bomb to explode after he had got away with the papers he hoped to find in the safe. It was cleverly thought out.

"He may have been waiting for several nights until an air raid gave him the opportunity he required.

"Under cover of the sirens, it was easy to make a certain amount of noise without being noticed and the organisers of the plot had, of course, no idea that we had discovered that the bomb destruction in poor Edward's house was not caused from the air."

"Yes, it was a good idea," Peter agreed.

He spoke strangely, I thought; his voice was quiet

276

and reserved as it so often was, but it seemed to me lifeless, as though he lacked any vitality or enthusiasm.

I wondered what he would have thought if he had known what a desperate night I had passed.

He had been unconscious when, finally, I had reached him among the glass-strewn debris in the study. It was the Foreign Secretary who told me that my screaming his name from the top of the stairs made him turn from the window just before the bomb burst.

Even so, the blast had flung him to the ground and flying glass had cut a jagged scar across his forehead.

The Foreign Secretary had been sitting by the fireplace and was unhurt save for a cut hand, and it was he who had insisted that Peter should be taken away immediately to the Westminster Hospital.

I had gone there and waited until after the doctors had seen him but I had not been allowed to go into him myself. They had given him an anaesthetic, and they insisted that I should leave him undisturbed.

And so I had gone home alone to find the house full of policemen taking notes and an almost hysterical Sybil who had arrived back from the country and was trying to get a coherent account of what had happened.

It was only when she had gone to bed and I was alone in my own room that the full horror of everything that had occurred threatened to overwhelm me.

"Supposing Peter had died?" I thought. "Supposing the bomb really had killed him—what would have happened to me?"

And then I knew that if Peter died, I did not want to live. I loved him as much as that!

How bitterly then I regretted that I had not had the courage to say what I had wanted to earlier in the evening—that I had not broken down the barrier which stood between us, however high, however impregnable!

"I love you, Peter," I said to myself, and repeated

277

those words over and over again as the hours of the night passed slowly.

I whispered them into my pillow, into the darkness of my room, and again as I stood at my window to see the first pale glimmer of the dawn break over the roof-tops and chimneys.

I had been dressing, determined to go to the hospital and see Peter whatever opposition I encountered, when a message came through that Peter had had a good night and that he wished me to meet him at ten o'clock at the Home Secretary's private house.

I had gone there, longing—with a yearning beyond anything I had ever known before—to throw myself into my husband's arms, to hold him close, to tell him I loved him.

Yet when we met it had been impossible and I could only greet Peter formally, hear his grave reassurances that he was quite all right, and listen to his politely expressed hopes that I had not been too uncomfortable overnight in the damaged house.

Now, at last, there was a chance of being alone together. I saw that the Home Secretary was ready for us to go and the car was waiting outside.

"You must look after your husband, Mrs. Flacton," the Home Secretary instructed me, "I had been telling him before you arrived that he must take a few days rest and quiet, away from the cares of office."

"I'll see to that," I promised gaily. "And Peter will have to think of somewhere nice to take me, for while they repair the study, the hammering will be unbearable."

"There will be plenty of time for them to do that," Peter interposed, then he added meaningly to the Home Secretary: "I thought of going to see the Prime Minister right away."

"I still think you ought to have a holiday," the Home Secretary replied, but my heart sank.

Downing Street was only a few minutes' walk away. Peter would go straight there and I would not see him alone before he spoke to the Prime Minister. Bravely, I interrupted Peter and the Home Secretary.

"Before you see the Prime Minister, Peter," I cried, "I want to speak to you . . . I must speak to you . . . alone."

My voice was agitated and the Home Secretary looked at me kindly; then he said:

"If you want a word with your husband, Mrs. Flacton, would you like to go into my own private sitting-room? There's a fire in there and you will not be interrupted."

"Thank you," I accepted, before Peter, who was looking embarrassed, could reply.

The Home Secretary led the way across the hall and opened a door. He showed us into a small, cosy room where there was a cat curled on the hearth-rug and a canary singing in a cage before the open window.

"No one will disturb you in here," he said with a smile, and left us alone.

Immediately, I was aware of a stiffness—almost a defiance—in Peter's bearing. It made me embarrassed and I stooped down to pick up the cat and hold it for a moment against my cheek.

"He's rather an old maid, but a dear," I said, referring, not to the cat, but to our host.

Peter said nothing—it was as if he stood to attention, waiting for me to reveal myself. The cat slipped from my arms.

"Peter," I began, and my voice was trembling. "Have you made up your mind about this post in the East? Are you going to accept it?"

"Yes. That is why I'm going to see the Prime Minister."

I felt as if he had stabbed me with some sharp instrument which pierced my heart and every nerve in my body. I had a wild desire to scream but I controlled myself and with an effort I stammered:

"Before you do that, there is something . . . I want to tell . . . you—something I want you to . . . know."

I couldn't look at him as I spoke. I put out my hands and held on to the mantelpiece.

"I think I can guess what it is."

"You can?" I exclaimed in surprise.

"You want to tell me that you have decided to leave me—that you love Tim Grant. Well, I can understand that, and if you tell me what you want, Mela, I will try to make things as easy for you as possible."

I wanted both to laugh and cry. I turned round to face Peter.

"You are wrong . . . so wrong!" I said. "I wasn't going to tell you anything of the sort. Tim's gone back to Scotland and before he went I knew that I didn't . . . love him, that I have . . . never loved him really."

Peter's expression did not change but I felt instinctively that he was tense, like a man who waits for a blow.

"Then what was it you wanted to tell me?" he asked.

Now I was overcome with shyness; I felt my voice die within my throat; I couldn't say the words—couldn't force them between my lips. I tried to speak yet no sound came.

"What is it, Mela?" Peter asked more gently.

Then in a voice so small and so strange that I hardly recognised it as my own, I whispered:

"I . . . love . . . y . . . you . . . Peter."

I couldn't look at him. I dared not raise my eyes to see the result of my confession.

There was a moment's pause, a silence so poignant that I could hear my own heart beating—and then Peter's hands were on my shoulders, gripping them fiercely and painfully.

"Say that again!" he commanded. "Say it again!"

I did not answer, and he put his hand under my chin and tipped back my head. I was forced to meet his eyes and what I saw swept away both my hesitation and my shyness. Peter's face was alight.

For a moment we stood looking at each other, and

then my arms were around his neck and I heard my own voice sobbing.

"I love . . . you, Peter—I love you so . . . terribly! You can't . . . leave me . . . you can't leave me now . . ."

He kissed me so wildly that his lips seemed to bruise mine, but I didn't care. I kissed him too, and the whole world was so golden and wonderful that I felt as if we flew together towards the sun.

"I love you, my darling," Peter said in his deep voice, and holding me so tight I could hardly breathe he added: "Tell me again—make me believe you—make me sure I'm not dreaming."

"I . . . love . . . you."

Only three words, but I felt as if I gave him my whole body, my heart and even something I've thought of as my soul.

"Oh my precious, my brave, wonderful wife," Peter said, and I felt he was almost in tears.

The tears were running down my cheeks from sheer happiness but Peter kissed them away.

"Don't cry, my sweet," he begged me.

"It's only . . . because it's all so . . . marvellous. I thought you didn't . . . love me . . . any more."

"How could you have been so foolish! I've been so abjectly miserable thinking you wanted to leave me that I kept wishing the bomb had killed me."

"Peter, how could you? I was screaming because I knew if that man killed you I wanted to die too."

"Darling—darling—darling."

I felt as if my heart was turning over and over in my breast when he spoke like that, and every time he kissed me a thrill seemed to run through my body making me feel and feel as no one has ever made me feel before.

"I adore you—you're so beautiful," he said, and his kisses grew more and more passionate until I felt as if there was a flame inside me.

281

I wanted him . . . I wanted to belong to him . . . to be part of him—to be really his for ever and ever . . .

How long it was before the door opened I have no idea . . . I was discovering for the first time what real love means when a man and a woman love each other passionately and with their whole being. Guiltily I slipped from Peter's arms as the Home Secretary put his head round the door.

"I'm sorry to interrupt you," he said with a smile, "but the Prime Minister is on the telephone. I told him you were coming round to see him, Flacton, but he says he would like a word with you now—right away."

"Tell him, darling," I commanded as Peter went towards the door.

"I will," he replied.

When I was alone I pressed my hands against my glowing cheeks and stood on tiptoe to look in the glass over the mantelpiece and tidy my hair.

I had no idea until that moment how much love can improve one's looks. If I had been pretty before, I knew that at the moment I was as beautiful as Peter had told me I was.

Peter came back into the room. He was smiling. As I ran towards him he put his arms round me and drew me close.

"It's all right, my darling," he said reassuringly.

"What did he say when you told him?"

"I didn't have time to tell him anything," Peter replied. "The Prime Minister wished to cancel the offer he had already made me of a ministerial post in the Near East."

"Thank goodness!" I murmured.

"He wanted to offer me another one instead."

I trembled and raised my head from Peter's shoulder. "What is it?"

"Don't look so anxious," Peter said, teasingly prolonging my suspense. "As a matter of fact, it is all due to you that I have been offered it."

"Due to me!" I exclaimed in bewilderment.

"Yes. The Prime Minister said he'd only just heard that my wife was a Canadian. He had also been told some very flattering things about you, and that was what persuaded him that I was the right person to be offered a new post which had only just been decided on by the Cabinet."

"Which is?" I asked, hardly daring to breathe.

"The post of Minister of Co-ordination between the U.S.A. and Canada. It will mean a good deal of travelling between the two countries. Do you think you will mind that, Mela darling?"

There was no need for me to answer. My arms were tightly round him and I was crying again—irrepressible tears of happiness against his neck.

"I have made only one stipulation," Peter said some minutes later, when he could stop kissing me.

"What is that?"

"That we should have a honeymoon first—and the Prime Minister has agreed. I want to take you away and have you to myself. I think to Cornwall; I know a little fishing village where we could be alone and where I could teach you to love me."

"I'd like . . . that sort of . . . lesson," I whispered unsteadily.

"We will leave this afternoon. There's nothing to wait for, and I want to get away at once—to have you all to myself. Oh Mela—I adore you—my darling— my own wife."

As we drove round Parliament Square and were turning in the direction of home, I remembered Rosy.

"Let's go and tell her," I suggested. "I'd like her to know how happy I am. It won't take us a minute and she will be so pleased. Do you mind?"

"I don't mind anything in the world!" Peter answered fondly. "I've got everything I have ever wanted next to me at this moment."

I snuggled against him happily. The sunshine glittering on the windows of the car seemed dazzling, as if it shone especially for us. We drew up at the block of flats where Rosy lived and went up together in the lift hand in hand.

As we reached the top floor Peter kissed me for a long time before opening the door and I felt almost dizzy with happiness and joy.

Rosy uttered an exclamation of surprise when she saw us.

"Come in, dearie," she said to me. "I have been thinking about you so much. It's all come right, as I was quite certain it would."

"How did you know?" I asked, almost disappointed that she had anticipated our story.

"I only had to take a look at your faces! Come in. We'll celebrate this in a glass of port—it'll do you both good."

I started to tell her everything, and, for the first time, Peter allowed me to reveal the truth about Uncle Edward's death. She cried a little when she heard how he had died and then we were all smiling again and Rosy drank our health.

"I'll come and see you as soon as I get back from Cornwall," I promised her as we said good-bye.

Then, just as we reached the door, she stopped us with a sudden cry.

"There! I knew I had something to tell you and I nearly forgot it. I suppose really I ought to have let you know about it before."

"Know what?" Peter asked.

Rosy fumbled in her handbag.

"This," she replied, and put a small key into his hand.

"What is it?" he asked in surprise.

"The key of poor Edward's safe. I ought to have told you about it long ago, but I give my word, it slipped my mind until the other day when we were spring-cleaning. He had it specially built behind that picture over there."

She lifted a picture off the wall, a rather bad oil

painting of some Highland cattle crossing a stream. Concealed behind it was the steel door of a safe.

"Your uncle put it in when he was changing houses," Rosy explained. "Sometimes he'd be working here until quite late at night and it was too much trouble for him to take the papers back to the office. I kept the key because I had various pieces of jewellery which he used to insist on my locking up in there. All of them had been given me by him and, to tell the truth, I haven't had the heart to put them on since he died."

Peter fitted the key into the lock, the door swung open, and I saw that the two shelves in the little safe were piled with papers.

I realised by the expression on Peter's face what he expected to find. I was certain that he would find them—the papers which were of such tremendous importance.

They had been in the safe all the time and yet so much had come to light—so much had happened in our search for them. In fact, unless they had been lost we might never have been married.

Peter must have been thinking the same thing because he looked at me and I felt my head leap at the expression in his eyes.

At that moment the front doorbell pealed and Rosy went to answer it, closing the door of the sitting-room behind her. Peter reached out his arms and held me close.

"I ought to be excited that we've found the papers," he said, "but all I can think about is you. I'm going to make two telephone calls and then we're leaving on our honeymoon."

"Two?" I questioned.

"One to the Prime Minister," he answered, "to tell him the papers are here and he can send someone to collect them."

"And the other?" I asked.

"To my house in Leicestershire," he answered. "It's only a small hunting lodge, Mela, but it was built in the reign of Queen Anne and is rather beautiful. There is a dear old couple there who look after it for me. She is a good cook and they will make us comfortable."

"It sounds heavenly," I murmured.

"When you are bored we can move on to Cornwall."

I laughed.

"Do you really think I'll be bored?"

Peter's hold tightened.

"No, I don't," he admitted. "I love you so madly, my precious, that I believe I can make you happy. Anyway, it will only take us about two hours to drive to 'Queen's Halt'."

"What a romantic name!" I exclaimed.

"Queen Adelaide slept there," Peter explained, "in a huge four-poster which bears her insignia. That is where you'll sleep tonight, my darling, and this time I shan't be across the passage."

The deepening of his voice and a sudden fire in his eyes made the colour come flooding into my cheeks.

"Sweetheart, you're blushing!" Peter exclaimed incredulously.

I hid my face against his shoulder.

"And once I suggested you were tough," he said wonderingly.

Then his arms tightened until they hurt, and in a very low voice he went on:

"Mela—I wasn't going to ask you—and you can refuse to answer me—but, darling, I have to know—have you—ever—?"

I put my cheek against his so that my lips were close to his ear.

"I know what . . . you're trying to . . . say," I whispered, "and Peter, I swear . . . to you by everything I hold . . . sacred . . . that . . . no one . . . no man has ever . . . touched me . . . like . . . that."

I felt him give a deep, deep sigh, then with his fingers under my chin he turned my face up to his. His eyes were blazing with triumph and some other expression which made me feel very shy.

"I knew it," he said, but quietly, almost reverently. "I knew it because no one could look so innocent and not be pure. Oh, Mela, you're all that I've dreamt of and yearned for—my wonderful, perfect wife."

Then he kissed me and the little room, the papers, everything seemed to disappear; we were whirling through space and everything was so incredibly glorious that I couldn't think any more, I could only feel and feel and feel an ecstacy beyond words.

Somewhere a voice was saying:

"I love you, my darling—my angel—my sweet innocent little love."

And another voice which was mine, yet almost unrecognisable, was whispering over and over again:

"I . . . love . . . you . . . I . . . love . . . you . . . oh, Peter. . . . I love . . . you."

ON SALE WHEREVER PAPERBACKS ARE SOLD
—or use this coupon to order directly from the publisher.

BARBARA CARTLAND

V2734	Open Wings $1.25 (#37)	
V3242	Out Of Reach $1.25 (#60)	
V2690	The Pretty Horse-Breakers $1.25 (#35)	
V3243	The Price Is Love $1.25 (#61)	
V2650	Reluctant Bride $1.25 (#34)	
V3020	Secret Fear £ (#23) $1.25	
V2429	Stars In My Heart $1.25 (#21)	
V2887	Stolen Halo $1.25 (#44)	
V2689	Sweet Adventure $1.25 (#17)	
V3189	Sweet Enchantress $1.25 (#58)	
V2920	Sweet Punishment $1.25 (#45)	
V2577	The Unknown Heart $1.25 (#29)	
V2996	Wings on My Heart $1.25 (#47)	
V2504	Wings of Love $1.25 (#25)	
V2749	We Danced All Night $1.25 (Autobiography)	